Fortunate Harbor

Books by Davis Bunn

The Miramar Bay Series
Miramar Bay
Firefly Cove
Moondust Lake
Tranquility Falls
The Cottage on Lighthouse Lane
The Emerald Tide
Shell Beach
Midnight Harbor
The Christmas Hummingbird
The Christmas Cottage

The Outer Banks Series
Fortunate Harbor

DAVIS BUNN

Fortunate Harbor

KENSINGTON
PUBLISHING CORP.

kensingtonbooks.com

KENSINGTON BOOKS are published by

Kensington Publishing Corp.
900 Third Ave.
New York, NY 10022

All Kensington titles, imprints, and distributed lines are available at special quantity discounts for bulk purchases for sales promotion, premiums, fund-raising, educational, or institutional use. Special book excerpts or customized printings can also be created to fit specific needs. For details, write or phone the office of the Kensington Special Sales Manager: Attn. Special Sales Department, Kensington Publishing Corp., 900 Third Ave., New York, NY 10022. Phone: 1-800-221-2647.

KENSINGTON and the K with book logo Reg. US Pat. & TM Off.

Library of Congress Control Number: 2024951800

ISBN: 978-1-4967-5422-6
First Kensington Hardcover Edition: May 2025

ISBN: 978-1-4967-5423-3 (ebook)

10 9 8 7 6 5 4 3 2 1

Printed in the United States of America

The authorized representative in the EU for product safety and compliance
is eucomply OU, Parnu mnt 139b-14, Apt 123
Tallinn, Berlin 11317, hello@eucompliancepartner.com

This book is dedicated to

FIONA FLOATE

Our Guide and Counselor
Dearest Friend

Fortunate
Harbor

CHAPTER 1

The Morehead City Hall was an awkward location for this meeting. As was how the mayor had scheduled the assembly for early afternoon. Rae Alden suspected both formed part of the mayor's reasoning. Atlantic Beach would have better suited most of the attendees. But the locals who wanted to come and shout and argue, the same group who had been fighting against this act for two years, knew their attendance meant becoming mired in afternoon traffic. The mayors and county commissioners were all in favor of this new hotel resort, and specifically chose this venue to keep as many of their opponents as possible fuming at home. Yes indeed, Rae decided. This was absolutely the place to meet.

Just the same, the assembly hall was almost full. She had found a chair by the rear left corner and hoped no one would recognize her. Rae had no real reason to be here, other than she desperately needed a word with her uncle, the sheriff of Carteret County. And Colton Knox had told her in no uncertain terms that between handling spring breakers and preparing for this meeting, if her business couldn't wait until Monday, then it had to be handled here.

Rae had hoped to arrive early, speak with Colton and then slip away. The last thing she wanted, the very last, was for someone in this group to recognize her. But her lunch meeting had dragged on, which had left her rushing across the bridge connecting Atlantic Beach to Morehead City with only seconds to spare.

Early in the locals' futile quest to halt the Fortunate Harbor project, Rae had been hired to file a legal brief on the group's behalf. Despite being in total sympathy with the locals and their objections, six weeks of digging into court records had revealed the utter futility of their protest, and Rae had backed out. She was still waiting to be paid for her time.

Then someone slipped into the chair next to her, and a voice said, "Rae Alden. As I live and breathe."

She steeled herself for the acidic comment that was bound to follow. Then she looked over and saw the man behind the smile. "I don't believe this."

Curtis Gage looked exhausted. And as handsome as ever. "Been a while."

"Twelve years."

His smile was canted slightly, a look that took her straight back. When they had been young and desperately in love, Rae had always thought Curtis resembled a mischievous ocean sprite whenever he smiled. A surfing sand-encrusted sprite, eager for the next good time.

Not anymore.

Rae flashed back to their last meeting. The sunburnt kid still semibroken over the loss of his father, his mother remarried and taking him away from the only home he had ever known or wanted. They had clung together in the desperate embrace of teens in love. Both of them weeping. Saying farewell. Promising to stay in touch. No matter what.

Twelve years.

Rae asked, "Does Emma know you're here?"

"That's the next stop on my agenda." He took in her rough silk slacks, sleeveless cotton top, gold watch, cork sandals, tan. "Wow, Rae, just look at you."

She was thinking the same thing. Curtis Gage wore a *GQ* version of weekend casual: gabardine slacks, silk knit shirt, alligator belt, Italian loafers that looked so supple he could probably roll them up like socks. If he was carrying any excess flab, she could not see it. His perfectly styled hair still held to that same remarkable blend of blond and brown, but now there were also premature silver threads. Finely woven lines emanating from the edges of his eyes and mouth testified to time's uncaring hand. If she had not known Curtis was twenty-nine, she would have guessed ten years older. The thought pierced her heart.

"What are you doing here?" she asked.

"My boss thought I should come and observe."

"Don't tell me you work for these people."

"Not the resort. The parent company's home office." He must have seen the fiery spark in her gaze, and added, "Sorry."

Before she could come up with a response, the mayor of Morehead City stepped to the podium, blew on the microphone, and said, "Let's go ahead and get started."

CHAPTER 2

Edgar Front, mayor of Morehead City, was a portly gentleman with the formal air of a pompous vicar. Edgar was a retired banker and looked the part. Unlike the beach-casual
attire of almost everyone else in the hall, Edgar wore a
starched shirt and trousers to a dark suit. A tie dangled over
his ample belly like a silk lure. But he was meticulously honest and so trusted he also served as senior county commis-
sioner. Edgar kept the region's books in perfect order. He
ran roughshod over both unscrupulous builders and time-
wasting bureaucrats with ferocity.

Three chairs were positioned on the stubby platform that
served as a stage for winter recitals. But the storm season was
behind them, spring breakers had come and gone, and the
late April evening held an unseasonable warmth. This was
Rae's favorite time of year. Not to mention how the afternoon was now spiced by the gentleman seated beside her.

As Edgar went through the long-winded process of introducing Rae's uncle and the third man seated on the platform,

Rae cast a few glances at this stranger who had once been the other half of her own heart's flame.

Then she noticed the hands. To be specific, the shallow crease on the left hand's fourth finger. The ring that was no more. Whatever it was that had caused the marriage to end, the hollow point at the center of Curtis's gaze now had definition. Some years-long battle had creased his features and erased the boyish excitement that had once defined him. In its place was . . .

Rae was suddenly charmed by the prospect of discovering who Curtis Gage had become.

Which, of course, was ridiculous. Beyond absurd.

She was, after all, one step away from becoming officially engaged to the second love of her life.

Her ideal mate. A nearly perfect man. Everybody said so. Almost.

Just the same . . .

Mayor Front gestured to the uniformed deputy standing by the rear doors. "No one else is to be admitted. If they can't be here on time, they're not welcome. There's been a lot of hot air expelled over this issue, and we're not having any more of it tonight."

The mayor's stern tone definitely rustled some outraged feathers.

Edgar glared at the muttering crowd, waiting. When they finally settled, he went on. "Sheriff Knox and his deputies are here to make sure everybody behaves. If you don't, you'll be expelled. If you make trouble, we'll invite you to spend the night as a guest of the county. Is that clear?"

The harsh no-nonsense introduction stilled the crowd, which now numbered so many they lined the rear and the sidewalls.

"Now some of you probably came here thinking it was as good a time as any to cause a ruckus. I'm telling you clear as

I know how, you're wrong. Those of you who came wanting answers, fine, you're welcome. Everybody else, now's your chance to leave." He gave the crowd another glare. "At my personal request, the governor has sent down Brian Sparks, director of the state's division of Parks and Recreation. Brian is also head of the parks' Trust Fund Authority. And he serves on the board of the nation's Wildlife Fund. I've known Brian for more than twenty years. He's a good man and he deserves your respect. Is that clear?"

Rae noticed the confusion on many faces, and silently agreed. She had come expecting debate, argument, perhaps some fireworks of a down-home variety. Her island neighbors were here to vent their opposition to the entire project. Instead, they were being ordered to behave.

When Edgar was certain the crowd was as close to being under control as they'd probably come, he turned and said, "Brian?"

He was a tall man, sun-blackened and very fit. He wore an ironed cotton shirt and a wool tie in the awkward manner of somebody who probably needed help making the knot. Rae put his age in the mid-fifties. The hands that gripped the podium were massive. He spoke with the calm authority of a man accustomed to being obeyed.

"Evening, folks. I'll do my best to answer any questions you have."

Harvey Sewell, a legal windbag of the first order, rose from his place on the front row. He introduced himself and began, "I am the official representative of the Friends of Fort Walton Park."

"I know who you are. State your question."

"I have filed an injunction on behalf of my clients—"

"That injunction was dismissed with prejudice last week." When a murmur of astonishment ran through the assembly, Brian added, "Dismissal with prejudice means the judge felt the case has no legal merit."

Rae positively enjoyed watching Harvey's features swell up like a frog ready to croak. She had come up twice against him in court. The man balanced a lazy attitude toward homework with an overabundance of windage. She thought the locals' choice of Harvey as her replacement was very telling. Rae was not especially in favor of the resort project, but the law was the law.

Harvey yelled, "I will appeal that decision!"

"Appeal all you like. It won't get you anywhere, and you know it." He scanned the crowd. "Next question."

One of the few women in the group whom Rae actually liked demanded, "How can you let them build on park land?"

Brian looked mildly astonished by the question. He turned and looked at the mayor, who said, "Told you."

Brian nodded once and faced the assembly. "Folks, I'm sorry to be the one to tell you this. But it's time you faced facts. There are four parts to answering this question. Firstly, the hotel has been open almost nine months now, and there's nothing you can do about it. Second, the consortium has completed almost all the residential development's roads and the first golf course. Seven homes are nearing completion. The oceanfront clubhouse will open in September. All the permits are in order, the governor has given his—"

That was as far as they let him go.

The trio on the stage let them shout for only a minute or so before Rae's uncle rose from his seat and motioned to the deputy standing by the rear door. The deputy opened the exit and spoke to someone outside. Immediately two more deputies entered the hall. The sheriff stepped down and walked the central aisle as the first deputy started up toward him, while the other two moved along the outer wall. Their unified presence had an almost immediate effect. The shouting invectives were reduced to angry murmurs.

Brian Sparks continued in the same calm manner, as if the

furor had never happened. Or at least had left him unscathed. "The third part of my answer is just as simple. Eighty-eight percent of the Fortunate Harbor's resort property has always been in private hands . . ."

Brian waited while Colton stepped toward a trio still on their feet. Rae's uncle jabbed his finger downward. When they were reseated, Colton lowered both arms. But he remained where he was, the gun-barrel gaze tight. Steady.

Brian started to continue, then saw a hand raised. "You there, go ahead."

A man Rae did not recognize said, "But the family willed all that land to the wildlife conservation fund."

"I know that's what everybody's been wishing had happened. Including myself. Around twenty years ago, the late George Cochrane made a handshake deal with my predecessor. Cochrane gave my predecessor his word. But he never actually got around to jumping through the legal hoops. When his widow recently passed away . . . When was it, Edgar?"

"Almost four years back," the mayor replied.

"The Cochrane heirs secretly sold the property to the consortium who built the Fortunate Harbor Hotel. We only learned about the transaction after the fact." He studied the audience, saw the shock on many faces, and added, "I was told you folks were advised this happened."

This time, it was the sheriff who declared, "They most certainly were." Colton pointed in Rae's direction. "By their former attorney, who is seated right back there."

As she rose to her feet, Rae had a bitter suspicion this was why Colton had insisted on their meeting right here. So she could tell the assembly, "That is correct. I informed the group's leadership and was dismissed for speaking the truth."

The mayor called, "Where are they seated?"

Rae spotted the Atlantic Beach mayor doing her best to

hide in plain sight. The middle-aged realtor was serving her fourth term and succeeded by being everybody's pal.

Rae decided to fib. "None of them are present."

Edgar gestured to the group at large. "Why didn't you tell the others assembled here?"

"The leadership ordered me not to say anything more about it," Rae said. "I was told Mr. Sewell would handle all related matters from that point on."

The lawyer bounced up and sputtered, "This is the first I've heard of any such—"

Edgar snapped, "Sit down, Harvey."

Rae took that as her signal. As she retook her seat, a gray-haired matron three rows up turned and hissed. "Traitor."

"Quiet!" Colton's command was not actually shouted. It only seemed so.

"That leaves the fourth portion to my answer. It is true that the park sold some of its land." Brian Sparks raised his voice to continue. "With the governor's direct approval, the division deeded six and a half acres to the consortium. The simple fact is, we need the money. As most of you know, the last hurricane effectively destroyed the park's beach access. In return for acreage that did not even contain a hiking trail, the consortium has rebuilt and expanded the beach frontage. It now contains two new crossovers, lighting, sewage, showers, parking for over a hundred vehicles, and a new structure that's been leased by a local restaurant. The total cost to the consortium was over eight million dollars. The grand opening was . . ."

"Two and a half months ago," the mayor offered. Edgar sounded beyond weary. "Many of the folks gathered here attended. Which means they heard me thank Fortunate Harbor for the part they've played in our region's future."

Brian gave that a moment. When no one else spoke up, he finished, "Folks, if you ask me, we need more deals like this.

The state's legislature continues to strip away the parks' budget. Our trust fund is basically empty. This way, everyone benefits." He ignored the rising mutters and told the mayor, "I guess that just about does it."

Mayor Front rose to his feet and called, "This meeting is hereby adjourned!"

CHAPTER 3

The meeting ended on that sour note. The woman who had condemned Rae started to make her way over, no doubt to add further vitriol. But Sheriff Knox stepped into the woman's path. Colton did not speak, because there was no need. The sheriff's looming presence redirected the woman toward the exit. She shot a final venomous glare in Rae's direction and left.

Colton pretended to inspect his niece. "No bloodshed or gaping wounds. I'd call that a success."

Only then did Rae notice that Curtis had slipped away unnoticed. "A different person might suspect you had me come so I could back your play."

"I admit the thought did cross my mind." Colton pointed them into chairs midway along the empty row. "Any particular reason why that woman was so riled?"

"I told her the truth."

Colton stretched out his legs, revealing polished Western-style boots. "Folks like that, if you accept their filthy lucre, they expect you to tell them what they want to hear."

"They still owe me nineteen hundred dollars."

"Don't hold your breath." He glanced at the exit. "Was that Curtis Gage I saw sneaking out with the crowd?"

"None other."

"Man's grown up." He checked his watch. "I can only give you a minute. Two alerts came in while the parks ranger was deflating some egos."

Rae launched straight in. "You said to inform you of any activity regarding the Cape Fortune estate."

Colton lost his good humor. "Has Landon Barrett shown up?"

"No, and that's the problem. His escrow account is empty, and the property taxes are overdue. Either I obtain the necessary funds or the estate will be seized."

"You still hold power of attorney?"

She nodded. "The agreement was open-ended. At Landon's instructions."

"When did you last get paid?"

"The funds ran out at the end of last year."

Colton's smile held no humor. "Some folks might say you're making a habit of taking on clients who don't pay."

Rae felt her face go red. "I didn't stop by so you could lecture me on how to run my practice. You told me to inform you of any activity." She started to rise. "Since you're so all-fired busy—"

"Slow down there. I'm sorry, Rae. I shouldn't have said what I did, especially today." He paused. "Now's the point where you accept my apology."

"I'll think about it."

This time, the smile was genuine. "Same old Rae."

"May I go now?"

"In a minute." He leaned in close. "This is strictly confidential. I was recently visited by two DEA agents. They stopped by my office and asked about Landon Barrett."

"When was this?"

"Seven weeks back, give or take."

"Colton, why am I only hearing about this now?"

"They informed me Landon Barrett is now part of a formal investigation, then specifically ordered me not to tell you. Those agents clearly didn't want to give Landon's attorney of record a chance to put up roadblocks."

Rae settled back. Crossed her arms. Blanked out the noise. Thinking. "Is my client the focal point of their investigation?"

"They didn't say. But from the little they told me, I think Barrett is a sidebar issue to something much bigger." He gave that a beat, then continued, "You and I both know there were suspicions surrounding Barrett from the get-go."

Rae did not respond.

"The DEA is probably worried he granted you power for some nefarious reason."

"Everything I've done for that client is totally aboveboard," Rae said. "All my work focused on the Cape Fortune property. Or rather, what's left of it after those two hurricanes."

"And that's exactly what I told the agents." When Rae did not respond, he went on, "Look at it from their side. There's a chance you and I are both taking money from the guy to help him do whatever it is they suspect him of doing."

Rae breathed around the enormity of what she was learning. "And you're telling me now because . . ."

"Whatever steps you decide to take, you need to make sure they're totally aboveboard."

"That's the only way I operate," Rae said.

But Colton was not done. "Now more than ever, Rae. There's a good chance those agents will put you and your activities under a microscope. Looking for any possible reason, however flimsy, to tie you up in federal chains."

CHAPTER 4

Rae had intended to go straight from the meeting to the county courthouse to take care of semitrivial matters that a larger firm would assign to a staffer. But she was the one-and-only. A young mother desperate to escape her twin infant daughters worked part-time, handling office work and keeping the practice's books. Otherwise, Rae was on her own. Which was precisely the way she wanted things to stay.

But the conversation with her uncle, the way Colton had stressed his warning and hammered in his concern, slowed her movements. She felt as if she was already under a federal microscope. Being watched, studied, judged.

She stopped at the coffee shop favored by many of the attorneys and courthouse workers. Ever since starting her solitary practice, there had been moments when Rae had felt overwhelmed by everything she didn't know. The practice of law was so different from school that Rae sometimes felt as if she had studied another subject entirely. One only slightly related to what she dealt with out here in the real world.

This was definitely one of those times.

Her initial response to Colton's warning was to grab hold of another attorney, put together a joint sale, have this outsider check her work, ensure everything was aboveboard. But the more she pondered, the more certain she became that something else was required.

She was still sitting there, reviewing options, when her phone chimed. She had a special tone for her aunt. Emma's health remained a very real concern, made worse by the woman's stubborn refusal to accept the medical assistance her worsening condition required.

Her aunt texted: Come for dinner.

Can't. Working.

Girl, this was not an invitation.

Same answer.

Curtis just left. I have news that can't wait.

Rae sighed in defeat. Six o'clock work for you?

Emma chimed a smiley face. Happy to have won. Again.

Rae left the café, crossed over to the courthouse, then halted midway around to what local attorneys called the minions' entrance. She stepped off the sidewalk and entered the shade of two blooming dogwoods. The spot was so often used by attorneys needing a quiet spot the ground had become hardpacked. As she dialed the familiar number, Rae wondered why it had taken her so long to realize this was the logical next step. Perhaps the only one.

"Dana Bowen's office."

"Hi, this is Rae Alden."

The words should not have shamed her like they did. But Rae had allowed the contact with her favorite professor to gradually fade to nothing. She could not remember the last time she had been in touch.

Despite the lapsed time, Dana Bowen's personal assistant recalled her well enough to brighten. "Oh, Ms. Alden. Good afternoon. I know Dana would like to talk, but she's in court all this week."

"I have something urgent that's come up. I need to speak with her on a legal matter. On the record. And on the clock."

The PA was aged in his mid-thirties and knew both law and his boss. "It has to be this week?"

"As soon as possible. Please."

"I know she would want to make this happen. Let's see. Depositions the day after tomorrow aren't supposed to begin until ten. I know Dana had planned on handling other business that morning, but I'm sure she would be more than willing to make time. How about eight-thirty?"

"Booked. Thank you so much." Rae cut the connection and carried her flood of relief into the courthouse.

She completed her work in half an hour. Less. Then she returned to the café, opened her laptop, and accessed her legal files by thumbprint and code. Rae spent the next two hours burrowing through everything she had on the long-overdue Landon Barrett, her power of attorney, and all the documents related to the property. She wanted to have everything there at her fingertips, ready for whatever Dana Bowen might toss her way.

Rae had been involved in Barrett's acquisition of Cape Fortune since the very beginning. Her success in bringing together the disparate owners and getting them to agree to the sale—and the price—was why she had gained Landon Barrett as a long-term client. She sought any hint of illegality, any item however small that might suggest a wrong move. Something that the DEA could use as a lever to pry open her life.

She found nothing.

For over a century, the property had belonged to a local fishing clan. Soon after the Second World War, the two brothers had argued, and the land had been divided. A generation later, it was rendered into six separate parcels, all still held by distant relatives of the original settlers.

Rae had no illusions as to why she had been selected to represent Landon Barrett. The man wanted a local. Someone who could speak with all these family members as one of their own. And it had worked. For a sizeable amount of cash, Barrett had managed to acquire the entire nine acres. Three hundred forty feet fronting the Intracoastal Waterway. Six piers, multiple dwellings, options for commercial and private usage guaranteed through its continuous use, going back to the island's early days. All so Barrett could build Cape Fortune, his dream home.

When the courthouse closed two hours later, she had identified nothing that explained why her client was being investigated by the DEA.

But Rae definitely had her suspicions.

CHAPTER 5

Curtis slipped from the assembly, eager to avoid the questions he knew Rae would have asked. His only alternatives were to avoid her altogether—which was totally not happening—or make this particular journey.

There was, of course, the possibility that Rae Alden had been transformed by the twelve years since their last meeting. He certainly had. But from what he had seen in the assembly, Curtis figured she had become an adult version of the teen he had loved. Feisty, intelligent, beautiful.

Curtis left Morehead by way of Highway 70 and crawled north, the afternoon traffic both heavy and very slow. He did not mind. There was nowhere he needed to be this evening. No one waiting for him. Not ever again.

He crossed the bridge over Harlowe Creek and entered Beaufort, one of the most beautiful places on earth, as far as Curtis was concerned. The town occupied a spit of land where three bodies of water intersected. Front Road overlooked the Rachel Carson Reserve and the islands of Shackleford Banks.

The town had been founded in the mid-eighteenth century, and remained calmly defiant of time's relentless flow.

Curtis snagged a space in the crowded public lot, then headed inland. His destination was two blocks away, where Broad Street met one of the local marinas. Here the world held to a different pace. Live oaks, magnolias, and blooming dogwood trees stood sentry to homes and shops older than the nation. Traffic was slow, almost apologetic. Tourists walked and gawked and reveled in a bygone era.

What had once served as the town's milliners and premier dress shop now housed the Beaufort Bookshop. Occupying the property's carefully tended garden was a crescent moon of whitewashed cottages that formed the Peninsula Guesthouse. Curtis climbed the front steps and opened the bookshop's front door, causing the bell to chime. The same bell that had greeted him all those many lives ago.

A lovely teen, perhaps fifteen years old, sat on the stool with both elbows planted on the countertop. She was the definition of bored. Curtis was halted by the sight, and the memories.

"Good afternoon."

She did not look up. "Just shoot me."

The left wheel of Emma Alden's chair still squeaked. She appeared in the doorway leading to the storeroom and greeted him with: "Great heavens above."

"Hello, Emma."

"Are you a ghost?"

"Some days, it feels like it."

The teen still had her face planted on her hands. "Tell me about it."

Curtis walked over, bent down, accepted the older woman's embrace. Then he returned to the counter and said, "I used to sit where you are."

Still, no movement. "Yay."

"Has Emma given you her spiel about staying open so tourists have a place to gather and meet the locals?"

"Only about a million times."

"Let me guess," Curtis said. "Your parents agreed to staff the bookshop a couple of hours every day in exchange for a lower rate on the cottage."

She lifted her head, but only so she could raise her arms and stretch. "The longest hours of my entire existence."

"Are they at least paying you for your time?"

"Ha." Back to slump. "Double ha."

"Which means they caught you doing something fairly awful."

"Our young friend broke curfew," Emma said. "She was due back at what, ten?"

No response.

"She insists she and a local lad merely wanted to watch a sunrise over the Atlantic," Emma said. "Apparently, her parents did not consider that an adequate excuse."

Curtis fished in his pocket. "You know the Fortunate Harbor Hotel?"

She glanced up, a microsecond of inspection, long enough to dismiss him as being of no interest whatsoever. "So?"

"How would you like to have access to their beach club?"

That brought her to full alert. "That costs, like, fifty dollars a day."

"Per person." He took a pen from the mug beside the register. "Unless you have friends in high places."

Emma wheeled closer. "You work for that lot?"

"The owners."

"I should bar you from my door."

"Too late." He wrote swiftly, then asked, "What's your name?"

"Beverly."

He handed her the card. "See what it says there? Contingent. That means your family can come with you, but only if you agree. Here's what I suggest. Emma needs you to keep working here, and you need to get paid. I'm sure Emma would be willing to shift your hours to the morning."

"If a certain young lady is able to crawl out of bed before one in the afternoon."

"For a chance to lounge poolside at Fortunate Harbor, my guess is she won't even need an alarm." To Beverly, "If your folks kick up a fuss about payment, you take the bus leaving from Front Street. Our logo is on the side. It runs once every hour and stops twice in Morehead City before heading for the resort. We operate the service for locals working at the hotel. Just show the driver this card. Which means if necessary you can go by yourself."

She was now on full alert. "Get out of town."

Curtis tapped the card. "This is good for the rest of your stay."

Emma said, "Now is when you thank the gentleman."

Beverly asked, "Can I bring my friend?"

Curtis looked a question at Emma, who replied, "She means the utter cad who kept her out all night. He reminds me of you."

"Probably not a good idea," Curtis said. He tapped the card once again. "Nine o'clock sharp, bright and cheerful and welcoming. When Emma asks, you hop. Agreed?"

"This is totally wild."

"Her parents are going to freak out," Emma said. "Seeing as how our dear Beverly was sent here on punishment detail."

Beverly released her day's first smile. "I know, right?"

Curtis watched Emma wheel her chair around and followed her from the shop. "Nice to meet you, too."

Emma parked her chair in the corner and used a cane to work around the kitchen. She did not invite Curtis to sit because she didn't need to. Emma Alden had been part of his world since he was five. All that time, she had suffered from arthritis. The chair was used on bad days. There had always been a lot of those.

Her late husband had been a big man with a booming laugh, a builder whose forebears had mostly died early from heart attacks. He had transformed their garage into the village bookstore and erected a series of two-room bungalows on their broad rear lawn, leaving Emma with both a source of income and a means of maintaining connection with their beloved hometown. A photograph of the man adorned almost every wall in their home.

Emma did not ask if Curtis wanted tea. When they were kids, he and Rae had often complained about the taste, but put up with it because of her homemade butter cookies. Her back to the room, Emma asked, "How long has it been?"

"Twelve years," he said. Several lifetimes.

"How did a dashing young man like yourself stay single?"

"I didn't," Curtis replied. "She died."

Curtis watched her pour boiling water into the waiting pot, set it on the kitchen table, and then bring over mugs and a plate of cookies that neither of them would touch. She settled slowly into the chair opposite his, leaned her cane against the table, poured the fragrant broth, and only then spoke. "When was this?"

"Almost four years ago," he replied. "Severe preeclampsia."

She sipped. Avoided his gaze. Calm and accepting. "She was pregnant."

"Just coming to the start of her second trimester. One day everything was fine. The next, seizures. The day after, a stroke. Two days later, I lost them both."

Her silence was the reason why Curtis had come. Enduring the hard confession, because of this woman's calm acceptance. Her ability to endure the impossible. For years.

She said, "Drink your tea before it goes cold."

Her signature brew was made by another local woman, an

herbalist who now served an online clientele that extended through the Southeast. Willow bark and dandelion and other elements that now spiced the kitchen's air. Sweetened with honey from another friend's hives. Curtis sipped and waited. And remembered.

Preeclampsia was a condition that usually did not occur until well into the third trimester. Most patients also suffered from a history of either hypertension or very high blood pressure. Lorna, his late wife, had neither. Curtis endured the hard moment, something that came far less frequently these days. Emma's kitchen became filled with the dark shock, the impossible transition. One moment, family. The next, a vacuum where their tomorrows had once resided.

Emma drew him back with, "You want me to tell Rae."

"Would you?"

"Of course." She reached over and took his hand. "My dear child."

The words became caught in his throat. He swallowed hard, managed, "Thank you, Emma."

She retreated back across the table, said, "Rae would worry this like a pup over her favorite toy." She sipped again. "You were right to come."

The silence held them for a time. He finally confessed, "This tea is actually very good."

"Don't sound so shocked." She refilled his mug. "I assume this means you're not hoping to rekindle things with Rae."

"Ha. No."

"Because she's the next best thing to engaged."

"I'm happy for her."

Emma's blank expression held any number of unspoken thoughts. All she said was "John Anders, her beau, keeps asking. Rae is gradually bending to the idea."

He tasted several responses with the tea, settled on, "What do you think of him?"

"Everyone says he is a wonderful young man. John's parents think she walks on water."

Curtis suspected Emma was ready to say more. If he asked. Instead, he decided on, "Changing the subject. Can you recommend a local realtor?"

"Are you talking about a place on the island?"

"No. Here in Beaufort."

"Don't tell me you're thinking of putting down roots. Not here." When he did not respond, Emma continued, "Do you have any idea how many folks you've infuriated with this new hotel?"

"You do realize it's not just a hotel."

"Even worse! Your buying a place in Beaufort is just about the most dreadful idea I've ever heard! You'll be tarred and feathered before your furniture is moved in!"

It felt beyond good to have a reason to smile. "No furniture. I'm living a furnished-apartment existence these days."

"I'm serious!"

"I know there's a problem. I just came from the assembly in Morehead City. And I have an idea."

"So you're not after buying a home."

"Maybe someday. Right now, I couldn't even say how long I'm going to be here."

"Will you tell me what you're thinking?"

"Yes. If you insist. But I'd rather wait and see if this particular dog has fleas."

She tried to smile and glare at the same time. "You used to say that a lot as a child."

"I remember."

She reached for her phone without taking her eyes off him. Hit speed dial. Waited. Then, "Gloria? Hi. I have a young man here in my kitchen who is wanting to waste your precious time."

"Thanks a lot, Emma."

"Gloria wants to know what this is about."

Curtis raised his voice. "Cash purchase of a specific Beaufort property. To be concluded as swiftly as possible."

Emma listened, said, "She's on her way."

Curtis waved to a smiling Beverly as he passed the bookstore and walked the sunlit lanes back to Front Street. The town suited him, and always had. Beaufort was not really cut off, in the sense of dangling at the end of roads leading nowhere else. But anyone heading to the beach either had to travel by boat or join the crawl through Morehead City.

As he had requested, the realtor's red Lexus SUV was parked by the Fortunate Harbor bus stop. The service had been put in place for hotel employees, then expanded to include locals wanting a free ride to the beachside park. Few took advantage of the service, of course, given how folks felt about the hotel.

The realtor was an immaculate woman in her late forties or early fifties, dressed in a suit that Curtis thought was beachside formal. Coral slacks and matching jacket, pastel sandals with cork heels, white silk blouse. Her hair was a natural blond going gray, her fingernails painted the same brilliant red as her car.

"Mr. Gage?"

"Curtis."

"Gloria Tanner. So nice to meet you. Your aunt is a treasure, I can't tell you."

"Emma is no relation. I've known her since I was a kid."

Her words held the local's silky down-home accent. "You're from around these parts?"

"I was. My family moved away. Now I'm back."

"And working for Fortunate Harbor."

"Actually, I'm with the parent company."

"May I ask in what role?" When he hesitated over the

question, she hastened to add, "I'm naturally curious, Mr. Gage. And I'm a realtor. Which means I sometimes step on toes without meaning to."

"It's a valid question, and really please call me Curtis. But I'd be grateful if you would treat what we say as confidential."

"Understood."

"I answer directly to the chairman."

"I see. Or rather, I probably don't need to."

"You are no doubt aware of the problems we've had regarding the adjacent resort."

"I couldn't live here and be as nosey as I am without knowing. And your job . . ."

"I'm just your basic problem solver."

Another silence. Then, "I hope you won't mind me wishing you good luck with that."

"I've always been partial to honesty." He swept a hand in the direction of the sunlit street. "Why don't we walk?"

They rounded the bend and started along the riverfront. This section of town still resembled the place he had loved as a child, a quiet backwater where two kids could roam freely and play games of adventure and mystery. They did not speak again until they had passed the marina and approached the dilapidated home.

Curtis said, "I'm interested in this particular property."

"In that case, let's just keep on walking." She held to the same steady pace, but everything about her radiated a new level of tension. "The owner lives across the street. See that house set back from the road? It belongs to Reddit Ryder. A purely vile and nasty man who lives up to the strangeness of his name."

Something sparked in Curtis's memory. "We used to throw pecans and crab apples at his tin roof."

"You're lucky he didn't shoot you." She cast him a tight glance. "Gage? Gage. Your daddy was the sheriff!"

"That's right. He was."

"Well, great heavens above. I remember you. Your momma . . ."

"Iris."

"Iris Gage. We were acquaintances. You folks had the farm just outside the Beaufort city limits."

"It was my grandparents' farm. My father built our home on a neighboring property."

She squinted at him, as if able to read between his words. "Your daddy's parents didn't deed him land?"

"My grandparents stayed furious with my late father until the day he passed. They expected their only son to farm the land that had been in their hands for generations. My father wanted to be a cop."

She walked slowly, mostly keeping her gaze on Curtis. "Sweetheart, I remember the day your father was shot. The whole town grieved."

He nodded. Curtis had no interest in dwelling on that particular memory. "Mom is Iris Staples now. Living happily with her dentist husband in Little Rock."

"I'm so sorry. I shouldn't have called you that. 'Sweetheart.'"

"Ms. Tanner . . ."

"Call me Gloria. Please."

"I am genuinely grateful to Emma for bringing us together. Now tell me about the place."

The house was, to put it mildly, an eyesore. None of the windows Curtis saw were intact. The roof bowed in the middle, like it had given up and now slumped in utter despair. "Old man Ryder uses the state of disrepair as revenge. He and his lawyer . . . Does the name Harvey Sewell ring a bell?"

"I just heard him speak."

"Well, of course you did. How did you think the meeting went?"

"As well as it possibly could have." He waved that aside. Later.

"Harvey Sewell is a weasel of the first order, and that's all I'll say about the man. Except he and old man Ryder were made for each other."

"He was old when I was a kid. Ryder."

"We're fairly certain he became pickled in his own vile juices sometime back. His daughter is an ER nurse at the Carteret County hospital. An absolute angel. She actually puts up with her daddy. Why, I have no idea. Or how."

Listening to the woman's easy manner was like walking through an open door. Curtis remembered so many other people and how they addressed the world. As if honesty in conversation was part of their birthright.

He said again, "The property."

"Because of the marina, all this riverfront you see here is zoned multiple use. Harvey Sewell weaseled his way through the zoning board and had the Ryder land approved for a condo development. We all assume it happened on a moonless night when the board was hoodwinked by ghouls. The sort of undead that count Reddit Ryder among their clan." She gave the riverfront land a single glance as they passed. "The prospect of a high-rise with thirty condos blocking out their river has the locals foaming at the mouth."

"How much does he want for the land?"

"Two and a half million dollars. And I'm telling you straight out, old man Ryder won't budge on price."

"How large is the property?"

"Just under three acres. But here's the thing." She waved her hand in the general direction of the next property, a lovely old-timey home shaded by multiple dogwoods in full bloom. Between it and the derelict place was a high stone wall. "That place belongs to the Oakley family. They've lived there so long you'd think they were here to greet Blackbeard. Or somebody. See how the boundary wall spreads like a fan? They basically own all the riverfront except a nar-row little split, call it sixty feet wide. Maybe not even that. Just enough for this dreadful excuse of a pier that's waiting for somebody stupid to come along and walk on it." She must have seen something in Curtis's face that concerned her. "And something else. That family will fight any attempt to build a structure that overlooks their property. You mark my word. They'll tie you up in knots. For years."

"I have no interest in building a high-rise."

She stopped, but Curtis kept walking. Which required her to almost run forward. "You actually intend to bid on this land? Despite everything I just said?"

"No bid. Outright purchase. Cash."

"Can I ask why?"

"Confidentially?"

"Mr. Gage. Curtis. Confidential is my middle name. It isn't on my business card. But it should be."

So he told her his idea.

Gloria's pace faltered, but she managed to keep going. "If I wasn't afraid old man Ryder was watching, I'd throw my arms around you and just bawl."

"You like it?"

"It's what this town has needed for years. You'll be the best friend of everybody in Beaufort who wants to see this section of town progress into the nineteenth century. Joke."

"Funny."

"Of course, there are a whole passel of locals who are dead set on anything that might move them out of the Steam Age. I suspect some of them are still lighting their homes with coal-oil lamps. But this news might actually sway them in your direction."

This time, it was Curtis who stopped. "Nobody can know."

Gloria lost her smile. "Confidential. Understood."

"I'm going to have a local attorney represent me on this. That is the only face people will see."

"Please tell me it won't be Harvey Sewell."

Curtis liked having a reason to smile. "I was thinking of Rae Alden."

CHAPTER 6

Curtis returned to his studio apartment in the island Ramada. The suites-motel stood two blocks from the ocean, partially renovated since the last hurricane struck Atlantic Beach. Curtis could have taken an oceanfront suite at the resort. He could have demanded a lot of things. They were all his due, but the Fortunate Harbor's hostile manager had done his best to make Curtis feel utterly excluded. Which was why Curtis remained where he was. In a modest place between the shore and the bridge.

He showered and changed into T-shirt, shorts, and slaps, then drove to the Shark Shack, a family-run fish restaurant that had already become a personal favorite. Curtis worked through dinner, returned to his room, and spent another three hours preparing his three documents. The first was a summary on his work, the issues, the way forward. The second was a costing of what he was about to spend, and how much he wanted to set aside for the rebuild and purchase of equipment to put his plan into action.

A lot.

Both of those documents were running commentaries. He spent most evenings adding to their content. The third was different. Each night he parceled out the most important bits, distilling them down to as few words as possible. His two bosses, father and daughter, insisted on daily updates. These had to be less than one page in length. At first, Curtis had sweated and strained over this ironclad limitation. In time, though, he had learned to like it. This restriction forced him to decide what was absolutely crucial, and what could be held back. There in case they asked for more details. Questioned his moves. Insisted on placing his work under the corporate microscope. The first few years after he started his current role, these inspections happened a couple of times each week. Sometimes daily. Now, almost never.

It was well after midnight when he finished and sent off his daily report. Curtis had no idea when or if it would be read, and by whom. That used to worry him a lot. Now he accepted the invisible leash as just part of his job.

He stripped and slipped into bed, then lay on his back, studying the ceiling and reflecting on the incredible journey that had brought him here. Back to the place that had once shaped his entire world. The only home he ever wanted. His very own island paradise.

Curtis woke with the dawn hour. Sleep had been a reluctant friend since his life fragmented. He made coffee and a fresh-fruit smoothie, drank a mug of both, then went for a swim in the motel pool. Back inside, shower, another cup of the two brews, dress, and go. Rushing into his morning routine was another part of his new world. Keeping his internal state intact was easiest when he held to a common routine, a steady pace, despite the constant transitions his job required.

The sun crested the eastern palms as he drove past the resort hotel's gated entry. Four employees were already working out front, picking up litter that had been dumped by passing locals. This was, Curtis knew, a daily routine and symptomatic of the problem he had been sent down to resolve.

Only today was different. Two of the employees were using shovels to scoop up what appeared to be fish entrails. Another used the portable water-truck to hose down the grassy verge. The sheriff's car was parked under the neighboring palms. Colton Knox toyed with his sunglasses as the hotel manager stood with his back to the road and waved his arms as he talked. Colton's gaze shifted long enough to watch Curtis pass.

Curtis continued north and pulled into the new beach-front public park. A few vans and SUVs were already there, most with empty surf racks. He rose from the car, recalling days when finding the best break defined the day's most important component.

Atlantic Beach had once framed his world. There was nowhere else he wanted to be, nothing he required that the Crystal Coast could not supply. Curtis stood in the strengthening light and reflected on those distant times. Such memories belonged to a different man. He might as well have been watching them on the big screen, part of someone else's drama.

The simple fact was, had he stayed he would never have met Lorna. There was nothing on earth, not even the tragic boundary that ended their time together, that could make him wish for a life that had never contained his late wife.

Six minutes later, the sheriff pulled in and parked beside his ride. Colton rose, settled his Stetson in place, and offered Curtis his hand. "I thought that was you, seated next to Rae at yesterday's shindig."

"Good to see you, Sheriff."

"It's Colton to you, son. Time doesn't change that." He had a cop's gaze, tight and hard and penetrating. "Emma called and passed on the news about your late wife. Wanted to say how sorry I am."

"Thanks."

"Smart move, stopping by her place. She'll make certain everybody who might otherwise pry will know to keep their yaps shut." Colton might have smiled. "Including one particular lady who lives to dig."

Curtis saw no need to reply.

The sheriff waved back in a southerly direction. "You're working for the hotel?"

"The parent group."

"Ah." Colton nodded. "So the rumors are true."

Curtis did not respond.

"Your sales team had their hands in the cookie jar."

"Say I was to agree," Curtis said. "How far would that go?"

"Son, the number of bombshell secrets I carry could sink the island."

"In that case, local architects complained."

"You're talking about the Dixon father and daughter."

"None other. They had two homes ready to start construction. Our former resort manager and his two sales staff refused to give final approval unless the Dixons offered an off-the-books commission. When the father complained, we turned to a detective agency we've used in the past, a retired FBI agent. He discovered the resort manager and his minions were also skimming funds off the initial land purchases." Curtis pointed to the Lexus pulling into the lot. "And that's all the time I have for dirt."

Colton waved to Gloria Tanner as the realtor rose from her car. "You ask me, you've made a good choice, working with this lady. She's solid as they come."

"Glad you think so."

The sheriff shook his hand a second time, started to turn away, then asked, "What exactly is your job here?"

Curtis nodded. It was the question he'd been hoping for. "I'm just your basic problem solver. In this case, it includes finding a way to bring the locals over to our side. You have any ideas on that score?"

Colton actually laughed. "You mean, other than closing your resort and burning down the hotel?"

"Preferably, yeah. I need to find some way to have the locals want us to stay. And grow. Any advice you can offer would be appreciated."

"I owe your father my life," Colton said. "That kind of debt never goes away. But don't go asking for what I can't give. Because my first reaction is, there's no way in heaven or earth you'll make that happen." Colton pulled out a business card and his pen. "This is my home number and private cell. Come over one evening, we'll grill some steaks."

As Colton pulled from his parking space and started away, Gloria stepped up and asked, "Am I allowed to ask what that was all about?"

Curtis returned the sheriff's departing wave. "Colton was just making me feel welcome. Sort of."

Gloria Tanner opened the SUV's rear gate, set her briefcase on a cardboard file box, and began setting out documents for Curtis to sign. The realtor showed a pleasant but no-nonsense manner that he found appealing. Curtis finished signing, listened as she explained the process they needed to follow in completing the sale, and filled out the deposit check.

That done, Curtis asked, "Mind if we take a look at another property?"

"My morning is booked. Will this afternoon do?" she replied.

"Now is better." He pointed west. "It's why I asked if we could meet here."

"Are we talking a lookie-loo or a semi-definite?"

"It carries the same urgency as this purchase," Curtis

replied. "Another cash buy. To be completed immediately, if at all possible."

"In that case, let me make a few calls and ask my junior associates to handle this other appointment." She revealed a lovely smile, equal parts coquettish and excited. "You may wish to step away. My two young ladies tend to scream when I wreck their schedules."

Instead, Curtis crossed the parking lot and took the dune crossover. He stopped by the lifeguard station, the construction so new he could still smell the fresh-cut timber. He checked his phone for messages and responded to a couple of emails. There was nothing from Amiya Morais, his immediate boss. Curtis took that as his signal to proceed. Full speed ahead.

The wind was gentle and blowing offshore. The waves were head-high and almost perfect, sizeable A-frames that broke in both directions, forming tubes that flowed from peak to shore. Curtis watched surfers gorge themselves on an early-morning feast and felt a thousand years old.

He was glad to be back in the Outer Banks, though he expected very little from his visit. His recollection of days spent on the Crystal Coast belonged to a different era, another man. The simple life he had known as a youth did not belong to the person he was now. These were someone else's memories.

Gloria appeared beside him. "Do you surf?"

"I did. Long ago."

She leaned back and pretended to give him a head-to-toe inspection. "You're young and fit. You should go for it. There's still time."

"Not today, there isn't." He started back. "Mind if we take my car?"

Once they were underway, Curtis said, "Thanks for making time this morning."

"I have a couple who've been dithering over a purchase,

hoping they can drive down the price." Her accent was down-home smooth, as if she delicately tasted each word. "All they've done is drive me and the seller around the bend. This morning was to have been our sixth visit to the property. With their lawyer this time, who at least is being paid by the hour. I might have intimated I was involved with another potential buyer."

"Which you are," Curtis said. "Just not to that same property. I hope."

Her smile was impish. "That little item might have been lost in the conversation."

He turned into the resort's newly completed central road. A female guard stepped from the gatehouse, recognized his car, waved a half salute and opened the barrier. "Changing the subject. What can you tell me about Dixon and Dixon Architects?"

Gloria lost her grin. "So the rumors are true."

Curtis took his time, pretending to inspect the four half-finished homes now lining the first lake. Beyond them, a landscaping crew was planting palms as a final ornament to their newly completed golf course. The first of three, if the resort ever grew to full capacity. Finally he replied, "Off the record?"

"We're not covered by attorney-client privileges here. But we should be."

"In that case, the answer is, our former estate manager and two salespeople were in it together."

"I hope you skinned those three," Gloria said. "Slowly."

"No comment."

"They were just one more reason why your project is loathed by so many local business people. You do realize they put roadblocks into any sale, particularly when an outside agent was involved." When Curtis did not respond, she asked, "Is that why you're here?"

He shrugged. "Tell me about the Dixons."

"Emmett Dixon and his daughter, Blythe, stand head and shoulders above all the other regional firms." Definite. "And they charge accordingly."

"Can you set up an appointment with them?"

In response, she brought out her phone and began texting. "I'm glad Emma brought us together."

"I was thinking the exact same thing," Curtis replied.

As Gloria worked her phone, Curtis left the resort by way of a clay-packed road dating back to the early-twentieth-century settlers. The scrub to either side still held vestiges of their crops—native corn, yams, collards, tobacco, fruit trees gnarled and stunted with age.

Gloria announced, "The Dixons aren't available until seven this evening."

"Tell them that's fine. Will you join us?"

"Delighted." A few moments later, she stowed her phone, looked up, and realized, "You're taking me to the Barrett estate."

"I am indeed."

"How do you know this road?"

The real answer was, he and Rae had walked this way for years. Back when the former owners had all moved away, and they could pretend the waterfront land was theirs alone. Rae always colored their walks with myths of bygone eras. All he said was "I've been down here a couple of times surveying the property adjacent to ours."

"Are you the resort's new manager?"

"More like a stopgap. I'll help resolve some issues, then be on my way."

Even on his third visit, seeing the home came as a shock. All but the garage, lager, and entry foyer stood on ten-foot pilings. It was the largest structure on stilts Curtis had ever seen. "What is this, five thousand feet under air?"

"Closer to six and a half would be my guess," Gloria replied. "That is, if the a/c system still worked."

The house was a tragic wreck. The three pilings supporting the northeastern corner had pulled completely free of the structure and now dangled like drunken flagpoles. Those beneath the vast waterfront patio were in similar condition. A sizeable portion of the structure was dangerously close to collapse. All but three of the windows facing their way were covered with plywood.

Curtis asked, "What do you know about the property?"

"Other than the house is pretty much a complete ruin, not a lot. Oh, I suppose with enough money the place could be repaired."

"I don't want the house."

"So this is not your idea of a future holiday home. Just waiting for a splash of paint and a decorator's touch."

"Not now, not ever."

"Let me make some calls." A delicate pause; then, "Just to be clear, you're treating this as another urgent issue?"

"I'd like to make an all-cash offer. Today, if possible. Which means I also need a reliable assessment of its value."

"The best appraiser in the county is a pal. I can probably get him to do an urgent survey, if you're willing to pay extra for him putting everything aside."

"Whatever it costs."

"In that case, leave it with me."

Curtis returned Gloria to her car, then drove to the resort office.

Behind the main gatehouse was a sizeable structure containing two glass-fronted offices and a large lobby with a model of the completed resort. Between the two buildings was a parking area for staff, a minibus, and six charging stations for golf carts. Visitors with or without appointments could not enter the property until the resort manager or a salesperson accompanied them. The electric carts and bus all bore the resort logo.

Curtis spent the day fielding issues with contractors and architects. When he had arrived three days ago and announced the former manager and salespeople were no longer involved, no one had expressed surprise or regret. Which was all the confirmation Curtis needed that they were right to let the trio go.

Two of the builders and their architects stopped by personally. The issues they raised did not require face time. Curtis knew they simply wanted to see if the resort was just changing people and not policy. Their expressions said clear as day, they were not putting up with more of the same. He did not try to explain or apologize. He simply responded to their concerns, doing his best to show that the situation was different. Permanently.

At five that afternoon, Gloria texted that she had information on the property and suggested they meet for a drink prior to seeing the Dixons. She named a bar Curtis did not recognize. He texted back, confirming, and locked up. But once in the car, he decided to take the long way around.

He drove back down the old packed-clay road, pulled into the Barrett drive, and walked down to the waterfront.

The entire property was lined with a bulkhead as battered as the home. The three piers all had missing planks. The central one had been nearly demolished by recent storms. It tilted and flowed like an incoming wave. Curtis knew the story of how the latest hurricane had made landfall south of Wilmington. Then just as the Crystal Coast breathed a sigh of relief, the storm swung around and took aim. The diminished storm passed just north of Beaufort, but when it reached the island's Fort Macon Park, it slowed. The eye rested directly over Barrett's home for almost two hours, long enough to wreak havoc on it and the neighboring park.

Curtis watched the sun begin its western retreat, turning the inland waterway into a shield of burnished gold. Ever since his arrival, he had been stopped in his tracks by such moments, when the region's beauty sought to awaken his heart.

He had no strong feelings about it, one way or the other. Very little had managed to impact him at a deep level. So much of who he was remained trapped in the amber of loss. He knew there were changes on the wind. He no longer feared the sudden strike of grief, brought on by the unexpected encounter with a happy family or a laughing child or a couple in love. These days, he had grown accustomed to simply feeling nothing at all.

And yet at moments like this, surrounded by the simple beauty of another Carolina dusk, he wondered if there was any chance of new beginnings.

When his boss had initially asked if he would take charge of this situation, Curtis had started to decline. So much of who he was, and what he had endured, started here. He had not been ordered down. Instead, his two bosses, father and daughter, simply asked. Could he possibly come and try to make things right with their first-ever North American project? Those exact words. Make things right. He had not wanted to come. And yet . . .

He breathed the tangy flavors of brackish water and springtime blossoms, of wild blackberries and magnolia trees in full bloom. And wondered if there was such a thing as healing. Or starting over. Even for someone like him.

CHAPTER 7

As Curtis passed the Fortunate Harbor Hotel entrance, his phone rang. The readout said it was his boss. He put on his blinker and pulled to the side of the road. Which meant winding his way around a Styrofoam cooler and rubbish tossed by locals returning from the park.

"Amiya, hi."

She started as always with, "Is now a bad time?"

"It's perfect."

"Thank you for your reports. They make for an exciting read."

"A lot is happening," Curtis replied. "And much faster than I expected."

"So tell me what you haven't included in your one-pagers."

This was one of their favorite topics, and had grown into as intimate a moment as Curtis allowed himself these days. He launched straight in, holding nothing back. Curtis started with the town hall meeting, how he had spotted Rae Alden and seated himself beside her, shifting from there to her aunt

Emma's, seeing the stopover as a way to avoid Rae's inevitable questions. But it had also allowed him to find the Beaufort riverfront property. Which brought him to where he was now. Seated in his idling car outside the hotel's entry, staring at yet more litter tossed by locals who wanted them gone.

Amiya responded as she often did, taking a silent moment to digest all she'd heard. Curtis risked being late for his meeting with Gloria, so he started the car and pulled off the verge and headed for Atlantic Beach.

Amiya Morais was a few months younger than his own twenty-nine, and the company chairman's only child. A sizeable number of the senior executives back in Delhi despised her. Curtis could not decide whether it was because she had moved from serving as her father's personal aide to running their new American operations, or because she was far more intelligent than they were, or because she was beautiful and rich. Or all of the above.

Amiya's parents had divorced when she was four. Her mother moved back to upstate New York and eventually remarried. But Amiya remained in close contact with her father and took aim for business school while still a teen. Curtis had heard snide comments among some of his fellows that Amiya had taken her father's name in order to sidle up to the old man. He knew this was false, because Amiya and his late wife had been the closest of friends. Amiya had wanted to work for her father, partly because she loved him, and partly because Kurien Morais lived for his work.

Finally she said, "Tell me more about this island house."

"Forget the house. The house is a wreck."

"It's the land. I know. Describe in more detail, please."

"It's shaped like an elbow, with the current home at the bend. The cove is mostly deep water and faces straight west."

"That is quite possibly the least persuasive description I have ever heard."

He pulled into the restaurant's parking lot. "It's all I have time for. I'm due to meet the realtor."

"I like the sound of her."

"Emma described Gloria as a friend for all the right reasons," Curtis said. "I think Gloria is exactly who we're looking for. A trustworthy and honest realtor who might become a real ally."

He expected Amiya to discuss the money he was about to spend, or what he hoped to accomplish with the architects that evening, or all the steps he would be taking the next day. Instead, she said, "I'm concerned about the trash being thrown at our hotel entrance."

"It's not just trash. Someone's been dumping fish guts. Which was when the sheriff became involved."

"That was the wrong move."

"I agree."

"Did you tell Simon?"

Simon Leroux was the hotel manager, a fussy gentleman in his late fifties. "We haven't spoken since our conversation when I arrived."

"Is that wise?"

It was as close to a criticism as Curtis normally heard from his boss. "I'll call him tomorrow if you want. But right now, he thinks I'm just focused on the resort. And for whatever reason, the man definitely does not like having me around. I'd prefer to have some reason for him to need my help. Be the one to reach out."

A silence; then, "Simon has let it be known that he is part owner of the hotel."

"You're joking."

"It was one of the sidenotes our detective included in his final report."

Curtis breathed around the news. Then, "You haven't told your father."

A laugh. "Daddy would fire him faster than he did our three thieves."

"We don't need to lose both the hotel and resort managers in the same week."

"Which is why Daddy doesn't need to know. Yet." A pause, then, "How are you, Curtis?"

It was the sort of gentle question that bridged the divide between Amiya being his boss and his late wife's best friend. The woman who had lived with them for almost five months after her own marriage fell apart. The friend who had held him at the grave site while he wept. The woman and her father who'd kept his life on course in the dark weeks that followed.

"It's been good coming back."

"Tell me how."

He found himself describing the late-afternoon vista and standing in the shadow of the storm-damaged home. He finished with, "Despite all the problems, there's a real potential here."

"Are we talking about the house or you?"

"I told you, forget the house. The property is just waiting for a new chapter."

She was almost laughing as she said, "Same question, Curtis."

He opened the door, pushing against the sudden flood of hope, and all the fears that sprang up. Curtis waved to Gloria, then replied to Amiya, "I'll have to get back to you on that."

Approaching Gloria's table, he could see the realtor was excited by something. Almost tense.

A waitress walked up before he was even seated, attractive and tanned and giving him the eye. "Welcome to the Full Moon. What can I get you this evening?"

He indicated Gloria's empty glass. "What was that?"

"A very nice Chardonnay. Ice cold."

"Sounds perfect. A round for us both, please."

When the waitress departed, Gloria said, "If you want a realtor's semiprofessional opinion, I'd say that particular waitress is interested in getting you a lot more than a drink." When Curtis did not respond, she added, "I believe the word you're looking for is 'hot.'"

"I need a realtor," Curtis replied. "Not a matchmaker."

"Honey, we Down-Easters are a full-service bunch. You come looking for one thing, you get the whole package."

The waitress returned with two glasses and another of those special looks and announced, "My name is Kitty. So you'll know who to ask for if you need something else."

Gloria watched the lady saunter off, then lifted her glass in a mock toast and said, "Meow."

The wine was frigid and oaky smooth and went down like it was oiled. There had been a time when the night's first drink held a promise of temporary oblivion. But the pills always wore off, and the booze never failed to disappoint. He had been almost glad to sober up. Nowadays those first few swallows were as far down memory lane as Curtis let himself drift.

Gloria set down her glass. "So you and your mother relocated to Arkansas, is that right?"

"Mom met William when he was here on vacation." He smiled at the memory.

The waitress was looking in his direction and responded with a smile of her own. Curtis shifted in his chair, which brought out a third smile from the realtor.

He continued, "In the space of those two weeks, my mom left her slow recovery behind and became this hyperexcited teen in love. William came back twice more that summer. The second time, they got engaged. The next time was to move us back to Little Rock."

"A whirlwind romance like that gives a lady hope." Gloria sipped from her glass. "You never made it back?"

"What did Emma tell you?"

She laughed. "To call her the instant you shared anything juicy."

"Which means she told you about me and Rae."

"Guilty as charged."

He pretended to watch a yacht make a slow-motion approach to the marina next door. "Those first few months, I missed Rae so much. William offered to pay for me to make a trip. I leapt at the chance. But that night, and the next, and the one after that, it all came back to the same question. Then what? I was seventeen. Was I ready to commit?" He stopped. Remembering.

Gloria asked quietly, "Then what?"

"From that distance, I saw what I hadn't wanted to accept while we were together. Rae and I were changing. We both did well in school, it was one of the things that drew us together. She was determined to study, graduate, become whatever, and come straight back. Live her life here. End of story. But now that I was away, even in those first couple of months, I began to see a bigger vista. For the first time ever, in the midst of all that heartache, I knew a bigger world was calling to me."

Her expression was soft, womanly. "And look where it got you."

And that, Curtis knew, was time to change the subject. "What about you?"

"Army brat. Both my parents hailed from a little bitty flyspeck thirty miles west called Wildwood. Daddy's last deployment was Fort Bragg. They retired down here. I did my best to run away, but it didn't take."

He had the distinct impression Gloria did not want to go any farther down that road. Which he understood all too well. "You might as well go ahead and tell me what's got you so excited."

"Maybe you should recharge your glass first. Give the lady watching you from the bar another lift to her evening."

"Gloria."

"Oh, all right." She was clearly enjoying herself. "Any-place like that, a big waterfront property that stays empty for so long, is bound to sprout rumors like weeds. But from what I've learned, in this particular case, the tales hold at least a smidgen of truth."

"Tell me."

She leaned forward. "The owner's name is Landon Barrett. I told you that already. I actually met him once. Big man, not nice, but a lot of wealthy second homeowners are not what you'd call salt of the earth. One reason why locals aren't especially happy to see your resort move ahead."

"To say the least."

"I know, right?" Her tone grew conspiratorial. "A banker friend must remain nameless because she'd get skinned alive for talking with me this afternoon. Landon Barrett's attorney is none other than your old pal Rae Alden."

Curtis was not impressed. "How does that help me acquire the place?"

"I'm not nearly done here. She says Barrett's property is giving Rae all sorts of headaches."

"What kind?"

"He left Rae with an account she was supposed to use for all related expenses. That was three years and two hurricanes ago. The fund is pretty much dry. And Landon Barrett has vanished. Nobody can find him. And they've tried. For years. Which explains the current state of Barrett's house."

This was news. "And?"

"Don't you dare give me that big-city sphinx act." She smiled. "Tell me that doesn't rock your boat."

He tried to hide his smile and failed. "What I said this afternoon about liking you. I take it all back."

"Oh, you. Anyway, your very own Ms. Alden visited the bank a few days ago, talking with my pal. She's worried about overdue property taxes that she can't pay."

"She's not my very own anything."

Gloria sniffed. "Apparently, Rae has pretty much decided she has no choice but find a buyer for the property."

This was definitely news. "Rae holds the authority to sell the estate?"

"I suppose you'll just have to ask the lady that yourself." She glanced at her watch. "We're due at the Dixons'. Finish that glass you've left to molder while I go ask the waitress for her phone number."

CHAPTER 8

The Dixon and Dixon firm was exactly as their private investigator had described. Curtis's group had employed former FBI agent Joel Blanchard on a number of occasions. Joel had spent over twenty years working on property crimes. He had two sons; one kept the books, while the other did Joel's online research. Joel was fast, discreet, precise, and on point. Curtis stopped outside the architect's entry and texted Joel, saying he needed to talk: ASAP. New project.

Then he followed Gloria inside.

The lobby was decorated with framed photographs of lovely homes, awards, drawings of prospective dwellings. Three *AD* covers were blown up to poster size. Gloria's phone chimed with an incoming message.

She read out loud, " 'We're tied up with a previous conference and need a few minutes.' "

"No problem. Do you have Rae's telephone number? I need to send her a heads-up."

"Well, of course you do."

"You can wipe that smirk off your face or you can watch me go find another agent."

"Oh, you."

Curtis accepted the paper with Rae's number, stepped back outside, and texted her requesting an urgent meeting. Tomorrow morning, if at all possible. The timing was crucial, and was in regard to a very important issue.

Joel Blanchard phoned while he was texting. "What's up?"

Curtis asked, "Are you recording?"

"Always."

"I need a rundown on two new issues. Both are time crucial, I need what you can give me tomorrow."

"All-nighters carry an extra charge."

"Understood."

"Will this require online research?"

"Absolutely."

"You don't know, you can't imagine, the moans I'll have to put up with. Go ahead."

"Rae Alden." Curtis spelled her name. "She's a local attorney. I need to know her recent background."

"Recent, as in . . ."

"A bit about her law school would be good, but mostly I want to know her reputation since starting her practice."

"Which means I'll need to connect with people directly. I need a couple of days."

"You can't have them."

A pause; then, "I'll have a basic workup by midmorning. What's number two?"

"Landon Barrett. He's a property owner adjacent to our resort. We want to buy his home. Barrett is missing. Rae Alden has power of attorney. I've just learned she intends to put the place up for sale."

"What does that mean, 'missing'?"

"No idea. I'm hoping to put an all-cash offer on the table tomorrow morning. I need what you can get me."

"Interesting." A pause. "Okay, I'll see what I can dig up. Call me . . ."

"Let's say ten o'clock, I'll text and confirm." Curtis saw Gloria step up to the entrance and wave through the glass. "I have to go."

CHAPTER 9

When Rae arrived at the architect's office, Blythe Dixon was pacing the front room. The lobby area fronted the street with internal wood-slat blinds covering tall windows. The blinds could be shut whenever the front room was used for a conference. They were open now, which meant Blythe spotted her approach. She used the hand not holding her phone to wave Rae inside, then point her back to the rear office.

Emmett Dixon was an ageless gentleman with skin the color of coffee and fresh cream. Rae had grown up with Blythe, a hyperintelligent and lovely woman now married, with two young girls whom Emmett worshipped. Atlantic Beach's premier architect was bent over the conference table separating father and daughter's desks from their support staff. His pianist fingers were delicately putting together the model of a home.

Rae declared, "If I could afford that place, I'd move in tomorrow."

"For you, special price," Emmett replied. He gently set the roof in place. "How are you, darling?"

"Fine. Why am I here?"

"Gloria called. She's bringing that resort fellow."

That was good for a pause. "Are you talking about Curtis Gage?"

"You know him?"

"Of course I do. And so do you."

Blythe chose that moment to step into the rear office and announce, "Gloria and some guy are walking down the street headed this way."

"That's not some guy," Rae said. There was no reason hearing his name should send her heart into overdrive. "That's Curtis."

"Come inside and shut the door," Emmett said. "Text the realtor lady and tell her we need another moment."

Blythe had always possessed the ability to text and talk at warp speed. "Who's Curtis?"

"You know. Curtis."

Blythe continued to use her maiden name, maintaining the family tradition and reputation. She held to her father's lithe build. But the woman's incredible energy had pushed her up rather than out. She stood almost a head taller than Emmett. It was rare that anything managed to freeze Rae's friend. Like now. "Not *the* Curtis."

"The very same."

"Girl, you mean to tell me *your Curtis* is running the resort?"

Emmett demanded, "You don't mean to tell me we're talking about Iris and Walter's boy."

"I admit it's weird, but yes. That Curtis. And for the record, he's not my anything. Any idea why they're here?"

"Gloria didn't say," Blythe replied. "Only that it's urgent."

Emmett said, "That man is here to stir up trouble. Bound to be."

Rae's immediate response was to defend her former beau. Which was ridiculous. "What makes you say that?"

Emmett responded, "You know about the detective that man had going through our garbage?"

"Blythe said you suspected something like that."

"This goes beyond mere suspicion. It's been confirmed by two people that man's investigator spoke with. Curtis Gage had a former FBI agent inspect us right down to our dental records."

"You accused their resort manager and two sales staff of taking bribes to move projects forward. If I was in their position, I'd want to know who you are." When Emmett didn't respond, Rae said, "I'm not clear on how you've decided Curtis was behind the investigation."

Emmett looked at her. "Maybe I was wrong to call you."

"Daddy, stop."

His gaze did not waver. Emmett Dixon was gifted, intelligent, and determined enough to be both Black and successful in eastern North Carolina. "That man of yours is down here working for the resort. There's only one reason for him wanting to meet us after hours. He's going to threaten."

Blythe was a strong enough woman to keep her father in line when necessary. Like now. "We don't know why he's here. We asked you to join us just in case." Her tone hardened. "Isn't that right, Daddy?"

Emmett pretended to inspect his model.

"Daddy."

"It's good of you to make time," he acknowledged.

Rae's phone chimed with an incoming message. She checked the readout, said, "Now that's interesting." She showed them the screen. "Curtis just asked me for an urgent meeting."

Emmett exchanged a long glance with his daughter, then quietly said, "Now's perhaps a good time to invite them in."

Yet again, Rae found herself drawn to the mystery enshrouding the man she once considered the center of her universe. Curtis remained standing by the doorway, not inserting himself, not uttering a word. Waiting.

Out of the corner of her eye, Rae caught sight of Blythe standing by her father's chair. Her lips were slightly parted, her eyes wide.

Rae swallowed her smile. *Oh yeah. The skinny surfer kid has grown into a beefcake.*

When Emmett did not offer any sort of greeting, Curtis did the gentlemanly thing and pulled out a chair from the table and held it while Gloria seated herself. He was dressed in another of those *GQ* outfits, knit shirt and gaberdine slacks. She thought his thin gold watch was a Patek Philippe, but couldn't be certain from this distance.

Emmett said, "We're here. Now what?"

Curtis remained standing, a pace to one side and behind Gloria's chair. "My company owes you a debt. I'm here to repay."

Emmett snorted softly.

Blythe said, "That's not what we were expecting."

"I can imagine." Curtis held to the stillness of a large cat. "For the record, the New York attorney who gave you such a hard time is no longer involved with our company. That is not the way we do business."

"What about your detective you had checking our dental records?"

Curtis showed neither surprise nor shame. "It was necessary."

"Was it, now."

"To discuss what brings us here tonight, we needed to be certain of who you are."

When Emmett did not respond, Blythe asked, "Who's your lawyer now?"

"I'll have to get back to you on that. We have decided to seek local counsel for all our Carolina activities." Curtis glanced at the model dominating their conference table. "In the meantime, the two plans you submitted to our former team are hereby approved."

Emmett's tone was glacial. "One of those clients has backed out, thanks to you."

"We are aware of that." Curtis met Emmett's gaze. "We want you to build the house as our new model. We agree in advance to your terms and conditions. This is an all-cash offer. How soon can you make it happen?"

Emmett opened his mouth, but no sound emerged.

Blythe said, "Why don't you have a seat?"

"Thank you very much." Curtis remained the total professional. Polite, firm, distant. "But I won't be taking much more of your time. There's just one remaining point."

Blythe asked, "Do you remember me?"

He nodded. "Blythe. Of course. So nice to see you again."

She nodded, visibly pleased. "Been a long time."

"You have no idea," Curtis replied.

She glanced at her father, who continued to give Curtis the squint eye, clearly not certain who this stranger was. Rae totally agreed.

Blythe said, "There's something else?"

"Yes. It's an offer you are welcome to refuse. Our intention is to become a good neighbor to everyone in Carteret County."

Emmett huffed a one-note laugh. "Good luck with that."

Curtis nodded agreement. "We have a long way to go. Which is why I want to have our relationship, yours and ours, become a new standard. Behind the resort gatehouse is the structure holding our management offices. I'd like to invite you to set up the front room as your satellite office."

Father and daughter were almost comic, two mirror images of the same confusion.

Curtis went on, "With no management or sales staff, we

need help, and we need it now. If you are willing, your firm will become the entire approval process for all new homes. We will supply you with written parameters. But the final decision rests with you." He gave them a moment, then added, "We can set this in place for the next twelve months, if you're in agreement."

Blythe's voice had gone all unsteady. "We'll need to discuss this."

"Of course." He looked at Rae. "That request I texted for us to meet. I cannot overly stress the urgency."

"I'm due in Raleigh tomorrow at eight." Rae's voice might as well have emerged from someone else. "I'll be leaving here at half past five. I suppose we could drive up together."

"Thank you. I'll be there." He walked to the exit. "Gloria?"

"I need to stay here and address another item with these fine people," the realtor replied.

He hesitated a moment, hand on the doorknob. Then, "Our aim is to be not just good neighbors, but honorable partners. I'd be grateful if you'd pass that on to all the architects and realtors in your orbit. The resort's former policy of handling sales on an exclusive basis is axed." To the room, "Thank you all for your time."

When the door closed behind him, Blythe quietly demanded, "What just happened?"

Rae did not speak, but silently she repeated Curtis's words: *I'll have to get back to you on that.*

"Something you should know," Gloria said. "This morning, Curtis Gage acquired Reddit Ryder's riverfront acreage in Beaufort. For cash. He met Reddit's price without a quibble."

Emmett huffed softly.

Blythe asked, "Do you know what he plans on doing?"

"Yes. He told me." A dramatic pause; then, "He intends

to build a riverside café and dockside inn. He wants it to model the same architectural structure as the Fortunate Harbor Hotel."

Rae nodded slowly.

Emmett looked over. "What?"

"My guess is, he told Gloria so she could tell you," Rae replied. "He wants you to design the new build. And he's letting Gloria mark up the sale."

"That's my take as well," Gloria agreed. "If you ask me, the man is doing his dead-level best to be as good as his word."

CHAPTER 10

Rae's alarm went off at four-fifteen, an hour earlier than usual. She rose and dressed in sports singlet and running shorts. While she was drinking her morning brew, her phone pinged with an incoming message.

From Curtis Gage.

Confirming his arrival in an hour. Thanking her for allowing him time to discuss an urgent legal matter.

His text was remarkably absent of anything remotely friendly. So unlike the normal sort of Carolina contact, where even the most pressing commercial issues were addressed with polite familiarity. Rae texted back that she had no idea when she would return, she might need to overnight, sorry.

His response was immediate. One word: Understood.

Rae wasn't sure how she felt about Curtis coming along. In the end, though, she decided it was an interesting way to transit from the past to today. As in, firmly set the super-heated teenage romance in her box of fond memories, once and for all. Take this guy at his word. Look at Curtis in the light of what she'd learned from her aunt the previous evening. About Curtis's late wife. And the family that never was. And how he now possessed scar tissue where his heart had formerly resided.

There were any number of things to love about calling Atlantic Beach home. These dawn runs were definitely high on Rae's personal list. The town's out-of-season population was around twelve hundred. The high season was still a month away, and Monday mornings like this held a breathless quality. The air was sparked with a salty chill. Even the birds sounded excited over the day that had not yet taken hold. Rae never ran with earpods. The ocean's faint whisper, the gulls, the silence, all this formed what she secretly called her island symphony.

Any question she might have had about Curtis and his motives were erased the instant she sprinted around the final corner and found him leaning against the fender of a late-model Cadillac mini-SUV.

He straightened at her approach, said, "I really appreciate this."

She leaned over her knees, waved in his general direction. A silent request for breathing space.

But Curtis kept pressing forward. "If you'll allow, I'd like to drive. Free you up to take notes, make calls, whatever is required to move this issue forward. I'll cover the cost of a limo for your return, including any additional stops you need to make, as long as it's required."

Rae straightened slowly, coming to terms with the presence of a man she no longer knew. "Ten minutes."

"Rae, wait." When she turned back, Curtis held out a dollar bill. "Just to make this official."

Rae climbed the stairs to her condo and quickly prepared for the day ahead—a bowl of yogurt and berries and granola left on the counter, taking a spoonful every time she came within reach. She showered and started to don what she had laid out before her run. Then changed her mind and went for her number one courtroom suit, the one used for impressing judge or jury or client. Or an old flame.

Since Rae's law school days, she had carried a vision of her someday home. She had actually bought a property on the outskirts of Beaufort, then sold it when a developer had offered her half again as much as she'd paid. The house would either be old and fully renovated, or new with an old-timey feel. It would possess a huge screened-in porch, protecting her evenings from snakes and mosquitos. She and her friends and her family would sit in rockers beneath slow-motion ceiling fans. They would enjoy the passing hours, sipping spiked lemonade and telling each other lies.

But a major component was missing from that dream, the secret reason why she had agreed to sell her property. Which was also why she remained where she was, living above a dress shop, one block down from her law office.

She liked how Curtis did not try and insert himself into her private world. She liked his calm manner, though it also left her aching at some very deep level. Rae had several clients who were military veterans. Several of the nation's largest bases were nearby, and any number of them retired along the Crystal Coast. Curtis reminded her of them, despite being less than half their age.

She gathered up the notes and laptop and the two files spread across her dining table, stowed them in her shoulder bag, checked her hair in the front hall's mirror, locked her door, and started down the stairs. Curtis was exactly where she had left him, leaning against the SUV and texting on his phone.

"You'd actually cover a limo from Raleigh back here?"

"It's already booked." He finished texting, pocketed the phone, asked, "Does this mean we can take my car?"

Soon as they were underway, even before they crossed the bridge, Rae knew he wanted to launch straight in. Talk about all the pressures that had him tense and running full bore at a quarter past five in the morning. Which was why she insisted, "I need a few minutes to review work related to my Raleigh meeting."

He offered a grudging nod. "Understood."

She shifted slightly, so she rested partly on the side door. She smelled a masculine scent, very faint, little more than woodsmoke on the wind. She opened a file and took a pen from her purse and pretended to review.

Ten minutes later, she admitted defeat. Rae closed the file, stowed it away, and said what was actually foremost on her mind. "We need to talk. And don't you dare pretend you don't know what I mean."

He glanced over. So worried now, he looked almost grim. But at least he didn't say no.

"Emma gave me a partial lowdown on what you've been through. And I'm really, really sorry."

Curtis merely shot her another look. He drove with his shoulders slightly hunched over. As if fearing an incoming blow.

Rae decided the only way this would work was if she launched straight in. About her least favorite subject. Herself.

She said, "Those weeks and months after your forced departure shaped a lot of who I am today. On the one hand, I never wanted to be hurt so badly. Not ever again."

"I understand that," he said. "Better than I could ever possibly say."

"I'm not blaming you. You know that, don't you?"

"Yes. But I'm sorry just the same."

Rae found herself thinking about John, her soon-to-be fiancé, the man who was so perfect for her. Ask anyone. It was the logical next point. But she couldn't bring herself to discuss it. Not with Curtis. Not now.

Instead, she said, "When I look back, those months after

burying your father become all mixed up with you and your mom leaving for Little Rock. I know that sounds crazy, the two events were over a year apart."

"No, Rae. That doesn't sound crazy at all." He was gradually relaxing now. Intent. A vague hint of the man she had once loved there in his gaze now. "It's how I see it, too."

Which made it very easy to continue. "It became this immense time of upheaval. My parents were getting divorced; my dad moved out; my mom thought I was just a brokenhearted teen."

"But it was more than that." Curtis was with her now. Fully engaged.

"Of course, she was right on one level. I was a teen and I was brokenhearted." Rae struggled to encase that hurricane-force tumult in a few words. "I began to ask all the questions I needed to answer if I was going to take control of my life. Begin forming the woman I wanted to become."

"All the hardship you faced split you from the girl you once were," Curtis said. "You were free to redefine yourself."

This was one of the traits she had most loved about him. How she could speak, and he understood not just what she said, but everything that remained unspoken. "One moment, we were so intensely together and in love; the next, your home was sold and your lives packed up and you were gone. In the bad moments, and there were a lot of those, I felt torn apart. But there were secret moments. Quiet hours, usually in the middle of the night, when I felt . . ."

"Tell me."

"I felt relieved. I'm sorry, that must sound so callous."

"It sounds honest, Rae. I felt the same."

"No, you did not."

He weaved his head back and forth, neither agreeing nor denying. "As long as we were together, everything I wanted had to do with us. Then you weren't there anymore. The longer we were apart, the clearer it became . . ."

This time, it was Rae who softly insisted, "Tell me."

"I wanted more. Maybe if we hadn't moved away, I would have been happy to stay here and live the island life. But the longer we were apart, the more I felt drawn to the world beyond those boundaries."

"It's why you didn't come back," she said.

He nodded. "It was. Yes."

"And it's why I didn't beg. When you stopped writing, why I didn't demand answers." Rae studied this man she almost did not recognize, and recalled how her aunt had actually wept as she described the pain Curtis carried. The loss of a wife and mother. The child that would never draw a first breath. She said, "I'm glad we had this talk."

Curtis breathed, "So am I."

Rae wanted to talk about the life he'd forged for himself. But to do so meant treading on the pain he clearly wanted to avoid. So she pulled out the yellow legal pad, turned to a fresh page, and said, "All right. Let's talk work."

Curtis responded almost instantly. "I have two problems. They're so tightly linked, it's tempting to think of them as one and the same. But they're not."

Rae imagined him standing by the car, watching the sunrise and preparing this, like he would a script. "And the first problem is . . ."

"How to bring the locals on to our side."

"By 'our,' I'm assuming you mean the Fortunate Harbor development."

"Correct." He glanced at her. "You don't represent any of the current legal proceedings against us, do you?"

"I don't, no."

"Three are still pending, correct?"

"After the assembly two days ago, my guess is they will drop two. Possibly all three. They were all nuisance claims, put forward by Harvey Sewell as reasons to milk the group."

A tightening of the skin around his eyes was perhaps as close to a smile as Curtis could come. "You don't like the man, I take it."

"He's the reason why the world is full of lawyer jokes," she replied. "Back to your problem one. My professional take is, you've got precisely zero chance of achieving your aim."

Another pursed breath. "My group's long-term goals all depend on proving you wrong."

She settled further. Adjusting to the idea of treating this man as a client. "What is your company's name?"

Curtis shook his head. "I can't answer that."

"Why on earth not?"

"For reasons I can't divulge, I am required to keep that confidential." His words were carefully spaced out, as if he read from a script. "I can tell you the name on the hotel's title. But it's a blind. A Delaware company with no other assets."

"Curtis, I'm your attorney. Which means I'm legally required to maintain strict confidentiality . . ."

He lifted one hand from the wheel. "If we move forward, you will definitely need to know. But not yet. And assuming we move forward, and you hear the reasons, I think you'll agree that secrecy is of paramount importance."

"Okay, one question. Is your group involved in anything illegal?"

"Absolutely not."

"Then why . . ." She stopped midsentence because of how his tension started building once again. "Never mind. Back to your problem one. I take it, you have an idea how to appease the locals."

"Not like, how all the hostility is suddenly going to vanish. But a first step toward proving us to be good neighbors. Yes, I do."

"Second step," she corrected. "I'd say the new beachside park is a move in the right direction."

He shook his head. "That was a trade-off. A solid corporate move. It brought the park service to our side. But the locals who are against us will see it for what it is."

Rae nodded slowly. Not so much because she agreed, which she did. Rather, Curtis was seeing this from an honest perspective. "So, what's your big idea?"

A glance. "This is where you come in."

"Go on, I'm listening."

"Did Gloria tell you about our acquiring Reddit Ryder's place?"

"Yes. But I'm not clear on why you asked Gloria to reveal this acquisition."

He offered another of those lightning-fast smiles. "Oh, I think you know."

"You want her to handle anything that comes from this, and the Dixons will be on point."

"Correct." He glanced over. "I can't tell you how much it meant for Emma to introduce me to Gloria. That is one great lady."

"On that, we definitely agree."

"Now that the sale is concluded, I want this project to break ground immediately. And the news to begin filtering into the community as soon as possible."

She worked through half-a-dozen questions, settled on, "Where's the money for this new café and inn?"

"I've left instructions with our banker. The escrow account should be set up by the time we arrive in Raleigh." He began tapping one forefinger on the wheel in time to his words. "Between the inn and the street, we're putting an oversized secure parking area. Right now, we're running a bus service from Beaufort and Morehead to the hotel. My plan is to also have a water taxi. Three times an hour, six to midnight. Free to all Catawba County locals. Electric buggies on the other end, running to the hotel and the park. If it works, I'm hoping resort owners and hotel guests will also leave their cars on the mainland. Erase any complaint about our adding to the traffic problems."

"Curtis . . . how much will all that cost you?"

"A lot."

When he did not go further, she pressed, "Okay, as your attorney, I need to tell you straight out. It's a great idea, but doing this and trying to keep your group's identity a secret is—excuse the legal terminology here—Curtis, it's totally off-the-wall idiotic."

Curtis did not respond.

"I don't care what your reasoning is. This mystery will soon be part of why so many people are against you. They'll insist your hotel and the resort are all built on illegal gains. Money laundering. Worse."

"I'll inform my superiors of your concerns." As formal as a judge. "That's all I can do."

She was tempted to argue, press, demand. But something in his expression told her it was a futile effort. "Okay, so on to problem two."

This time, his smile lingered. "This is where things get interesting."

CHAPTER 11

Rae was still pondering her drive-time conversation when she was escorted into Dana Bowen's office. Which was beyond wrong. But there was very little she could do about it. The PA asked if she wanted anything, assured Rae the firm's senior partner would not be much longer, and departed. Having Rae wait inside the empty office was just like Dana. Wanting her to know that even on a day short on extra minutes, Rae was not just welcome, but trusted.

Three minutes later, the door opened and Dana walked in. "Rae. What a genuine pleasure."

Rae stood and accepted the half handshake, half embrace, which Dana swiftly offered.

Dana Bowen was everything that Rae might have wanted to become. If only the Crystal Coast had not held her fast.

Dana was North Carolina's preeminent corporate attorney and part-time professor at Wake Forest Law. She swung around her cluttered desk and seated herself. "I want to hear about everything. And I want us to plan a long, leisurely lunch. Preferably after a full eighteen holes. You do still play golf?"

"Badly."

"But today is not the day, for which I am deeply sorry."

"It's so good of you to fit me in."

Dana pushed a trio of files to one side, clearing the center of her desk. A habit that took Rae straight back. A sign Dana was shifting to full-bore intent. "Okay. Tell me what's brought you here."

"Day before yesterday, I met with the county sheriff, my uncle, a man I've known my entire life. He informed me that the DEA recently interrogated him regarding a property where I am the attorney of record."

Dana Bowen was a solid woman, very precise, perhaps the most intelligent person Rae had ever met. Thirty-plus years of corporate litigation resulted in Dana possessing an almost perfect poker face. "Are you under suspicion?"

"They did not say. Only that Colton was not to inform me of their meeting. Which he didn't, until I told him about the issue that's brought me here this morning."

The attorney's crystal-gray gaze was not so much cold as penetrating. "An ongoing investigation by the DEA is not why we're meeting."

"No."

She rose from her chair. "Just a moment." Dana left the room, returned, seated herself, said, "Go on."

Relating the core issue took less than ninety seconds. Even so, it was long enough for the room's atmosphere to shift into a new level of tension. Rae actually found herself relaxing into the pressure. It felt beyond good to have someone share her unease.

Dana had been Rae's favorite professor at law school. She had been one of the very few teachers to transition her lectures from classroom to real life. What it meant to be an

attorney practicing law. The risks a big case carried. Just
like now.

When Rae finished, Dana launched straight in. "Your
power of attorney carries no restrictions. You're certain of
this."

"I went back over the original documents and the adden-
dum last night."

"Let me make sure I understand. Landon Barrett originally hired you to serve as attorney in the purchase of his
Atlantic Beach property with the very strange name."

"Cape Fortune. Named after the bay that his property
fronts."

"You then handled a pair of further acquisitions, when he
purchased the adjoining land."

"Four and a half acres in all," Rae confirmed. "After that
were a couple of minor issues he asked me to handle. Then
the sale of a business in New Bern. And a car rental company based in Fayetteville."

"This was followed by Mr. Barrett granting you limited
power of attorney to cover all necessary expenses related to
the upkeep of his home and land whenever he went away."
Dana was basically resuming her professorial role, feeding
back to Rae the details she had just shared. "Followed nineteen months later by an extension of said document, granting you full and unfettered powers to handle any and all
Carolina-based legal issues whenever he was away."

Rae waited. Here it came.

"This is rare, but not unheard of. You have proven to be a
valued and trusted member of Mr. Barrett's business and
private interests. How much time did he spend in his Atlantic Beach residence?"

"Three, maybe four months each summer."

"And the rest of the year?"

"His primary residence is listed as an apartment on Park Avenue."

"You've tried to contact him there."

"Mail, email, phone. Multiple times. After last autumn's hurricane, I traveled up. I couldn't find anyone who had seen or heard from him."

"So the man effectively vanished over three and a half years ago."

"Four years this August."

"During which time, his Atlantic Beach home has been struck by two hurricanes."

"The first took off part of his roof. Even with the insurance payout, making the necessary repairs reduced his accounts to almost nothing. I threatened the insurance company with a court case. We settled." The memory was a bitter pill. "The house was left in a fragile state because the money simply wasn't there to do everything needed."

"Then last autumn our coast was struck by the hardest blow in decades."

"Tore out windows," Rae said. "Demolished his bayside deck. Shattered three of the northeastern supports. The place is uninhabitable. I brought in two local contractors. Both said it would be cheaper to tear down and rebuild."

"Which leads us to the immediate issue. You hold power of attorney over a ruined house. Your client's accounts are empty. The property taxes are in arrears. The county has now sent formal notice threatening to seize the house. Which leaves you with no option but to sell the property." Dana began nodding slowly, her gaze shifting over the office's far wall, as if reading her summation. "While this is happening, federal agents have questioned the local sheriff about your relationship to the missing client." A pause; then, "You were right to come, Rae."

"I'm so glad you could see me."

"We need to make a careful and well-documented—" Dana was halted by Rae lifting her hand. "Yes?"

"There's one thing more. I have a potential buyer."

"What, already?"

"Since half an hour ago. His name is Curtis Gage, and he's asked me to represent him. Curtis is part of a group and is ready to make a cash purchase. Today." She pointed behind her. "He's waiting in your lobby."

When Rae emerged from the office, Curtis was nowhere to be found.

The secretary positioned by Dana's door offered, "Your guest asked to use the empty conference room."

Rae opened the door to find Curtis seated at the head of a polished oval table. He was bent over and making notes in a small leather-bound notebook, his ears holding white pods. His phone was positioned beside the pad, the screen showing a woman's face. He nodded to something she said, spoke too softly for Rae to hear, then touched the screen and cut the connection.

Everything about the scene was wrong.

Okay, not wrong. Just entirely different. Rae tried to synch what she witnessed with the man she had once loved. And failed.

There was no hint of the sunburnt surfer, the man who held an ability to infect everyone around him with the joyous thrill of life. The ragged shorts and salt-encrusted slaps and rainwashed T-shirt that defined his wardrobe, the shagged haircut, the steady crystal-sharp gaze . . .

Gone.

This stranger was so intent on his notebook he was unaware of her observation. He wrote, pondered, wrote. Turned the page. Studied the blank sheet. Wrote again; this time, a string of numbers. His handwriting was tight, precise. Very self-contained. Very intense. Very . . .

He sighed, closed the notebook, leaned back, and realized she was there in the doorway. Instantly Curtis rose to his feet. "I'm sorry, I was just . . ."

"Working." She stepped forward. It was time to treat Curtis as the client he wanted to become. "You need to understand what is happening."

"Can we move forward with the property sale, that's really all—" He was halted by her upraised hand. "Sorry."

"As an attorney, having the legal authority to act on behalf of a client and using this power are two different things." Under different circumstances, Rae would have smiled at her own words. They came straight from classes with Dana Bowen. "I am able to sell you the estate. My proper disposal of the property has reached a critical point because his accounts are zero, and because the owner has disappeared."

Rae did not realize Dana had entered the conference room until she heard the older woman ask Curtis, "Do you know the current owner?"

"No."

"You have never had contact with him or his representatives before this moment?"

"Absolutely not." Curtis looked from one woman to the other. "What's going on?"

"The sale must happen because property taxes are overdue," Rae continued. "Unless I take this step, the authorities are obligated to place a lien on the estate. I have a duty to preserve my client's assets. This responsibility is more important than holding on to the house."

Curtis demanded, "Is that a yes to the sale?"

"There are extenuating circumstances regarding this estate," Rae said.

"What does that mean, 'extenuating'?"

This time, it was Dana who replied. "Can you provide us with concrete evidence that you are ready to move forward with the purchase?"

Curtis pointed to the phone still resting on the table. "Give me the sale price and I'll have the funds in escrow within a couple of hours."

Dana asked, "Rae?"

"A professional surveyor has valued the property at around three million."

"When was this?"

"Last week."

Dana told Curtis, "You need to come up with your own valuation before we can move forward."

Curtis pointed to his phone. "I hope to have that in a couple of hours."

"Just one moment." Dana now used the ironclad tone Rae had last heard when her former professor had been arguing a case before the federal bench. "Because of issues we cannot divulge, we are required to establish a legal record of these proceedings."

Curtis frowned. "You've lost me."

"We have questions that must be answered to my full satisfaction before any sale can move forward. I suggest we meet here this afternoon. The judge trying today's case has something else on his afternoon docket. I should return by two."

Curtis showed impatience. "This is a strange way to treat a cash buyer when you're facing—"

"Yes or no," Dana said. "I'm due in court."

"I suppose . . . yes."

"I will see you here at two. Be on time." Dana started for the door. "Rae, walk with me."

CHAPTER 12

When Rae and Dana emerged from the office building, a midnight-blue Lincoln Navigator was parked by the entrance. A dark-suited woman rose from behind the wheel and called, "Is one of you Ms. Alden?"

Dana asked, "What on earth?"

"Yes, I'm Rae Alden."

"Ma'am, I'm to tell you that I've been booked for the day. Can I take you somewhere?"

"I don't believe this." To Dana, "Compliments of my new client."

Dana motioned to the young attorney who had accompanied them downstairs. "Take my car and meet us at the courthouse." She slipped into the rear seat beside Rae, settled her case on the middle space, said, "Well, well, well."

"Curtis offered me a limo if I'd let him drive us up. Give me the chance to take notes. I thought, you know, he meant for the ride home."

Dana asked the driver to take them to the federal courthouse, then asked Rae, "What exactly do you know about this new client of yours?"

"We grew up together. His father was sheriff before my uncle. Walter Gage was killed in the line of duty. Curtis moved away when he was seventeen. We lost contact. Yesterday was the first time I've seen him in twelve years."

"At the best of times, I don't like mysteries involving new clients."

"I agree totally."

"So here's what I suggest. We treat this afternoon's meeting as a formal deposition. I'll arrange for my PA to tape the proceedings. She is a sworn officer of the court. This will serve as a counterpoint to any questions we might face in the future."

The band of tension Rae had been wearing since speaking with her uncle continued to ease. "I can't tell you what it means, hearing you include yourself in this."

Dana smiled. "You're handling this very well, I must say. If I had been handed such a situation at your age, I would be in total meltdown."

"Getting there."

"Nonsense."

"About this afternoon. Curtis has said his superiors insist on an extreme level of confidentiality. He's told me he can't even divulge who the ultimate owners are."

"What Curtis and his superiors want and what they get are two very different issues." When Rae remained silent, Dana pressed, "Remember why we are here. The federal authorities are involved. Any hint of impropriety could cost you your license."

"I need to sell this estate. Curtis represents a cash buyer."

Dana glanced at the driver, then asked, "What if he also represents the reason why the Feds are sniffing around?"

"I suppose it's possible. But the issues surrounding my

client's property have been developing since last year's hurricane. Curtis arrived yesterday."

Dana tapped the top of her briefcase, an almost inaudible drumbeat. "So we will be completely up front with our situation and ask him to do the same. Because it is necessary for your own safety. Not to mention clearing the way for a clean transaction."

"That makes perfect sense."

Dana did not speak again until their driver halted in the courthouse red zone. She then told the driver, "Step outside and give us a moment, please."

"Certainly, ma'am."

When the driver exited the vehicle, Dana said, "The property's missing current owner."

"Landon Barrett."

"What can you tell me about him?"

Rae had suspected this was why she wanted a private moment, and was ready. "As big a mystery as Curtis. Bigger. The questions I had regarding my client only grew with time. I worked for him almost four years, and I never felt like I had a handle on who he really was."

"Did Barrett ever indicate or even suggest he was involved in illegal activities?"

"No. Never."

"So describe the man."

"Tall, so skinny he was almost skeletal. But strong. Very unattractive, and didn't care. He was always well dressed, but the clothes, I don't know . . ."

"Tell me."

"I had the impression he bought what somebody else told him to wear. On him, the clothes were almost clownish." She closed her eyes and saw the man so clearly, he might have been standing beside the driver. "He'd show up wearing these expensive suits that just hung on him. Big gold

Rolex with the diamond face, but it rattled on his wrist. His shirts and ties never matched."

"Interesting."

But Rae wasn't done. "His hands were so big, they belonged to a different man. Mid-fifties. Spoke with a light accent, I always assumed it was Jersey or Bronx, you know, one of the outlying boroughs—but he'd taken elocution lessons to get rid of the worst."

"You never asked him?"

"Not a chance." Definite. "With me, Landon Barrett was very soft-spoken. Very polite. Just the same, he scared me. Everything he said or did seemed like he'd measured it out, thought it through carefully."

"I don't follow," Dana said.

"Like he was learning a role. That's the impression I had, right from our very first meeting. This was Landon Barrett practicing to be a nice guy."

Rae opened her eyes and realized Dana was watching her now. Nodding. "You suspected he hid a different face."

"Barrett never gave me any reason to think that. But yes. I always suspected that down deep Landon had a dark side. Dangerous."

"Deadly," Dana suggested.

Rae did not respond.

"Anything else?"

"No. Well, one thing." Rae felt as if the missing owner was watching her expose his hidden depths. "He couldn't get enough of my tales about pirate treasure and the buccaneers who called the Outer Banks home."

Dana was unimpressed. "He liked legends. So?"

"They're not legends. And that's what appealed to Barrett." Rae stared at the empty front seat. "He'd invite me to these cookouts. A dozen or so guys with accents and attitudes to match, you know? Ladies with big hair and a lot of makeup. Sooner or later, Barrett would draw me over to his bar, shoo everybody out to the patio and the grill, and have me retell some of the stories about pirates and Fortunate Harbor. The last Christmas before he vanished, I gave him a framed print of a treasure map showing what local experts considered to be the pirates who most likely used Crystal Coast as their safe haven. I treated it as a sort of joke, you know? He hung it behind his bar."

"All right, I've heard enough." She reached for the door, then said, "Everything you want to know about Curtis Gage, this is your chance. Your job today is to design our inquiry. Set out all the unresolved legal issues as a series of questions that I will ask on your behalf."

"Understood."

But the older attorney wasn't finished. "Which means we are both billing this gentleman for our time, correct?"

"I suppose . . . yes."

"Nothing is off the table. Remember, you're preparing for a worst-case scenario. Your erstwhile client will be speaking on the record. If the Feds invade our space and come hunting for your scalp, this will serve as your one-and-only get-out-of-jail card."

Curtis waited until the limo pulled away, then crossed the adjoining parking lots on foot and entered the indoor-outdoor North Hills Mall. The upscale central avenue was filling with early shoppers and business people from neighboring structures over on break. He bought a coffee, then found an empty trio of benches partially sheltered by potted palms. As he settled, his phone rang with an incoming number he did not recognize.

"This is Curtis."

"Mr. Gage, it's Holly? The driver? My boss said something about you wanting to know what the ladies talked about?"

He had asked the limo service for a report, but had not held out much hope. "Hundred-dollar tip, did they tell you that as well?"

"You bet."

"So let's hear it."

She did a fairly decent job of repeating the discussion between Rae and the Raleigh lawyer. Curtis knew the driver missed some items and didn't care. The core issues were clear enough.

The coming interview was not about him.

They were covering bases. Because the Feds were involved. When the driver finished, Curtis asked, "Did they mention which agency was investigating them?"

"Not that I heard. But like I said, the Feds aren't after those two ladies. It's the property. A missing guy. Or something like that."

"Thanks, Holly. This is most helpful."

"One thing more. They can't figure out who you are. It was kinda vague, but the one lady you used to know talked about you leaving one guy and coming back somebody else."

Curtis nodded. They had that right. "I'm texting the agency now, telling them to add the hundred to my bill."

He cut the connection, sat staring at the nearest plant, readjusting his day. While he was still deliberating, his phone rang again. Joel Blanchard, the private investigator, said in greeting, "I need more time."

"Give me what you have," Curtis replied. "I'm facing a crucial decision and going in nearly blind."

The former agent did not protest further. "So we'll take the lady first."

"Rae Alden."

"She checks out. Top of her class at Wake Forest Law, *Law Review,* interned with a federal judge, which is an indication of a lady on the rise. Was recruited by two big-time firms, but returned to her hometown and set up her private office. Handles mostly small issues, typical of a local lawyer. Has a solid rep, by all accounts. She represented the group opposing your hotel, but when she realized you guys were totally legit, she alerted her clients and backed away. Even the local cops like her."

"Her uncle is county sheriff."

"Yeah, I got that, too. That guy, Colton Knox, is a straight shooter by all accounts. Back to the lady. I've run several investigations in small towns. There's a real chance these questions I've been asking will get back to the target."

"Understood."

"You're okay with that?"

"I'd prefer it not to happen. But it's a risk we need to take."

"Okay, then. This is where we enter the swamp."

Curtis nodded to the palms. "The property."

"Not the place. The current owner." Blanchard's tone hardened. "Because of the time issue, I went straight to my agency contacts. I'm concerned I might have burned bridges."

"Do what you can to repair things. Add it to our bill."

Blanchard eased off a notch. "There's not a lot I can say for certain at this point."

"Anything you can supply is helpful."

"Then we'll start with the lady lawyer. Landon Barrett probably hired her because she's local and has a solid rep. The property in question had been split up between various relatives, all of whom were feuding. Rae Alden managed what apparently was considered an impossible feat. Brought them together, sealed the deal, and kept them happy in the process."

Curtis heard it in Blanchard's voice. "You like her."

"Hard to admit when it comes to any attorney. And that's not what I'm being paid for here. But my gut tells me the lady is a keeper."

Curtis listened to the surrounding noise, the commercial

cavern filled with an almost musical echo. His mind flashed on an image from long ago, Rae seated in the bow of an old fishing trawler, watching for dolphins as he motored out through the Bogue Inlet. Back when they thought such days were theirs forever. He found somber satisfaction in knowing the lady had stayed true to the nature he had both admired and loved. Another breath, and he returned to the present with, "Which takes us back to the current owner."

"About him, I have very little concrete info. He's been missing for some time. How long is vague, somewhere around four years. All I can say for certain is, the man's file is flagged."

"By whom?"

"Not the FBI. Which means I can't access. Might be Homeland. But I doubt it."

"Who do you think?"

"Gun to my head, I'd say it's DEA. There's a certain razor edge to their secrecy. Like they don't trust the other agencies even when the law says they must."

Curtis nodded understanding. "You're concerned they're going to track you down."

"If it's DEA," Blanchard replied, "it's only a matter of time."

"Tell them everything. Sooner or later, we're going to need to clear this anyway. Might as well be now."

"So you're going ahead, despite all this?"

As if in response, his phone chimed with an incoming call. Curtis checked the screen, saw it was Gloria, and told the investigator, "I'll have to get back to you on that." Curtis ended the call, connected to Gloria and said, "Give me one minute."

"I can call later."

"No, it needs to be now." Curtis shot a text to Amiya, requesting a quick phone chat soon as she could manage. Then he clasped the phone with both hands and leaned back. He had known any number of such moments recently, coming into a difficult situation and finding himself abruptly confronted by the totally unexpected. The bigger picture that included a massive risk. A make-or-break decision that impacted not just the project, but his own future.

The thrill was indescribable.

It was as close to a full-on high as he came these days. Riding the wave of risk, charting a course on meager data. Trusting his gut.

Since recovering from the months of booze and antidepressants and whatever illegal drug he could find, Curtis rarely even took aspirin. More than a glass or so of wine risked dredging up the memories. What he once had. The pain of loss. The grim intent he'd known, searching for an empty grave.

He was secretly proud of himself and the way he'd found a way forward. Even though he'd lost the ability to taste life's delicate flavors.

Moments like this felt like a reward for the struggle.

Curtis lifted the phone. "Sorry, Gloria."

"It's just fine." Her voice held the breathless quality of an excited teen. "I have the property assessment."

"Go ahead."

"It's probably not what you were hoping for. But the gentleman I use, he's considered the best on the Crystal Coast." A delicate pause. "I'm afraid he's rather expensive. He had to drop other work to do this first thing."

"I'm scheduled to make a formal offer at two this afternoon." That is, if they decided to go ahead. Despite everything. "Speed is crucial."

"Well." Another breath scented by the prospect of a major sale. "Barry thinks—that's his name, Barry Welker. He's fairly certain this would be the last remaining property of its size along the southern Outer Banks. And because of its history as a commercial fishing center, it carries the deeded right for multiple use. Plus, it's situated adjacent to your resort—"

She was cut off by his phone ringing. Curtis had assigned a special tone to calls or texts from his bosses. It sounded like a giant gong.

"What was *that*?"

"A text from my home office. Hang on." He checked, saw Amiya was available for the next few minutes. He told Gloria, "Skip the windup and go straight to the meat."

"Base line, three and a half. This market, as high as four point seven-five."

"Thank you, Gloria. This is most helpful."

Her voice lifted a full octave. "So, are we proceeding?"

"I need to speak with my superiors. In the meantime, a further question."

"Go ahead."

He carefully tested the words. "I'm catching hints of illegality associated with the property. I have no idea what the reality is, or whether a purchase might taint us or the resort."

She lost her excitement. Whoosh. Gone. "You want me to check this out?"

"Only if you can do so without alerting the market to our interest. You understand?"

"Perfectly."

"A few well-placed questions, only to people you can trust. I'm slated to meet with people this afternoon who can hopefully shed light on this issue. Why don't we plan to meet tomorrow morning and compare notes."

He hit speed dial for Amiya, who answered with, "I'm seated in the back of a very uncomfortable limo, and my youngish driver is dancing on the curb outside my door."

Curtis jumped straight in. "There's a bad smell attached to the property we want to acquire."

"In what way?"

"No idea. Something related to the current owner."

"Who is missing, is that right?"

"Yes."

"So walk away."

"We could. But this represents a one-of-a-kind opportunity."

"For this goodwill mission of yours."

"That's actually a sidebar. An important one. But the more I think about this, the more I feel like we can do something much bigger with this land."

"Yes? Go on. I can watch this staffer do his New York polka for another minute."

Curtis needed two for the telling. Soon as he was done, that very instant, she said, "I like this very much."

"There's a downside."

Amiya chuckled. "You mean, besides the unknown bad odor."

"Because of that. If we go ahead, I'm probably going to be forced to reveal who we are."

She responded with a minute pause, then said, "I am not yet refusing you point blank."

He did his best to explain in briefest detail what he suspected would happen. Just the same, it took another four minutes.

Amiya observed, "My father will probably say this is very not good."

He wanted to press. Tell her how important this move might be. But he knew and liked and respected this woman and her father. If she needed time, Curtis resisted the temptation to push, and waited.

Amiya asked, "When are you scheduled to meet with them again?"

"Around two this afternoon."

She sighed. "And now you are going to wreck my afternoon."

"Amiya—"

"Stop. I understand. You were right to call." Another silence pared down to New York timing; then, "If you're correct in your assessment, if this is indeed what transpires, I need to observe."

"Does this mean—"

"It means I will observe. You will call and put me on speaker and I will assess. Then, and only then, will I decide." There was the sound of a door opening. "And I really must go now."

CHAPTER 13

Having the limo wait while Rae and Dana entered the courthouse held a decadent flavor. Rae had hoped for another semiprivate moment with the Raleigh attorney, but the instant they passed through the glass-and-brass doors and entered the marble-clad lobby, Dana's assistant and three strangers in their best courtroom suits crowded in. Dana bid Rae a sparse farewell and turned her attention elsewhere.

Just the same, Rae found a distinct pleasure to this utterly unexpected turn of events. Rae had planned this as a get-it-done journey. Meet Dana. Lay the just-in-case foundation to shield her if the DEA came knocking. Enjoy a moment reconnecting with her favorite professor. Use this unexpected development as an opportunity to build a new professional relationship.

And return to her small life on the Crystal Coast.

Instead, this had become a day full of surprises. Required in order to fulfill the charges she had accepted by taking on this particular power of attorney. For a missing client. And his property that had been reduced by two recent hurricanes to a very expensive pile of rubble. And who now was the subject of a DEA investigation.

But wait, there's more.

So now her newest client wanted to pay cash for this very same property. Which was not, officially, actually, for sale. Yet.

And then there was the kicker.

This very same new client also happened to be her first flame. The love at the center of her sixteen-year-old existence. Who had then vanished, only to reappear after twelve mostly silent years.

And hey, guess what. This guy has gone from easygoing beach bum to representing some very rich, very mysterious people. And to top it off, Rae's assignment for the next few hours was to formally prepare a series of questions so her all-time favorite prof could peel this guy like an onion. And if Curtis wanted to be her client, he was going to pay for the privilege.

Her phone pinged as she entered the courthouse café. Rae slid into an empty window booth, ordered coffee from a passing waitress, and checked the readout. Her boyfriend and semi-fiancé had texted. John Anders came from old Down East money. Both his parents were professors at the University of North Carolina in Greensboro. They were content and haughty in their regional existence. John had, to say the least, issues. He scorned their ivory-tower complacency. He despised their gatherings of like-minded intellectual snobs. He never actually said it, but he thought his folks were flabby and complacent and lazy, cruising through life at a near-idle speed because they could. Rae thought they were wonderful, but had learned not to say as much.

John had grown into a man his parents simply could not understand. His mother actually referred to him as their beloved cuckoo, secretly deposited in their nest by a roving pixie. They held on to Rae with almost comic desperation, treating her as their last remaining hope to maintain connection with their son the stranger.

John had scraped through university on a tennis scholarship. He occasionally served as instructor at the new hotel. He repaired boats at a relative's marina, taught sailing, crewed for two nationally ranked teams, and lived for his trips to do the impossible. Right now, he was with a clutch of like-minded fitness freaks, hiking the Tehachapi Mountains in California's Mojave Desert.

His text said he was headed out for the day's big hike. They planned to overnight in a local roach motel, eat a meal that didn't come from ready packs. He'd try and call if they had cell service. Hoped she was well and enjoying a fine day. Bang and gone.

Rae tried not to be irritated with his casual offhand manner, which was John's typical method of dealing with her world. They were perfect for each other in so many ways. Sadly, their professional paths were not among the reasons why they were meant to be together.

As so often happened when they were apart and trying to communicate, Rae pushed aside all the unanswered issues, opened the shoulder bag that served as both purse and briefcase, and pulled out a legal pad and her laptop. Then she glanced through the window by her booth and caught sight of her limo idling by the curb.

Oh yeah. Definitely a day for the books.

An hour and a half later, Rae left the courthouse. She wanted to try and beat the heavy lunch crush at her favorite Raleigh spot, the Irregardless Cafe. Despite the early hour, a crowd was already lining up for tables when she arrived. There were probably better ways to grab a rushed hostess's attention than a single woman pulling up in a limo, having a uniformed driver open her door. But this worked well enough.

Rae pretended to ignore the stares and took her place in line. But a few moments later, the hostess announced there was a window table available for one, if that was acceptable. So back she went, through a restaurant full of curious gazes, to what was probably the premier spot. Rae ordered and asked if it might be possible for her waiter to take the driver's order and put it on her bill. Then she filled her sunlit table with computer and phone and pad and notes. Just another day at an off-site office.

Following what was perhaps the most fun she'd ever had at a working lunch, Rae returned to the limo in time for a pair of conference calls. Nothing major, just serving her coastal clients, keeping tabs on a pair of slow-moving cases, riding through Raleigh in style.

Magic.

When Rae entered the law offices, Dana's assistant was already setting up the conference room. Rae seated herself in the lobby and resumed work. Five minutes later, Curtis entered, greeted her, and stood by the outer window, texting. Two strangers playing at their professional afternoons.

The law offices occupied three high floors in a building adjacent to the North Hills Mall. The large outer lobby was a remarkable blend of austere luxury and comfortable furniture. Rae paused from her work and inspected her surroundings. She tried to imagine what it might have been like, had she taken this direction. Dana's firm had actually recruited her, along with a Charlotte firm on the rise and an Atlanta powerhouse. But Rae had never doubted her direction. She was a Down-Easter, an island girl born and bred, destined to remain in the finest place on earth. Her Crystal Coast hometown.

Yet, watching this group of professionals move smoothly through another busy day tugged at her. Here on display was everything Rae's one-woman firm would never contain. Was her dream come true worth not being part of something this potent?

Which brought up the other unanswered dilemma. How she had broken off two previous relationships as they approached what Emma called the marriage stage. Both times, her beaus had refused to promise they would remain permanently fixed in this one place.

Rae glanced down at her phone. There on the darkened screen was the text she didn't need to read again, the latest hello-goodbye from the man who wanted to become her fiancé. John was as firmly fixed to the Crystal Coast as Rae. A big reason for why they were together.

Leading to the question for which she had no answer. Were the reasons for her relationship with John enough to see them through, well, life?

Rae was genuinely relieved when her phone rang. She checked the screen and was astonished to find that it was her aunt. "Emma?"

"Hello, darling. Is now a bad time?"

Rae cupped her phone, leaned over, and spoke softly. "I'm sitting in an elegant lobby waiting for a meeting to start. You won't believe who's standing by the window, not talking to me."

Her aunt replied, "Which is why I'm calling."

"What?"

"I just got a call from Colton. Nola's heard from two friends. Somebody's been asking about you."

Nola was Colton's wife—Rae's aunt—a woman Rae counted among her very finest friends. "Why exactly are you the one telling me this?"

"Because Colton made inquiries. He wants you to know this wasn't some possible new client wanting to check you out. 'Probing' was the word Colton used. He said you'd understand."

"Colton thinks it's the Feds again?"

Emma was clearly enjoying herself. "That was his first thought. And the reason he called me and not you. But what he's learned left him wondering if perhaps it's time to hire a private investigator."

Dana chose that moment to step from the elevator. She stood in the lobby long enough to complete a phone call, surveying the two of them in the process.

Rae followed Dana's gaze over to where Curtis stood by the window, his back to the room, texting. Rae's body straightened with a professional outrage. This was precisely what she needed. A reason to set aside whatever had once existed between them. See this from the perspective of now. Accept the man was a complete and utter mystery.

"Do me a favor and tell Colton I owe him and Nola a huge thanks."

"Was it Curtis?"

"I can't say for certain. But I think yes."

"That dog." Emma was almost laughing now. "That scurrilous mongrel. How dare he?"

"I have to go. Thank you, Emma. So much."

Dana waited until Rae rose from the sofa; then the older lawyer asked, "Everyone ready?" When her PA stepped from the conference room and offered Dana a thumbs-up, Dana said, "Why don't we get started."

Soon as she was seated in the conference room, Rae took her sheet of questions and wrote a new one across the top of the page, bearing down so hard she punctured the paper. Rae handed it to Dana and watched the attorney's expression turn grim. Beyond glad that Dana now shared her outrage.

"Are we recording?" When the PA nodded confirmation, Dana looked across the table at Curtis and demanded, "Have you instructed someone in your employ to investigate Rae Alden?"

"Joel Blanchard is a former FBI agent who specialized in white-collar crime," Curtis confirmed.

"Why did you feel this was a necessary step?"

Curtis hesitated. Just a fraction. But clearly measuring his response. "We're discussing a multimillion-dollar transaction. Tied to a resort where we've recently confronted improper dealings among our own employees. It's only logical that I supply a formal confirmation of the individual responsible for this sale."

It was Dana's turn to hesitate. Rae nodded silent agreement. Curtis responding so directly caught her somewhat off guard. It didn't make things right, not by a long shot. Just the same . . .

Dana glanced at the sheet of questions. Then, "Moving on. We need to have a clearer understanding of who you are and who the group is you claim to represent."

"I represent a cash buyer," Curtis replied. "Is that not enough?"

"In this case, no."

"I approached Ms. Alden to discuss the sale of a property. Nothing more. Can I ask for the particulars involving this . . . 'case,' did you call it?"

"All you need to know is, the sale can only move forward if and when we are fully satisfied with your responses."

Curtis drew out his phone and set it on the table before him. He touched a number, hit the speaker tab. A woman answered before the first ring.

"Yes?"

"It's as we discussed," Curtis said. He described the setting, named Rae and Dana, then said, "If we want to proceed, we have no choice but to answer their questions."

Even over the cell phone's miniature speaker, the woman's voice held a silken quality. Elegant as a French perfume. "You still think this is so important?"

"We need the property," Curtis said. "And something else."

"Go on."

"Sooner or later, this information will need to come out."

"My father would definitely prefer this to happen later. So would I."

"I know that," Curtis replied. "But right now, in this place, we have the opportunity to build allies. This goes far beyond the property's ownership. We are at the point of needing to equip ourselves for the next phase."

Silence.

"The timing may not be as you and your father wish. But moving forward now offers us a guarded entry."

"An interesting way to define this hour," the woman said. "'A guarded entry.'"

"Guarded in that these attorneys are both charging me for their time. Which means everything that is revealed here remains confidential." Curtis looked across the table. "Is that correct?"

Dana glanced at Rae, received her nod, answered, "It is."

"They are now bound by confidentiality," Curtis said. "And something else. We are forging a second item, something your father holds as important as his secrecy."

"And that is?"

"Building trust." Curtis met Dana's gaze and continued. "As you can see, what you're asking forces us to make a highly crucial decision. I need you to explain precisely why this breach of my employer's confidentiality is so important."

Dana glanced at Rae. She did not need to think this one through. Rae told the older attorney, "Go ahead and explain."

Dana matched his formal tone. "Am I correct in assuming your investigator uncovered the DEA's ongoing interest?"

"Joel learned some agency had flagged the file," Curtis replied. "He suspected it was the DEA."

"This requires us to adhere to professional guidelines in case there is evidence of a future potential conflict," Dana said. "Because her client has gone missing and she serves full power of attorney, Rae Alden is effectively serving as principal. This results in the DEA's concerns being directed at her, as well as the absent owner. If the DEA decides laws have been broken by the current owner, and these are tied to the property, Ms. Alden could be held liable."

Curtis shook his head. "That doesn't affect us. We want this estate. Who owned it before us is not important."

"It is if we say it is," Dana retorted.

Whatever he was preparing to say was cut off by the woman on his phone saying, "Curtis."

"Yes?"

"I've heard enough. You may proceed."

He was clearly caught off guard. "Do you need to check with your father?"

"I already have. Tell them everything they need to know."

"We're both a little confused, Rae in particular," Dana began. "The image she presented of you was, well . . ."

"Different," Rae offered. "Extremely."

His response was immediate. "I don't feel comfortable answering personal questions."

The unseen woman's voice emanated from the phone. "Curtis, please, this may actually be a good place to start." When his only response was to drop his gaze to the phone, she went on, "Curtis Gage was recruited straight out of Columbia Business School, where he graduated top of his class. My father had instructed the agency to identify six recent MBA graduates with a specific set of skills and personal traits. Curtis is the only one of those six who is still employed by our group."

Curtis settled his right hand by the phone. Every shift of his fingers revealed a damp smudge on the table.

"A year after he started, Curtis was appointed my father's personal assistant. This is a highly coveted role in our group. It is actually how I began my entry into our group's higher echelon. This marks the individual as someone intended for a senior executive role. Fourteen months later, Curtis was named director of one of the group's smaller divisions. He was . . . How old were you, Curtis?"

He did not respond.

"Well. In any case, he was the youngest division chief ever. My father trusts him implicitly. As do I."

"And your father is—"

Curtis spoke without lifting his gaze. "Not yet."

"Curtis—"

"If the property sale is not moving forward, we don't need to divulge your identities."

The woman hesitated, then said, "It appears we have reached an impasse."

Rae was the one to decide. "We're gathered here and recording this session in case the DEA moves forward with their investigation. We have to show them there is no hint of impropriety."

Dana said, "There are two areas of extreme risk. We must demonstrate that Ms. Alden has been completely aboveboard in the sale, taking no undeserved commission or misappropriating funds. And secondly, we need assurance that the buyer is not perpetrating whatever illegal operations the current owner might have been involved in."

"Very well," the woman said. "Curtis, proceed."

"The family's name is Morais," Curtis said, and spelled it.

"Originally of Calcutta. Twenty-two years ago, they moved their headquarters to Delhi. The CEO is Kurien Morais. The lady on speaker is Amiya Morais, the CEO's only child. Ms. Morais is directly responsible for the family's new North America operations."

The woman added, "The Fortunate Harbor project is the first step in what we hope will become a major new division."

Curtis continued, "Three generation ago, they were South India's largest shipping company. Now they own warehouses, distribution centers, trucking firms, and a large chain of Walmart-style stores operating throughout the Indian subcontinent."

"And ships," the woman added. "Mostly bulk transport, some container vessels."

"Their move into resort hotels is fairly recent," Curtis said. "They acquired the Nayer Hotel chain, sixteen properties, all five-star, located throughout Southeast Asia and the Middle East." He stopped then. Stared at the phone. Waiting.

Amiya Morais said, "Two years ago, my father's elder brother was kidnapped. My father was shot in the attack, but survived. We paid the ransom. My uncle was never found."

Dana said, "I'm so sorry."

Amiya continued, "Years before this incident, my father had decided to try and establish a foothold in the United States. We are all convinced our family's safety and our company's future requires this."

"The attack on Kurien and his brother only accelerated the process," Curtis agreed. "The exact opposite of what these opponents are after."

Amiya went on, "It is absolutely crucial this information not be made public. We have several other North American projects we are considering. Decisions on those will only take place once Fortunate Harbor is running smoothly."

Curtis added, "Some very powerful members of our own organization oppose this shift to North America. We don't know for certain, but we suspect they are looking for a reason to stifle this move before reaching its full potential."

Amiya added, "They are very concerned this will disrupt their power structure. Which is why the Fortunate Harbor project is not directly connected to the existing hotel chain. We can say that we are simply testing the waters. Nothing more. Just the same, they are opposed. Angry. Very, very angry indeed."

"They're searching for a way to sabotage our efforts," Curtis said. "Keep us from showing a profit. Prove to the main board this entire North America venture is a total failure."

"If they hear this new property is available, they'll pay whatever you ask to make it theirs," Amiya continued. "They will do whatever they can to wreck our venture. I would not put it past them to build a competing hotel."

"They will not care about upsetting the locals," Curtis added. "I can't stress that too highly."

When the two of them went silent, Dana nodded slowly. Her response carried a courtroom formality. "We are both very grateful for this gift of trust."

Curtis demanded, "Does that mean we can move forward with the purchase?" When the two women hesitated, he pressed, "Our realtor's appraiser has valued the property at between three and four and a half million dollars. We are hereby offering a million-dollar premium on the top estimate. Five and a half million. But we want to make this happen today—"

"One moment please," Amiya broke in. "Curtis, please take me off speaker."

He cut the connection and lifted the phone. "Go ahead."

Whatever he heard pushed Curtis from his chair. "When, now?"

A silence; then, "Are we clear to proceed with the purchase? Right. Understood. Two minutes."

Curtis lowered the phone, but did not resume his seat. He told Rae, "Something's come up. I can't accompany you back, you'll need to take the limo."

Rae thought he had gone through an almost violent transition during that phone call's short space. The man was now beyond tense. Iron hard, fiercely intent.

"Okay."

"Are we good to go on the property?" His speech was not just accelerated. Each word was precisely carved.

Rae sorted through several responses, and settled on, "There's the matter of payment."

In response, Curtis reached into his back pocket, drew out a check, and wrote hurriedly. "This is my personal account, but it gives you a paper trail. I'll have the funds in place in an hour." He passed it across the table. "Is that acceptable?"

Rae shifted the check over so Dana could see it clearly. As if she needed confirmation that Curtis had just handed over a check for five and a half million dollars.

"Rae?"

"I'll have the papers drawn up and ready for signing tomorrow morning." She looked up. "For the moment, yes, I agree to your price and the sale."

"Outstanding." He glanced at the phone, studying the blank surface. "My boss has decided she needs to come down. Or maybe her father is insisting. Amiya will want to meet you. Can you make time for us tomorrow morning?"

"I'll have to work on my schedule, but I think . . ." She checked her phone schedule, saw the one unchangeable appointment was not starting until the afternoon. "Let's say ten, and I'll have the documents ready."

"Excellent. Let's meet in the hotel's main restaurant." He addressed Dana, "I need a private space."

Dana gestured to the PA. "Turn off the recording, please, and show Mr. Gage to the empty office next door."

"Thank you both." As he followed the young woman from the conference room, he offered them the day's first smile. "I can't say this was a pleasure. But I'm glad we met."

CHAPTER 14

Soon as Curtis left the conference room, Dana declared, "Nothing about that entire episode is what I expected."

"That makes two of us." Rae fought against a wave of unease. "Was I wrong, agreeing to the sale?"

"Absolutely not." Very firm. The senior attorney serving as adviser. "You are being forced into finding a purchaser, and fast. The gentleman in question has offered you above top-market estimate, but only if we proceed immediately."

"It means so much, hearing you use the plural there," Rae said.

"And I, for one, am delighted to be a part of this." Dana rose from her chair. "Let me show you out."

As they passed through the law firm's lobby area, the secretary-receptionist handed Dana a cluster of yellow message slips, three of which were rimmed in red, indicating matters of some urgency. Dana jammed the papers into her jacket pocket. She entered the elevator and stared at her reflection. "May I give you my take on this?"

"Dana, of course."

The elevator pinged. They exited into the lobby, crossed the marble-tiled foyer, and entered the afternoon sunlight. Dana stepped to one side as a trio of chattering office workers left for the day. When they were alone, Dana said, "This might have started as a property sale. Curtis might have had a former federal agent check out your sock drawer. All because of . . . What is the estate called?"

"Cape Fortune. It's an old legend of pirates." Rae stopped when Dana waved the air.

Dana watched the limo driver open her door, rise, straighten her jacket, and wait expectantly. "I'm glad this is happening to you."

"Okay, now you've lost me."

"The very first time you spoke up in class, I thought to myself, this lady is made for great things. When you turned down my firm's offer so you could return Down East, I feared you had made a terrible mistake. Now . . ."

"Dana, what?"

"I stand ready to serve as your number two in any capacity you may feel necessary. Night or day." She offered Rae a butterfly's embrace. "Have a good trip home."

Rae did not walk to the waiting limo so much as float. She drew out her phone and pretended to scroll through messages. When the driver settled behind the wheel, she asked, "Just hold it here a second, please."

"Certainly, ma'am."

Rae could not say exactly why she remained stationary. Only that it felt right to digest what had just happened before she began moving into whatever came next.

She was still seated there when Curtis emerged.

Whatever he had experienced inside the empty office, it resulted in a seismic change. He stopped on the top stair next to Dana and swayed slightly. The man was clearly buffeted by unseen winds. What was equally interesting was how neither person spoke. Or moved. They remained standing there, watching her.

Rae told the driver, "We can go now."

As they pulled away, Curtis offered her an oddly formal farewell. He lifted his right arm and held it stiffly in a ninety-degree angle.

Dana remained there beside him. Motionless.

Rae was tempted to swing in her seat and track them as long as possible. But that did not feel appropriate. The two of them had acted like high-level diplomats, offering their honored guest a professional farewell. Rae watched the driver swing them into eastbound traffic and wondered at why it left her so unsettled. Even frightened. As if they could see farther ahead, around the next bend, to the dangers and shoals and threats that awaited them all.

CHAPTER 15

Curtis followed the attorney's PA from the conference room, entered the neighboring office, and waited for the young woman to close the door. He stood in front of the empty desk, listening to the a/c's quiet sigh. The raw pain of divulging his past had grown somewhat muted over time. It had actually felt rather good for Amiya to answer their questions.

Amiya had taken on numerous such diplomatic-style roles while Curtis had served as her father's aide. The executive infighting had never touched him before that appointment; then suddenly he was in Delhi and part of the parent group's inner circle. From that very first moment, some of the company's leadership had viewed him as a threat. Their response had been vicious, shocking, even frightening at times. India was a land of extremes. The attitude of some executives in a multibillion-dollar corporation reflected the brutal struggle they had endured to reach the top tiers. Amiya's intervention had saved him. Several times.

Curtis had often suspected she had served as guardian and

interpreter at her father's request. Such tactics fit the man. Kurien Morais could remain aloof, take no sides, and play no favorites. Everyone knew Amiya was leaving for America, looking for acquisitions marking the Morais Group's entry into the largest market on earth. She needed allies while building a toehold in this new and untested terrain. Which was also why Curtis thought his opponents had finally, reluctantly, granted him a temporary pass. So long as he didn't stay too long, or grow too close to the old man.

He had not spoken with Kurien since the abduction.

Curtis had reached out twice, once after Kurien was released from the hospital, again the week before they buried Kurien's younger brother. Later that same week, Kurien's PA had instructed him to step back. Curtis was forbidden to attend the funeral. He was to stop reaching out. Delhi was closed to him.

Two years later, it still hurt.

The time in Delhi had been a transformative period. Curtis had never understood the concept of loyalty before then. Not really. Kurien Morais had remained aloof, mostly silent, granting Curtis no direct reason to develop the deep affection he still held. The head of Morais Enterprises was regal in his approach to all his executive staff. Serving as the man's aide for six months was both a test and a gift. In some respects, Curtis never truly understood the full extent of the man's reach until after Lorna's death. Standing there in the Raleigh law offices, Curtis returned to the same realization that had lit any number of dark nights. He had survived and found meaning in his days because of Kurien Morais and his daughter.

The phone rang.

Amiya demanded, "Curtis?"

"I'm here."

"Are you very much alone?"

He knew instantly that something had raised Amiya's stress level. Whenever things grew especially tight, vocal traces of her birthright reappeared. Otherwise, she spoke with a slight New England lilt, a music that had seen him through so much.

"They've given me an empty office. The door is closed."

"Daddy has been held up. He will join us . . . Just a moment, please, I need . . ."

In the silence that followed, he reflected on how strange their connection might appear to outsiders. How this lovely woman was both his boss and a true friend. How the two relationships fit together seamlessly. Because of who she was.

"All right, I'm back," Amiya told him. "I'm so worried. I haven't spoken with Daddy for almost a month. He's never been distant like this before. And then he insists we speak, the three of us, this very moment."

Curtis watched dust motes drift in light streaming through the west-facing window. "I wondered about that, too."

"He listened to our conversation with the attorneys as well."

That was a genuine shocker. "Why didn't you tell me?"

"He said not to. Again, the reasons are beyond me. And before the conversation, when we spoke at long last and I asked him about breaching the confidentiality, do you know what he told me?"

"I have no idea what your father could have said."

"I was to drop everything and fly to North Carolina. Not tonight, not tomorrow. Then and there, Curtis. I spoke with you and the attorneys on the way to Teterboro."

"You had a driver overhear what we discussed?"

"My secretary drove us. Judith is a terrible driver, by the way. Just horrid. When she pulled up in front of the terminal, I was tempted to do like the pope, drop to my knees and kiss the pavement."

"Where are you booked?"

"What an odd question. The resort, of course." A pause; then, "You are not staying there?"

"No."

"Why on earth not?"

"I told you. Simon, the manager, considers me a foe. It seemed best to keep a distance."

"Wait, here is the pilot. I am moving to the plane." There was the sound of conversation Curtis couldn't be bothered to hear, then a rush of airport sounds—jet engines and louder distant voices—followed by silence. "I am flying into New Bern's airport. We'll be landing in—" There were a trio of clicks. "Here is Daddy."

"Curtis, are you there?"

"Yes, sir, I am." He checked his watch, realized his hands were shaking. Three o'clock in the afternoon, East Coast time, was half past midnight in Delhi. "Good evening."

Amiya's father had never been comfortable with small talk. His meetings were often a few minutes long. Less. Kurien began, "You and I share the burden of great loss. The weight we both carry, it is so heavy, no?"

Curtis would never have allowed anyone else to open these wounds. But with Kurien, there was no need to deflect. "I've never been able to speak with you directly and express—"

"Now is not the time, my friend." He coughed weakly. "I asked my daughter to include me in this conversation so that I might listen to what you have said, and what remained unspoken. I heard many things that brought me great comfort. You are healing, and you will soon become healed. That I heard most clearly of all."

The words and the man both confounded him. Kurien's weakened state was glaring. He had always addressed the world in a calm and soothing manner. Even his rages carried a distinct undertone of regret. Now, though, his voice held the fragility of a broken reed.

"Sir . . ."

"My own coming transition is different from yours." A weak cough; then, "I am failing, my dear young friend."

There was a quick sob, a choking sound. Amiya.

Kurien went on, "I have three requests and no one else I can trust them to. That is also what I heard in today's discussion. How I can rely on you."

Curtis found himself infected with Amiya's sorrow. It choked off his ability to respond.

Kurien seemed to have found what he needed in the silence. "Here then are my requests. Three of them, as I said. First, I want to begin the transition now. While I have time and energy to appreciate the tomorrow that may be soon lost to me."

"Daddy . . ."

"Hush now, my dearest child. There isn't time for this. Soon, but not now. Curtis?"

His voice sounded strangled. "I'm here."

"Find me a home. Somewhere private. Not the hotel, you understand?"

"I'll get on this immediately."

"That was the easy part. Here is the difficult. The challenge. Two things. First, do what is refused to me. Accept that you are healing and move beyond your loss. Ready yourself for a new tomorrow."

The need to clench down on the flood caused Curtis to bend over, tight, struggling, sinking slowly until he knelt on the carpet.

"Do not allow fear of this unknown to trap you. Strive to walk the road ahead with eyes and heart open. Live a full life for us both."

Amiya was sobbing now. Curtis found harmony in the sound. A woman capable of weeping for him as well.

"And finally, tomorrow I am formally naming Amiya my successor on the Delhi board."

"Daddy, no!"

"I have done my best to shield her. Our executive board will remain in charge of the operations here. She will serve as overseer from our new U.S. base. She will also vote my shares in the parent group. Upon my death, she will inherit them. You understand what this means?"

"Your nephew." Curtis forced himself to stand. "He doesn't like me."

Kurien might have laughed, or perhaps he simply cleared his throat. "That does not go nearly far enough. Ajeet despises you. Almost as much as he loathes the prospect of Amiya taking charge of any portion of our group. You understand?"

"If Ajeet thinks your daughter might soon be taking control, he will come after her."

"Not directly. That is not Ajeet's way. Who knows what form the opposition will take? Or when they might decide to strike." He paused for a weak but wracking cough. "So. My third request. I am asking you to take care of my beloved child. Help her. Be strong for her. And that is enough for now. I arrive in two days. You may give me your answer then."

The line went dead.

CHAPTER 16

Curtis emerged from the office building to find Dana standing on the top step, staring at where Rae's limo idled at the curb. He stood to one side and slightly behind the older attorney, wanting to hide how he remained rocked by unseen winds. When the limo pulled away, Curtis managed to lift his arm in farewell.

When Dana remained standing there, staring at the sunlit vista, Curtis took that as his cue. "Thank you for the role you've played."

The senior attorney did not speak. Nor did she look his way.

"I suspect you understand what is at stake here," Curtis continued. When Dana remained silent, he went on, "My superiors will probably find it necessary to investigate your background as well."

Dana started back inside. As if she had heard precisely what she required.

Curtis said to her departing back, "Glad we had this conversation."

*   *   *

Curtis became caught in Raleigh's rush-hour traffic and needed three-quarters of an hour to reach the city's eastern perimeter. Soon as the highway opened up, he punched the accelerator. The two-hour drive should have made for a perfect opportunity to digest, reflect, plan. But that did not happen. As he passed the Garner exit, he became trapped by the unexpected. This was the real risk of looking back. Having other elements spring from his internal cage. Only, this time was different. His recollection carried the lilting melody of a woman's true nature. Revealed at the most impossible of moments. Forming a new definition of who they were, and how things remained.

Friends.

In the early days after losing his family, Curtis had consumed empty hours, like he did the booze and antidepressants. Three weeks passed, his unpaid leave a gift from Kurien, who only called once, but texted or emailed every few days. Never more than a few words. Telling him to take what time he needed. Twice, Curtis submitted his resignation. Twice, the CEO simply insisted he come back when he was ready. Both times, the gift and the kindness almost broke him.

The realization grew in stages. It started as a feeble voice that cried softly before dawn, when his nightly doses had run out and the aftereffect dulled his sorrow. By the fourth week, however, it had grown into a dominating uncertainty.

If he did not change direction, and fast, he would soon follow mother and child to the grave. And nothing would have disappointed his late wife more.

He called Amiya.

Afterward, he felt ashamed it had taken him this long to reach out. Ever since Amiya's marriage fell apart and she spent those five hard months in their guest room, she had referred to Curtis's wife by one word only.

Sister.

Amiya had answered before the first ring, her voice almost instantly there. Like she had spent four weeks with her hand poised over the phone. "Where are you?"

The power contained in that connection wrenched him so hard, he could only manage one word. "Lost."

In response, Amiya took over his life.

She moved him into a furnished apartment a block from their offices. Hired a temp to come in, cook a meal, add order and shape to his day. Ditto for the personal trainer. A dawn workout that Curtis still maintained. It was either give up on the booze and the drugs or endure a daily retching agony.

Curtis threw himself into work. From zero to redline in one desperate week. Kurien and his daughter responded with assignments that tested his limits, broke his boundaries, redefined what he could manage. A week in their temporary New York office, a week on the road. On and on. Six months of grueling challenges. His personal trainer phoning in, holding Curtis to the daily predawn routine. Forcing Curtis to treat the hours with the same steady discipline as he did his breathing.

He was vaguely aware that Amiya had cleared out his and Lorna's home. Buying storage units for everything that had belonged to his late wife and their shared dreams. Lorna's home office. Clothes. Personal items.

Crib. Baby clothes.

She had movers strip out every stick of furniture and box up all his personal belongings. Then she waited. Granting him the opportunity to return to their former home when he was ready. So he could enter the place and study the empty canvas. Decide on next steps.

He put their place up for sale the next day.

Eleven months passed.

Somehow his boss had known Curtis was ready before he

could see it himself. Amiya had been standing in his office doorway when Kurien called on Curtis's private line. For the first time since the funeral, his boss asked Curtis how he was faring. And then said it was time for the next step.

They sent him to France.

The wine regions of Bordeaux, to be precise.

The journey had been at the top of Lorna's bucket list. Something they had been planning as their next vacation. Temporarily put on hold when she became pregnant after two years of trying.

Sixteen glorious days. Early June, France's finest season. A cycling tour with guided chateau visits. Wine tastings. Five-star resorts. Michelin-star meals. The tour service took care of his luggage and all peripheral issues. Incredibly expensive. A pure unadulterated indulgence from start to finish.

Amiya must have talked about it with his late wife. There was no other way Kurien could have known. His boss had called that day to tell Curtis he needed to do this. Take the trip for both of them. Say farewell to his previous life in a way that would honor Lorna and his child. Speaking the words with such care and respect that Curtis wept for the first time since leaving the cemetery.

Of course, he went on the trip. How could he not?

New Bern Airport's proper name was Coastal Carolina Regional. Not even the people who worked there used the title. The private air terminal was closed for refurbishment, so Curtis waited in the main arrivals hall surrounded by a sea of green. The U.S. Army Reserve's main training camp was just outside town. Between New Bern and the coast were five other major bases: Marine Corps Air Station at Cherry Point, North Carolina National Guard, Coast Guard Sector Field Office and Station, Marine Corps Landing Field, and USMC Camp Lejeune. The main arrivals terminal was a loud, happy place, full of family reunions and military coming off leave.

Amiya's appearance caused a major stir, but a polite one. Curtis liked how old-style courtesy was still a point of this region's life. People stared, whispered, moved on. Curtis liked that a lot.

At first glance, Amiya was the same as always. She was dressed in a tailored silk-and-cotton business outfit colored in multiple shades of dark silver-gray. Her coppery raven hair was pulled back to show off diamond-stud earrings. Long legs and pianist's hands. Low-slung heels. Fashionable, functional. Her statement of choice. She had a dozen nearly identical outfits.

But Curtis knew at first glance it was all a thin veneer. Inside, the woman was barely holding it together. Her cheeks held the stains of exhaustion, stress, poor sleep, tears. Her smile of greeting was tilted, her dark eyes glazed.

He pecked the proffered cheek, took hold of her carry-on, and said, "You look fabulous."

"I'm hot and I'm wrinkled and I smell like somebody who's been at her desk since four-thirty this morning."

"You smell like a French perfume ad." He pretended to start for the exit, then stopped and asked, "This is all your luggage, right?"

"You know perfectly well I have never—in my entire life—traveled light." She pointed to a uniformed pilot who emerged from the luggage portal pulling two oversized cases. "You are a terrible person and tomorrow Daddy will fire you. I will watch and I will be very happy."

Amiya paused when they emerged from the terminal. She looked around, then up at the dusk-tinted sky, and breathed deep.

Curtis watched her, smiling. "A little different from Manhattan."

"Another universe."

Once they were settled in the car and underway, Amiya said, "I don't want to talk about what we need to discuss. Not now. I'm exhausted."

He nodded agreement. "It's been a long day for me as well."

"Tomorrow it is." She pried off her shoes and settled her feet on the dash. Long hair spilled over the seatback. Her eyes gleamed as she glanced his way. "How has it been for you, coming back?"

He had always enjoyed the lady's delicate, almost musical accent. Even when she pried where no one else was allowed entry.

"Smooth. I've been so busy, there wasn't much time for memories."

"So it sounds. Still, it didn't worry you, this return?" When he was slow responding, she pressed, "This must have been different from your one-day visits during the hotel's acquisition. Facing a crisis situation at the resort, pulling you back into the orbit of people you knew before Lorna. Not to mention that woman from your past."

"How do you know about Rae?"

"Lorna told me. Don't look like that. We talked about everything." She poked his shoulder with a pianist's finger. "How you were lucky to escape that woman's clutches."

"It wasn't like that at all."

"This 'Down East vixen.' That was how Lorna referred to her. She was jealous of this Rae woman."

"That's the stupidest thing I've ever heard you say," Curtis replied.

"And now she's an attorney. Who happens to be handling a property you say we simply must acquire."

"Because we must."

Amiya settled back, catlike. "So, when do I view this perfect property?"

"Tomorrow." This was how it was between them. How it

had been since the very first day he had emerged from that dark cave. Amiya insisted on keeping his late wife part of their conversations. Their lives. Curtis went on, "The estate fills a gap I didn't even recognize until I was standing there."

"Tell me about it."

"I've told you twice already."

"Not about the land and the damaged home. You said it held memories, yes? Tell me about those."

He looked over, took in the wide-open gaze, the liquid flow of her hair, the finely sculpted features, the skin that glowed like sourwood honey in the dusk. And there in that moment, separated from the crushing flow of so much, he recalled, "It was where I fell in love."

She sighed with pure womanly pleasure. "Oh, I do so relish a good story. Did you tell Lorna?"

"Let me think." Curtis felt the smile stretch his features into unaccustomed angles. "Did I tell my wife how I fell head over heels in love with another woman in a particular spot she'd never seen? Hmmm. No, I don't think the matter ever came up."

"And here I thought this would be just another boring drive through Carolina flatland." She faced the sunset highway. "Tell me your secret tale, Curtis."

A series of long-dormant memories became overlaid upon the drive. "Rae and I were snorkeling the waters off Cape Fortune, looking for pirate gold."

"You're making this up."

"It's true. Every word."

She glanced over, studying him. Amiya must have found what she wanted, for all she said was, "So. Pirates."

"Rae was crazy keen on the Carolina pirates. She was born and raised in Beaufort. The town was founded in 1700. About twenty years later, so the legends go, pirates hunting the Spanish galleons started using the Outer Banks as their way station. The place they'd go between expeditions, far from the battles, a safe haven where they could lay low and store their booty. The legends Rae chased were about a lot of them, we're talking at least a dozen. The only two I remember were Stede Bonnet and Edward Teach."

"That name—"

"Stede Bonnet was the Gentleman Pirate, and Edward Teach was known as Blackbeard. There's a house six blocks from where Rae lived, one of the oldest in the state. The official name is Hammock House. But all the locals call it Blackbeard's Home." Curtis pointed through the windshield, out beyond the empty road. "Blackbeard's ship, the *Queen Anne's Revenge,* was sunk off the coast in 1718. The inlet used to be called Topsail, because for years you could still see the masts and highest sails from there."

Her response was a silent gift. This exhausted and semi-shattered woman curled onto her seat. Leaning against the side door. Shifting so she could watch him full on. Becoming comfortable in a manner that Curtis suspected had not been hers to claim for a long, hard time.

He went on, "No one knows when Cape Fortune got its name. But the legends, man, Rae could make them live." Another genuine smile. "My family had a miniature spread west of Morehead, what used to be called a truck farm. It was my granddad's place; my folks built their home on scrubland at the land's farthest boundary."

"Why there?"

"I've told you this before. A misguided sense of loyalty to a family who hated my dad becoming a cop."

"Correction. You've mentioned something and then changed the subject. So another day I will ask and you will tell me the whole sordid story, yes? But for now, back to your first true love."

"Rae and I met in grammar school. Early on, we made what we called a secret camp in the woodlands separating our home from our grandparents—"

"What kind of trees?"

He glanced over, relishing the chance to free her at least momentarily from all the burdens she brought along. "In case you were wondering why I don't tell you stories? It's because you're always interrupting."

She reached over and poked him in the ribs. "The trees."

"Loblolly pine, mostly. Some cyprus and hickory. And dogwoods."

"So this became your childhood haven. Yours and Rae's."

"Right. There was this tiny clearing deep in the woodland, where you could pretend the outside world didn't exist. Or at least didn't matter. We'd build a campfire and Rae would tell these stories, making the legends real. I couldn't get enough of them."

Suddenly the recollections were so vivid, Curtis could smell the woodsmoke. He was back there again.

His smile was a constant thing.

Amiya said softly, "Tell me."

"Rae called this time of year the lightning bug season. I'd stretch out by the fire and watch sparks rise and dance with the bugs. The past and those pirate crews weren't some distant tale. They were alive. There with us. Dancing in the fire's shadows."

When he went quiet again, caught by all the bygone eras, Amiya said, "Cape Fortune."

"If the pirates used any haven near the Bogue Cut, it would have been Cape Fortune." He glanced over. The woman's gold-black gaze only made the memories more intense. "The property surrounds a small bay shaped like the business end of a giant spoon. Entering from the inland waterway meant passing between two sharpish points. The bay itself was sheltered from all but the strongest winds, and the deep water goes almost up to the shoreline. A couple of places, we never actually touched bottom. The water is fairly clear for a brackish cove that close to the Atlantic. We used to go every couple of weeks. The family was gone by then, holding on to their share of the property, but never doing much with it. The original homestead was a jumble of old pilings and broken glass and weeds. Rae asked for a metal detector for her twelfth birthday, can you imagine?"

"I'm trying," Amiya said. She was smiling now. Despite everything.

"That day, we were in her daddy's boat, the tide charts spread across the gunnel. She had talked to some of the old fishermen, trying to figure out the currents that might have been the same three hundred years ago. I basically didn't care how crazy it all seemed. I was just having the time of my life. We were free diving in maybe thirty feet of water, using garden rakes to push through the bottom silt. By the third dive, there was so much gunk in the water I couldn't see my hands, much less something that might have been worth bringing up. Then, all of a sudden, there was this clink."

Amiya leaned forward, so intent it didn't matter she was perched across the central well. Her seat belt's shoulder strap was in the way; so with an impatient gesture, she slipped it off. Curtis wanted to tell her it wasn't safe, but just then, the memories were all consuming. For both of them.

"I shifted the sand with my fingers and came up with something. No idea what it was, only it was round and big. About half my palm in size. I couldn't find Rae, the muck was too thick. I yelled loud as I could, got a mouthful of silty water, and rose to the surface, choking."

"You found it," Amiya said, so close her breath was a heated rush. "Pirate booty."

"I didn't know at the time. But yeah. A Spanish gold doubloon. Gold doesn't lose its luster underwater, and that thing, man, in the sunlight, it was bright as a mirror. Then Rae popped up, her eyes big as the doubloon, shrieking with so much joy and excitement. After years of searching, there it was. The proof she probably thought she'd never find."

"Despite everything," Amiya said. "She was right. And you made it so. For her."

"The look she gave me, the way she held me there in the water . . ."

"The kiss," Amiya said. "Tell me she kissed you."

He just smiled all the harder. "Suddenly I was fearless and invulnerable. Holding that coin . . ."

"Holding her."

"It felt like my entire world just opened up to a new reality."

"And suddenly you were in love." She watched him a long moment, then swung back around, slipped the seat belt into place, fit herself into the seat, and realized, "Amazing. We're already there."

CHAPTER 17

The hour before dawn, Curtis woke from a dream he could not clearly recall. He and Kurien had been discussing the future. The old man had been very worried. As he rose from the bed, Curtis felt nearly consumed by the man's fears. He knew there was no chance of getting back to sleep, so he slipped on shorts and jogging shoes, and went for a run.

The soft footfalls formed a rhythmic pattern that had seen him through so much. During his first months of recovery, it had become as close to a healing meditation as Curtis had been able to find. When the weather was truly awful, he had often been the first client waiting for the gym doors to open. Walking straight to the treadmill, dropping his street clothes in a heap, stepping onto the machine, going full blast. Desperate to run away from the dark.

Now was very different. The air held a salty perfume, so precious he tasted the same soft joy he had known during the evening drive. He was beyond glad that Amiya had joined him. The news of Kurien's health had rocked his world.

He had desperately needed her presence just then. Help him recover from the prospect of losing the man he admired most in the world. Share this moment with someone who understood what the loss would mean.

The morning's humid heat was gathering by the time he returned. He showered, dressed, pulled a smoothie from the fridge, and seated himself at the laptop. When Curtis had first arrived in Morehead City, he had gone directly to the resort and introduced himself to the manager and his deputy. Their coldly polite response to his presence was exactly what he had expected. Joel Blanchard, their private investigator, had warned him of bad blood between the hotel director and many locals. Curtis had resided at the Ramada ever since.

Now that Amiya was here, he needed to relocate.

His corporate status granted him unfettered access to all the hotel's confidential files—accounts, bookings, time sheets, the works. Fortunate Harbor Hotel was officially listed as sold out. But Curtis could see three rooms were still available. This was common practice with most five-star establishments. A few extra rooms were held back, in case a regular guest or VIP made a last-minute request. They were welcomed and charged the maximum room rate.

Amiya had taken the last available suite. Curtis booked himself into a standard room overlooking the main parking lot. By the time he ate breakfast and packed, the Ramada's day staff were on duty. He checked out, explained work was taking him away unexpectedly, and said he'd be back later for items still with their laundry service.

He arrived at Fortunate Harbor an hour and a half early. Curtis pulled into the hotel's main parking area, cut the motor, and just sat there. His bones felt welded to the seat. The conversation with Kurien represented changes beyond his control. Once again he heard the three requests uttered by that frail and failing man. Kurien had not merely passed on a dying wish. He had uttered a life's challenge.

It was only now, sealed into the car's stifling heat, that Curtis realized what had really woken him that morning. The man Curtis admired most in the world was asking him to move beyond. Begin life anew. Because that was the only way he could even possibly do all that Kurien wanted from him. Those three spoken requests, and all the challenges the old man's words represented terrified him. To try, to give it his best, meant fully emerging from his safe haven. And even if he did, there was every chance he would fail.

He remained there, perspiring and worrying and stressed, until his phone rang. "Hello?"

"I've been standing on my balcony, waving at you for *hours.*"

And there she was, leaning out far enough to peer around the building's corner, her free hand making shadows on his windshield.

"Interesting," he replied, "since I only got here five minutes ago."

"Liar. I've gone for a swim and I've walked the beach and I'm bored and I'm desperate for a decent coffee."

"There's this amazing new development called room service."

"You're terrible. People will talk if they see me pound on a strange man's car window. Come get me."

"It's probably best if I meet you in the restaurant." He opened his door. "I'm on my way now."

Rae's night was serrated by lightning strikes. Or so it felt. Every hour or so, she was jolted by a flashing image. She was back in the conference room, seated across from this stranger who had once been the love of her life. She was standing on the office building's front steps, listening to her former professor redefine her future. She was returning home in a limo, restructuring her day so she could meet the daughter of a billionaire Indian who also was her new corporate client.

And so on.

Which was why Rae was already awake when John called at a quarter to six.

"Babe!"

Rae had never much cared for the way he said that word. This morning, in particular, it echoed with hints of having been spoken to any number of young lovelies. Ladies whose names her erstwhile fiancé could not be bothered to remember.

"Good morning, John."

"Sorry about the hour!" His enthusiasm was nearly explosive, a suggestion of the energy John barely managed to keep contained. "This was our one night not camping, which puts me in phone range. We got in sooo late! And some beers were involved. At least I'm pretty sure they were. It's three in the morning here and I'm still foggy."

"I was already awake. How are you?"

John Anders was quite possibly the most handsome man Rae had ever known, and certainly the fittest. He ran with a global crowd of long-distance runners, hikers, climbers, people whose passion for the impossible drew them into a very tight and happy niche. He spent hours and hours planning his treks. Like this one. Two weeks hiking the Mojave Desert mountains. Rae knew because maps and data sheets had adorned his apartment's walls and every flat surface.

Peakbaggers, such treks were called. Rae had gone with him. Once. She considered herself to be immensely fit. She had lasted three days.

Rae told him, "I'm good. Sleepy."

"We're off for a predawn start, watch the sunrise from

Quail Mountain, see the light come to Joshua Tree." He laughed with childlike excitement, John's finest quality. "How's the same old, same old?"

Rae could actually hear the snap. An audible break, sharp as shattering crystal. "*Don't you call it that!*"

"Hey, babe, take it easy—"

"How *dare* you belittle my world? These are *my* passions!"

A silence; then, "Maybe calling you so early wasn't such a good idea."

"How would you like it if I told you to go climb your stupid hill?"

Suddenly she was crying.

"Rae, honey, sweetheart."

She forced her breathing under semi-control. "I'm fine. It's just . . ."

"What?"

"Yesterday was possibly the best and biggest day of my career. A real game changer." A trembly breath. "I'm still exhausted. That's all."

"Then I wake you up and say the totally wrong thing. Which makes me a double idiot."

Right then, all she wanted was to get off the phone. "You're on vacation. Idiocy is allowed."

"So I'm forgiven?"

"Yes. Go climb your silly hill."

She tolerated another abject apology, wished him a good day, then responded to his affectionate words. Heard nothing, felt less. She dropped the phone to her lap and sat there on the edge of her bed, dripping tears.

Rae knew what was happening because she had witnessed similar moments among that group. John would show up in the lobby, one of his mates would ask what was the matter.

John: *I just made my lady cry.*

Friend: *What did you do?*

John: *I said the wrong thing.*
Friend: *Which was . . .*
John: *I wish I knew.*
Friend: *Do I ever know what that's like! Come on, let's go bash some peaks.*
End of story.
For them, at least.
As Rae prepared for her day, one thought in particular returned to her bruised mental state. How nice it would be to talk about this with Curtis. She recalled the way he had listened to her during their drive. How he heard what she could not put into words.
How he cared.

Rae arrived at the Fortunate Harbor Hotel feeling both bruised and fragile. She could not say what about the conversation with John had shaken her so. There had been so many times when John's interest in her world had seemed, well, feigned. As if a good-hearted man was doing his best to understand when Rae spoke Mandarin.
This morning was different. Why? She had no idea. Rae hoped it wasn't simply because Curtis had reinserted himself into her picture. She was ninety-nine percent certain the man held no interest whatsoever in rekindling their relationship. She was also one hundred percent sure it would be the worst move ever. They were both different people. They had moved on long ago. There was no going back. Certainly not for her.
Just the same.
Their conversation on the inland journey, the simple pleasure of being in the company of a man who understood her. Who treated their conversation as so important he willingly set aside his own urgent issues. And *listened.*
Their time together resonated on a very deep level.
Rae had always found honesty with herself, no matter how difficult, to be an essential part of living the life she

wanted. This was not simply having her relationship with John fractured by just another imperfect moment. It was . . .

Was she intent on breaking up? Adding John to the list of failed romances? Despite everything others said about him?

And was this actually, down deep, about Curtis?

Rae had been to the Fortunate Harbor Hotel any number of times. Several of her clients had used it as a temporary base while moving into homes whose contracts she had overseen. She and John had twice eaten in the restaurant. The food was awesome, with prices to match. She loved the place more with every visit. Despite her internal baggage, today was no different.

The project had originated as the vision of a Raleigh consortium. They all had places along the Outer Banks and saw a need for this sort of high-end resort. But they also loved the Crystal Coast's unique charm, the simple way it hid wealth and power behind barefoot strolls and easy days. They envisioned a hotel that married the finest five-star quality with this down-home charm. The architect's concept was a remarkable marriage of Outer Banks simplicity with the finest of hurricane-proof materials. But as often happened, the consortium's finances took a severe tumble long before the project reached completion. Even the locals who had grumbled over these Raleigh folks coming in and messing with their world grew fearful they would be left with a nearly finished eyesore.

Which was when the new mysterious owners stepped in. Local opposition solidified around the idea that New York money was shouldering into their community. Bullies just waiting to foist their will on the Down-Easters.

The prospect of these locals learning the hotel was now owned by an Indian consortium almost had Rae smiling. Despite everything.

Curtis had texted to say they were on the restaurant's veranda. She took the path around the main building and stopped where broad stairs rose to the rear patio. Square parasols sheltered the tables like canvas flowers. The sound of happy families was musical. She spotted Curtis and a beautiful woman seated with Simon Leroux, the hotel manager. She had met the hotel boss several times, and disliked him more with each encounter.

Simon introduced himself by stressing the proper way to say his first name— "See-Moan." According to chatter among locals, he was a recent transplant from somewhere exotic. Réunion was the name that popped up most often, an island off the African coast, where he had run another of the chain's resort hotels. The local business community was forced to be nice to the guy. Rae thought *See-Moan* was just another part of the hotel's PR problem.

Rae stopped where the rising sun struck the first canopy and sheathed her in shadows. She watched as Leroux leaned over so far, he looked ready to crawl into the woman's lap. Fingers of his right hand tapped the table, millimeters from her wrist. He spoke with quiet urgency, pushing hard.

Rae thought Amiya's response was regal. She did not move. She did not draw back. Her face showed nothing whatsoever, a calm mask that might as well have been formed from sunlit wax.

Then it struck her.

Rae was glad she could remain unseen. The image was blisteringly vivid and required time to digest. She studied the two of them, Amiya Morais and Curtis. And realized she had been asking the wrong questions.

Curtis was not simply the boy she had known and loved, grown and matured and developed in an unexpected direction. He had been completely and utterly reshaped. There before her was the answer to an age-old question, could a man ever change. The answer was most definitely yes, but only if fate dynamited him, rendering his former world to ashes.

The question now was, who had Curtis Gage become? Because looking at the two of them seated there, Curtis and Amiya, she realized they were in utter parallel. This was not merely their polished exterior, the way they both looked drawn from some Hollywood set. Nor their magnetic appeal fashioned from a mix of looks and sheen and money and power. This was something much deeper. Whoever Curtis had become, he was a man who existed in utter harmony with this strangely exotic woman.

He showed no more reaction to Simon's urgent pressure than Amiya. Curtis listened with singular focus. He matched Amiya's expressionless response. He gave nothing away. Just as he had in the law office. Except when Dana probed his past. The fracture had appeared then, a single hint of what he had apparently endured.

Rae was very glad for this shadowed moment. She studied herself as much as the trio. Wondering.

Did she have any interest whatsoever in rekindling a romance from long ago? Did he?

She had no idea. All Rae could say at the moment was, this very different individual was dealing with issues that appealed to her. At a heart level, she felt as though there simply wasn't room for anything more.

Which led to the second question.

Did she want to involve herself more deeply in what these people represented? Because this lay at the heart of what the Raleigh attorney had said. Rae was certain of this.

The answer to this was unequivocal.

Rae watched the trio and felt her future beckoning. Observing that tableau sparked an excitement that resonated through her entire being.

Amiya turned her head slightly and spoke a single word.

It was enough for Curtis to rise and walk toward her. Only then did Rae realize they had been aware of her presence all along.

"Thank you for coming," Curtis said. "Sorry to make you wait."

"I can come back later."

"No need." His gestures were formal, the tiniest of bows, a minute wave of one hand ushering her forward. "Please join us."

Simon greeted her arrival with a look of irritated surprise. "*You.*"

"Good morning, Mr. Leroux."

Amiya rose to her feet. "Thank you so much for your time, Simon."

The hotel manager struggled to hide his anger over being dismissed. "You'll discuss the matter with Kurien?"

"As I explained at the outset, my father will be unavailable."

"But this is a crucial—"

Amiya silenced him with a flash of something; Rae had the impression of a frigid door being slammed shut. "If you think it might be of some small benefit, I will try to re-arrange my own schedule and participate."

The hotel manager realized he had overstepped the unseen boundary and fumbled over his reply. "Madame, most certainly, of course, I meant no—"

"Excellent. You will have my response tomorrow." She offered her hand. "I wish you a good day."

Simon offered a fractional bow, spun around, and departed without acknowledging either Rae or Curtis.

Amiya offered Rae her hand. "You must be Ms. Alden."

"Rae. Hi."

"And I am Amiya. Such a pleasure, I can't tell you." The slightest of smiles. "Especially how you rescued us from a conversation that should have been over half an hour ago."

She watched how Curtis first held the woman's chair, then her own. Amiya glanced up and said, "Remind me why Simon is in charge here."

"It was your father's decision."

"I doubt that very much," Amiya replied. "This smells of my dear cousin's subterfuge."

"No comment." Curtis asked Rae, "Coffee? Breakfast?"

"Tea," she replied. "Green, if they have it."

"You really should have an OJ," Amiya said. "Fresh squeezed. Every glass. And a croissant that comes straight from the baking oven."

She tried to match the woman's ceremonial manner of speech. Rae knew it was a feeble effort. But still. "That sounds lovely, thank you."

Instead of signaling to one of the waiters, Curtis crossed the patio and entered the restaurant shadows. Personally seeing to her needs.

Amiya said, "Simon is hosting our first-ever gala in five days. He's heard my father is coming. Simon is desperate for him to serve as official host."

"The big banquet," Rae said. "I've been hearing about that for weeks."

"It's far more than just a banquet," Amiya said. "May I ask what's being said?"

"Something about you charging a thousand dollars a table."

"A thousand dollars per place," Amiya corrected. "And it has been sold out for almost three months. All the money is going to charity. My father is footing the entire bill. Which includes music by a Grammy Award–winning jazz band. Six courses from a Michelin-star chef flown in from Chicago. Wine pairings that culminate with Château Cheval Blanc. And some snobbish wine critic boring everyone with an introduction to each pairing between courses."

"I actually don't know what to say," Rae replied. A thousand dollars. "You're really sold out?"

"Such an event becomes a calling card for the superrich," Amiya said. "Plus, we are offering free tickets to the resort's homeowners."

"It makes sense, Simon wanting your father to play host."

"That is not happening." There was a hint of the same closed door to Amiya's reaction. Then she lifted her gaze and smiled a welcome as Curtis approached. "And here comes your breakfast."

He was followed by a smiling waitress, who settled tea and croissant and OJ and linen napkin and sterling silverware at Rae's place. Only when the waitress departed did Curtis seat himself.

"Taste the croissant. Is that not the most perfect use for butter in the entire world?"

"It's delicious," Rae agreed. "The problem is, I can feel it going straight from my mouth to my fanny."

Amiya laughed, a bell-like melody that drew smiles from other tables. "Listen, why don't you come to the gala? As our guest, of course."

Curtis said, "Amiya."

"Yes?"

"Simon will freak."

"Good."

"You are actually wanting him to perform a manic dance in front of a booked-out hotel and all his staff."

"It serves him right. Don't you agree, Rae?"

She pulled off another feather-delicate shred of croissant. "Something you should know. Simon has been telling some of your local suppliers that he's soon to become part owner."

Curtis shared a glance with the lady, then asked, "We've heard vague rumors. Could you tell us precisely what's being said?"

"I've heard it from several sources. Apparently, Simon likes to emphasize this, show how important it is for these people to stay on his good side."

"Daddy has granted partial ownership to several of our most successful hotel managers," Amiya said. "But he has never mentioned this as an option with Simon. I would know."

Curtis added, "In any case, it's far too early. The hotel still hasn't broken even."

"I hate to say it, but this meshes with my concern over Ajeet having a hand in this." Amiya waved it aside and asked Rae, "Did you hear how that man sniffed at your approach?"

"I'm glad to say I missed that."

"And his greeting. '*You.*'" She told Curtis, "No one deserves to freak out more than Simon. Go tell him to rejoin us. We will make his freaking a public event."

"Not on your life."

"Hunh." To Rae, "Can you imagine the gall of this man? How can Curtis possibly refuse a direct order from his immediate superior?"

"It's easy," Curtis replied. "I've had a lot of practice."

"I shall instruct Daddy to eliminate your bonus for this entire year."

"Your father doesn't pay bonuses."

"No? Well, good. He probably assumes you'll be such a perfect . . . What is the word I'm looking for, Rae?"

"I am legally obliged to pass on that one."

"A wise move, counselor," Curtis said.

Then as Amiya continued her easy patter, drawing Rae into their moment, it struck her. Amiya's banter was a cover. Her gaze, the way she looked his way . . .

The lady was definitely interested in Curtis. And not just professionally, no matter how she might couch her words. A woman knew.

What was more, Rae suspected her former beau was blind to the fact.

Rae allowed herself a momentary inspection. Was she upset? Jealous? Happy for them? What?

She had no idea.

All she could say with any certainty was something about this realization only heightened her fractured conversation with John.

Amiya brought her back into focus by asking, "Would you like to bring your young man?"

Rae hoped her own expression was as calmly blank as her voice. "Sorry, John's away for another ten days."

"Well, I suppose the two of us will simply have to make do sharing this lone escort."

Curtis showed a genuine astonishment. "I'm not going to Simon's gala."

"Of course you are."

"Amiya, that guy considers me a louse from the home office."

"Well, he has that at least partly right."

"Me showing up on your arm will make things ten times worse than they already are." Curtis looked genuinely worried. "And I don't dance."

"Nonsense. I've had you step on my toes any number of times."

"And my tux is seven hundred miles away."

"I'm sure there's a wedding rental somewhere around here," Amiya replied. "No doubt they'll have something in your size. Electric blue, perhaps. With spangles on the lapels."

"Amiya . . ."

She reached over and settled a long-fingered hand on his wrist. Took off her sunglasses. Regarded him with the serious calm of a strong-willed woman. And said, "Curtis. It's time."

Something in her words and manner pushed him back. He would have taken his arm away, but she held him fast.

"How long has it been since you allowed yourself to relax, enjoy, simply take the night off?" When he did not respond, she answered for him. "Almost two years. When my father sent you on the tour of Bordeaux wine country, no? And before that? Four years? Five?"

Curtis did not respond. Rae could not tell if the man even breathed.

She held him fast for another moment, then solemnly repeated, "It's time." Amiya leaned back and released him. "Now then." Speaking briskly. "This will no doubt require fitting in a new table. And if Simon wants me to attend, it will obviously need to be at the head of the room. Or the center. He may decide. How many place settings are there to each table?"

"Amiya . . ." His protest was stifled by the look she shot him. "I think . . . twelve."

"So. You and me and Rae. I think we should also invite the architects, father and daughter, yes? And Simon, of course. That's . . ."

Rae offered, "Six."

Curtis reluctantly suggested, "Gloria Tanner is—"

"The realtor. Perfect. Does Gloria have a significant other?"

"Divorced," Rae replied. "Single mother. Between relationships."

"So now we are seven." Amiya addressed them both. "We have a public relations issue here. Who else can we include that might help us win over the local community?"

"My father's former partner," Curtis suggested. "Rae's uncle. Now sheriff of Carteret County."

"Will he come?"

Rae said, "Colton will absolutely hate it. But his wife, Nola, will be over the moon. He'll come kicking and clawing the earth, but he'll come."

"Excellent. Which makes nine, correct? Three more."

"The mayor of Morehead City has been an ally of mine," Rae said. "He's not exactly on your side. But he's open to persuasion."

"Excellent. And his spouse?"

"Miriam's shrieks of excitement will be audible on this patio."

"Nothing like a little excitement, is there, Curtis?" She ignored his glum silence. "Which leaves one. Who can that be? Anyone?"

He nodded slowly, looking at Rae. "My dearest friend growing up is Rae's aunt. She is an unofficial leader of the Beaufort community."

"You have to let me tell her," Rae said. "Emma will die. Just keel over on the spot."

"And that's our twelve." Amiya made an underhanded shooing motion. "Why don't you go make dear Simon's day?"

Curtis looked ready to argue, but in the end, he pushed his chair back and stood. "Thanks a lot."

When he disappeared inside the main building, Rae took that as her cue and reached for her briefcase. "I have the Cape Fortune purchase documents ready for your signature."

"Leave that for Curtis." Amiya continued to watch the door through which Curtis had entered the hotel.

"I thought that was why you traveled down."

"Ah." Amiya swung back. "Which means Curtis must still be referring to himself as some midlevel corporate lackey."

"Actually, he never really said what his title was."

"When it comes to anything in the United States, Curtis Gage is my father's right-hand man. I suppose you could say I am his superior. But neither of us is concerned about such issues." She resumed staring at the open doorway. "Curtis has full signatory powers. Without limits. He will handle everything to do regarding the resort until we find a suitable replacement as manager."

Rae mentally gave a silent *wow*. Then, "Understood."

"I fear he may well need to take over the hotel as well," Amiya mused. "I've been concerned about the decision to bring in Simon. He has done an admirable job with the hotel itself. But I fear he has become part of why we are having such difficulties with the locals."

Rae took her silence as an invitation. Or request. She decided to answer honestly. "There's a group of locals who will never forgive you."

"But the hotel was already here," Amiya protested. "And in bankruptcy. We simply spruced things up and brought it online."

"When the original developers ran out of money, these folks considered the entire project dead and buried. A few hurricanes and the empty structures would be lost to a king tide," Rae replied. "Then here you come, bringing this five-star resort to life. Not to mention the new five-star housing estate. Which includes land they see as stolen from the state park."

Amiya was intently focused on Rae now. "Tell me why they are so opposed to our project."

"You'd have to be here for a while to understand. This area has for years been a very unique Carolina haven. There's a lot of money here. A great deal of power. But you would never know it. Most of the families who buy homes along the Crystal Coast want to strip away everything that defines them in the outside world. They wear cutoffs and slaps. They are nobodies in the extreme. And they love it."

Amiya was nodding now. "And here we come."

"I have to tell you, the way you've redesigned this place, with the smallish buildings and the understated luxury, it fits in a lot better than anyone ever expected. But these locals, they'll never forgive you for rocking their island world."

"And Simon?"

"There's a second group, you could call them fence-sitters. They'll go either way. Then they meet Simon. His attitude pushes them into joining the ones who want you gone."

Curtis reappeared then, looking very grim. Amiya watched

his approach and greeted him with, "The man is singed, but I can't detect any third-degree burns."

He remained standing. "We need to leave soon if we're going to make our appointment with the architects. Rae, I think it would help a lot if you could join us."

"All right."

He eased himself down, as if coming off a hard slog. "Do you have the documents regarding the property sale?"

"Right here." She lifted the file from her shoulder bag and set it on the table between them.

"Amiya, do you want to check them over?"

"Thank you, but no."

Curtis signed, initialed, signed some more. He handed her the file, did his best to smile, and said, "Pleasure doing business."

As they rose from the table, Amiya asked, "Curtis, would you mind terribly if I traveled into town with our attorney?" She offered Rae a singular look. Woman to woman. "I think it's time for us to become better acquainted."

Neither of them spoke until Rae pulled through the hotel's main gates and drove into Atlantic Beach. This time of day, beachside traffic was heavy, but mostly heading in the opposite direction. Amiya lifted her sunglasses and used both hands to rub her eyes. Rae thought she handled the burden of exhaustion well.

Amiya said, "I thought it was time I offered an apology for Curtis using our investigator to check you out."

"Hearing about that was a shock," Rae agreed. "Why did he?"

"It is a practice my father has employed for years. Perhaps it doesn't suit this place and time. We'll see. But for now, Curtis did the right thing. We are not simply buying a property. We are trying to build a new network of trusted allies. And we don't have much time."

"This time, pressure . . . I'm not clear on what's pushing you to such extremes."

"My father arrives tomorrow." Something about that statement sent a tremor through the woman's entire frame. She pressed one hand to her mouth, breathed, then said, "You need to hear the rest from Curtis. Please."

"Sure thing. Let's change the subject."

"Thank you, Rae."

She was tempted to ask about Curtis, but decided this was not the time. "Can you tell me a little about yourself?"

"Certainly. My mother is from upstate New York and met my father on holiday. I was born in India and lived there until a few days before my sixth birthday. My mother left India and returned to New York. Why she insisted on my coming with her is still a mystery. Even then, I knew she had little interest in being a mother. But something happened between my parents that left her with a bitter fury she still carries. I have no idea what that might be. She refuses to even hear his name. My early pleas to stay with Daddy sent her into such a rage, I can't tell you. After a while, I stopped asking. When I was nine, my mother married a wealthy financier and became what she still is today, a Manhattan socialite. After that I was raised mostly in boarding schools. We meet every now and then and remain polite strangers."

Rae liked the woman's demeanor, her apparent willingness to be completely open. Even when it cost her. "And your father?"

"I spent my summers in Delhi." Her body relaxed, her demeanor shifted. "When my mother tried to make things difficult, Daddy took her to court. My mother never once asked me how things were for me in India. A car service took me to the airport. A kindly driver handed me over to a kindly flight attendant."

"That sounds so sad."

"It was heaven. Spending those months with Daddy was—"

And then, without warning, Amiya was weeping. She stripped off her sunglasses, tossed them on the dash, and mashed her hands to her face.

Rae pulled into an empty space and reached behind her. She searched her bag and pulled out a pack of wet wipes. "Here."

"I must look a sight."

"Your makeup could use a touch here and there." She pulled down the visor and opened the sleeve, revealing the mirror. "Take your time."

Amiya sniffed, blew her nose, pulled out another wipe. "You certainly run a full-service operation."

Rae found it the easiest thing in the world to confess the reason why. "I'm only carrying them because my boyfriend made me cry this morning. I brought these just in case there were aftershocks."

" 'Aftershocks.' I love it."

Rae watched as Amiya worked on her face. The silence was remarkably comfortable. Two friends sharing a hard moment.

When Amiya flipped the visor back up, Rae asked, "How can I help?"

"And that is the perfect question." Amiya reached across the central console and took hold of Rae's hand. "Do whatever Curtis asks. His words are mine. Even if I disagree with him, I will not override his decisions. I am not here to second-guess his moves."

Amiya's fingers were still damp. And cold as ice.

"Noted."

"That surprises you."

"Hearing you two in the conference, and there on the patio, I had that impression. But I didn't, you know . . ."

"Expect me to actually put it in words?"

Rae nodded.

"Daddy trusts him. He relies on Curtis. How can I possibly do any less?"

Rae heard the undertone. The affection. She was tempted to get it out in the open, but she could see Amiya's hold on control was beyond fragile.

She shifted the car back into drive. "We better be going."

CHAPTER 18

Rae stopped by her apartment so Amiya could have an opportunity to fully repair herself. It was a natural component of Carolina courtesy, ushering her inside and offering to make them a pot of herbal tea. Amiya exclaimed over the apartment's beauty, and repeated over and over just how grateful she was for this shared moment. She stood by the hall's entrance, listening with solemn intensity as Rae put the water on to boil and described growing up drinking her aunt's homemade brews.

Rae knew the woman was very close to breaking down again. After Amiya entered the guest bath, Rae stepped to the side window and wondered at a life where another woman's simple act of kindness would be reason to weep.

Rae texted Curtis, said they had become held up by a discussion that proved more important than expected. They'd be a few minutes late, she would explain later; in the meantime, they should go ahead and start without them.

Amiya emerged soon enough, her hair brushed to a silken

glow, her face immaculate. There was, of course, nothing she could do about the shattered gaze.

Rae poured two clay mugs of Emma's brew, handed one over, said, "I've texted Curtis."

"So did I." A sip. "This tastes as wonderful as it smells."

"Growing up, Curtis used to moan every time we approached Emma's. How he might as well boil weeds growing in her backyard." She sipped around her smile. "He would have drunk lye for another batch of Emma's cookies."

Amiya dropped her gaze to the mug. "Curtis."

There it was again. The temptation to poke her nose into something that was not and probably would never be any of her business. So Rae put on her professional voice and asked, "How can I be of service?"

But Amiya was not having any of it. The lovely, strong woman whispered, "I desperately need a friend."

CHAPTER 19

Curtis refused to enter the Dixons' main office without Amiya. There was no reason to begin. Everything was founded upon her presence. Thankfully, Gloria had other business with the father and daughter. Curtis remained stationed by the front window, texting on his phone, putting out minor fires. Until he saw them.

The scene was completely unexpected. The two women, Rae and Amiya, stood at the closest intersection. They were so involved in what Amiya was saying, neither noticed when the light went green. Tourists slipped around them, a steady colorful flow, but they just stood there. Rae's face held an almost funereal cast, so different from her normal gung-ho energy, and Amiya was scarcely any better, solemn as a judge. Then a passing tourist jostled Rae's shoulder, and she jerked as if being forced from some desperate dream. Amiya stopped talking. They stood there through another light, the both of them captured, immobile.

Then they embraced.

When they separated, Rae settled a hand on the other

woman's shoulder and basically guided Amiya across the street. They continued toward the office, stoic and silent and so intensely focused on whatever they had discussed, neither woman noticed him watching.

He stepped back into the room's shadows and waited as they approached the door and stepped inside. Both greeted him with calm and solemn masks, as if whatever had just taken place did not include him.

Curtis knocked on the inner door, stepped back so Amiya and Rae could enter first, and waited while they went through the introductions. He held first Amiya's chair and then Rae's, as formal an act as it was natural. He stepped back, or started to. But Amiya shot him a look. He pulled out the chair on her other side and seated himself.

Amiya began. "Curtis assures me that you are to be trusted. I hope you have decided to accept his offer regarding the establishment of a secondary office and that of serving as the resort's approval process for new builds."

Emmett glanced at his daughter, who replied, "We are honored to accept. Right, Daddy?" When her father remained silent, she continued. "Thank you very much."

"Until a new resort manager is appointed, Curtis Gage is responsible for all operations. I hereby approve all his actions in advance. From this point forward, I will serve as an observer."

Emmett spoke for the first time. "Why is that?"

"Two reasons. There can be only one key decision maker, if we are to move forward as fast as we intend. And need. Speed is crucial. Second, for the moment, I must remain involved in overseeing issues related to our parent group."

She looked at him. Curtis met her gaze and felt as if the mystery he had witnessed on the sidewalk now entered this meeting. There was something different to the way she watched him now. Her lips were parted, her gaze a bottomless well. Curtis had the fleeting impression . . .

She wanted to kiss him.

Absurd. Crazy. Idiotic.

Just the same, the thought set his heart to racing.

All she said was "Please proceed."

Curtis gathered himself and told the room, "We need a home. It should be as close to new as possible. Buy, rent, whatever works."

Gloria pulled pad and pen from her purse. "How large, and for how long?"

In response, he asked the two architects, "If time was more crucial than cost, how long would you need to build the house you already have planned out?

"These days, it's very hard to say," Emmett replied. "Eighteen months to two years would be my initial guess. Maybe longer."

"There are huge supply chain issues," Blythe said.

"And labor constraints," Emmett said.

"We currently have three different homes under construction that we simply can't finish," Blythe said.

"Marble tiles. Appliances," Emmett said. "New exterior wind-rated sliding doors. The buyers are yelling. We're yelling. It doesn't help."

"The suppliers can't even give us a date for when the items will be delivered," Blythe said. "The manufacturers often can't get the necessary parts. Everybody involved is beyond stressed."

"Say we dropped any specific requirements," Curtis suggested. "Roof, tiles, colors, kitchen, everything. Whatever top-rated materials you can get your hands on without delay. Speed without sacrificing quality. Go with whatever is immediately available."

"Spend whatever is necessary to bring in your best skilled labor," Amiya added.

"Pay a top contractor to put everything else aside and

focus exclusively on this project," Curtis said. "How long then?"

Father and daughter exchanged a long look. Emmett asked, "Eleven months?"

"With no back talk or discussions over costs and components? And remember, all the permits are in place," Blythe said. "I think we could do it in seven."

Emmett snorted. "Now you're into pipe dreams."

"Eight, then." To Amiya: "We can't promise, mind. But I think seven or eight is doable."

"We agree," Curtis said. "Right, Amiya?"

"Absolutely. Please prepare the documents."

Curtis told Gloria, "If you have a suitable rental, it's probably best if we ask for a minimum rental period of nine months."

"I know just the place." The realtor was already smiling. "Why don't we take a little trip?"

As Curtis and Amiya departed with the realtor, Rae paused in the Dixons' front office and pretended to check her phone for messages. Blythe passed by the interior doorway, phone to her ear, and shot Rae a grin. She and her father were already talking with building contractors and their principal suppliers. New project, blank check, multiple other opportunities springing to life. It was exciting.

Then a thought struck her.

Rae stepped back to the entry and rapped loudly on the open door. Once she had Blythe's attention, she asked, "Did anybody tell you about the gala?"

Both faces went blank.

"The dinner at the hotel everybody's been talking about," Rae said. "We're invited."

Blythe said to her phone, "I'll call you straight back."

Emmett just hung up.

Blythe said, "That gala is, what, a thousand bucks a pop?"

"Right. We're all going to be at the head table. Guests of Amiya."

Emmett said, "Is it true Chris Compton and his band are playing?"

"Who?"

"Daddy's favorite trumpet player after Wynton Marsalis," Blythe said.

"Who?"

Emmett said, "Lady, you need to get out more."

"Daddy, hush." To Rae, "What are you wearing?"

"I haven't gotten that far."

"Well, you better, unless you've got something hanging in the back of your closet that I haven't seen."

Emmett asked, "Is there a dress code?"

Blythe said, "You've heard the same as me, Daddy. Formal."

"That does it," Emmett said. "I'm not going."

"Don't give me that. You're actually passing up a chance to hear Chris Compton, eat that fine food, meet new rich clients, all because you hate wearing a tie?"

"A *bow* tie. And a tux. Which I don't own."

"Hmph." To Rae, "He's going. Now when are we shopping?"

Emmett pointed to his phone. "In case you've forgotten, we've got work to do."

"Will you give it a rest?" To Rae, "How about later today?"

"Works for me. Can Emma come?"

"That fine lady is invited, too? This day just keeps getting better. Daddy, stop looking like you're having prunes for lunch. You tell Emma we'll be by directly."

CHAPTER 20

Rae called her aunt and enjoyed one of the finest conversations they'd had in years. By the time she cut the connection, Rae's smile felt almost permanent.

She remained where she was, standing by the Dixons' front window, watching the island world drift by. Reliving the morning's big moment. Buoyed and burdened both.

There were two parts to the recollection. The first happened while she and Amiya were still in her living room, drinking tea, defining this new component to their world. Friends.

Amiya confessed what Rae already suspected. "I fear I am developing very deep feelings for Curtis."

Rae sorted through several responses, and settled on, "You *fear* this."

She nodded. "I also fear Curtis does not feel the same. That he has permanently defined our relationship as friends. Nothing more. Permanently." When Rae did not react, Amiya asked, "How do you feel about this?"

This time, Rae knew exactly what needed to be out in the

open. "Okay, first of all, you need to understand something about me. Since we're talking like, you know . . ."

"Like we are already the friends I hope we shall become," Amiya said.

"I missed my share of the subtle gene. If you ask me something, expect a straight answer."

Amiya settled on one of the kitchen stools. "How utterly refreshing."

"So there are two answers to your question. First, how do I feel about our having this conversation? The answer is, I like it more than I can possibly say." Rae was drawn onto the neighboring stool. There for the full confession. "My life here is wonderful. I hope the Crystal Coast is my permanent home. But it's also limiting. You and Curtis represent an opportunity to expand my horizons. Far beyond anything I ever thought might happen."

Amiya took her time responding. "Curtis and I."

"Which brings us to the second part of your question."

"How you feel about Curtis."

"The answer to that is harder. I don't know *what* to feel. Curtis is not the same. Neither am I. Despite the fairly terrible conversation that started my day, I still have a great deal of affection for John. What does this mean?" She breathed around the enormity of this conversation. "I wish I knew. I really do."

"Your honesty is a gift." Amiya's words carried a gentle solemnity now. "This much I can tell you, if it helps with your coming to terms with the man he is now. Curtis has barricaded himself into a very tight cave. A place and way of life where he feels safe. I'd like to help him leave that behind."

Now that the truth was out, Amiya had become immensely calm. Almost distant. Relieved of one great burden. "I can't tell you how nice it is to speak of such things with a woman who knows him. And still cares for him."

"I do," Rae confirmed. "And I probably always will." She gave that the moment it deserved, then added, "But the longer we talk, the more I feel like our relationship, the one in this new version of who we've become, will never move beyond friendship."

Amiya took a long, slow breath. "Thank you for trusting me with this."

"I only just realized it myself."

"Again, thank you." She made a pretense of checking her watch. "Perhaps we should go."

But Rae found herself moving slowly, careful little motions, washing the cups and pot, filled with an unexplained need to say, "I'd like to talk about John."

"Your fiancé."

"And that right there is my problem in a nutshell," Rae said. Folding and refolding the kitchen towel. "He's asked me to marry him. Three times."

Amiya revealed an ability to time her motions to Rae's. A synchronized departure in slow motion. "And you have told him?"

Settling the purse on her shoulder took forever. "I'm not ready."

Rae said what she always did while describing her relationship with John. How he was the most fun she had ever known in a man's company, how this did not change with time. How he did not appear to be the kind to stray, a rare quality among coastal men. How he balanced Rae's gung-ho attitude with a calm steady strength. How he was proud of her desire to work, to achieve, to grow beyond the island's limits . . .

It was not until they left the apartment, and Rae was locking the front door, that she finally said the *other* thing. The reason she had kept from everyone. Until now.

She said to the whitewashed door, "John is safe."

"Ah." Amiya used each descending step as punctuation. " 'Safe' is such an easy word. Just tuck all the things we don't want to look at more closely. Everything locked up inside those four little letters. *Safe.*"

They pushed through the exit and started down the sidewalk. The sunlight felt blinding. Or perhaps it was how Amiya managed to draw out Rae's secret worries. The reasons why she had not accepted John's proposal. The elements she managed to hide even from herself.

Until now.

"Safe for me meant the perfect man to have on my arm," Amiya told her. "He would never challenge my position. He would support my rise to the top job. He would do this and be that. I had it all planned out. Just another project I needed to complete. And I did. We married, the perfect man and I. *Safe.*"

Rae forced herself to move forward. So slowly the tide of tourists broke and fluttered by on either side. She told Amiya, "I hate the way you say that word. It's like a stab to the heart."

"It certainly was for me. My safe little man fit me like a finely tailored suit. But soon enough, the trappings came off. A year and a half after our perfect wedding. That was when I discovered my perfect man's other side. What he did with his secret hours wasn't even the worst part. Or how he had planned this all along. Or why he kept his dark element hidden until he had established his legal hold. Or even how I was forced to divorce him in secret, and make him rich in the process. Because to do otherwise would mean shaming my father's good name. Bad as all that was, what hurt me worst of all was how I had wanted to define my future using that terrible word, 'safe.' If Curtis and Lorna had not been there to catch me, I would probably still be lost."

Rae arrived at the crossroad and could go no farther. She knew the light changed and other pedestrians were forced to flow around them. It made no difference. The calm way Amiya spoke only stabbed deeper.

"Here is what life's cruelest lesson has taught me, my dear new friend. Like it or not, you must be honest. What is that word hiding? What secret fear or ambition or your own dark elements are you desperate not to expose? Because if that is what your version of safe contains, make no mistake. In a marriage, sooner or later, your secrets will all come out."

CHAPTER 21

Curtis followed Gloria's Lexus SUV across the bridge connecting Atlantic Beach to the mainland, then north on 70 and into Beaufort. Most of the late-morning traffic flowed in the opposite direction, toward the bridge and the beach. They made good time.

He drove alone.

As they left the architects' office, Amiya had offered the Dixons such a warm farewell, even Emmett unleashed a rare smile. She then asked Gloria if they might ride together, and shot Curtis a look that said clear as words that he should follow.

He minded, and he didn't mind. On the surface, all this was excellent progress, his boss making friends and influencing everyone with whom she had contact. Just the same, he had questions. As in, what had Amiya and Rae talked about? Because something had happened. The look she had given him, back there in the office—he'd have to be blind not to know there was a definite change in the wind.

He minded, and he didn't mind.

The new high-rise bridge connecting Radio Island to Beaufort entered the town at Gallants Point. Highway 70 then made a sweeping turn west by north, exiting the peninsula much farther inland. Running parallel to the highway was the older Live Oak Street, from which branched off several residential havens, well removed from the heavy tourist traffic that dominated the town's southeastern reaches.

Their destination was a single-story home on North Shore Road, fronting Gibbs Creek. It had been built in the late 1970s and the side facing the road still held a modest and dated appearance. But the current owners had gutted the interior and added two stubby arms framing a new infinity pool. Walls facing the waterfront now held sliding glass doors that vanished into cubbies, so as to offer an uninterrupted waterfront vista. Working fireplaces adorned the living-dining area and master bedroom.

The viewing did not take long at all. Curtis had assumed these three meetings—Rae and the Dixons and finding a suitable rental—would take all day. Instead, they were finishing up in time for a late lunch. Curtis tracked the two women back to Gloria's SUV and mentally began filling the now-empty afternoon. So much needed doing. Two issues, in particular, were time sensitive. First and foremost, would Kurien require round-the-clock specialist care? If so, there were a number of other issues that couldn't wait—hospital bed, nurses trained for residential duty, and so on. They were taking the place furnished, but there was bound to be specialty items he should have on hand.

The second issue was security. While Curtis had been in Delhi, Kurien had never bothered with a full detail. There had been a lone staffer with military training who had served as driver and personal aide. But that was before the attack.

Kurien's brother had been even worse about personal safety. He had scorned the very idea of armed guards, and had referred to them as human hood ornaments. Both brothers had played cricket, trekked the high country, loved the sea and work and family and life. Which made Ajeet's suspicious and narrow-minded nature all the more baffling.

Curtis had no idea what sort of changes had been put in place since the kidnapping. He wished he had thought to ask these things when they had been talking.

Gloria opened the vehicle's rear hatch and used a box of files as her temporary desk. As she set out the rental documents, she described the Charlotte couple who had spent years transforming the home in preparation for their retirement. But an unexpected promotion took them to Oregon and delayed their move to Beaufort. They wanted top dollar; they wanted a huge deposit; they wanted this; they wanted that. Until Curtis arrived, Gloria had thought it would be impossible to meet all the owners' demands.

Amiya stood to one side and waited as Curtis signed the documents and wrote out two checks, one for the deposit and another for the first three months' rent. As they accepted the keys and said farewell to Gloria, Curtis was about to suggest they tell the Dixons that their build time was no longer so crucial. If Kurien was as weak as he sounded, another move in less than a year might actually cause the man harm.

But Amiya was giving him another of those looks.

She showed a rare ability to leave him utterly unsettled. Stripped bare. Like she was inviting him to dive right in and . . .

He asked, "What is it?"

She tasted several responses, or so it seemed to Curtis. But all she said was "Everybody has been telling me about Aunt Emma. You, then Rae, now Gloria. Do you think I might meet her?"

He was certain that was not what Amiya had been thinking. But something about the moment, the *look,* left him mentally incapable of pressing. "Of course."

"Should you call?"

"Not with Emma. My guess is, she's already expecting us to stop by."

Once they were underway, he continued to struggle with how to frame a simple question. As in, what was going on?

Then Amiya interrupted his conflicting thoughts with a question of her own. "Do you remember when you first came to Delhi, and I walked you down the central corridor in Daddy's home?"

Something about her solemn tone, the coming reunion with Kurien, the slow drive through familiar streets, brought the memory up in sharpest detail. "All those old photographs."

"Five generations of my family on display. Back to the days of the Raj. I felt it was so important, introducing you to the people whose invisible hands shaped and molded my world."

The musical note to her voice carried something new, yet familiar. Like he was being reintroduced to something long forgotten. "Will you tell me what's wrong?"

She remained quiet for a time. When she spoke, Curtis had the impression she had shelved his question. At least for the moment. Amiya went on, "I feel like this is what's happened today. I am walking through the corridors of your past. Being introduced to the places and people who framed your beginning. New-old images drawn from both now and a different era."

She waited until they had pulled into the bookstore's parking area to speak again. "Curtis, have you ever wondered how we came to acquire an unfinished hotel on the Outer Banks of North Carolina?"

He cut the motor, swung in his seat, asked, "What kind of question is that?"

"The kind I want you to answer."

"Amiya, of course I know."

She refused to meet his eye. Instead, she slowly shook her head to the sunlit windshield. "You only *think* you do. You assume we sent commercial realtors on a nationwide hunt. Find us a five-star waterfront resort with ample land ready for development. That's what you think."

"Because that's what happened."

She continued shaking her head, a fractional shift, slow as a metronome. "It happened because Daddy and I talked. Two months before the realtors informed us of Fortunate Harbor, he and I met in Delhi and wondered if you might be ready. If you would ever be. Daddy knew what I wanted. And he thought it was time. I was so afraid to hope, Curtis. But Daddy said, 'Have them see if there's a property near his birthplace. See if he can come to terms with the prospect of new beginnings. Make peace with his past and accept a new version of his future.'"

His heart had become a thundering force, a beat so strong it drowned out everything except Amiya's voice. She, by contrast, held to an ethereal calm. Reading from a script months in the making. Years.

He knew she was waiting for him to speak. And would sit there studying the shadow-scripted glass until he did. Ask the question she wanted, *demanded,* that he pose. He had no choice. Far more than the car's rising heat forced out the words: "What is it you wanted?"

"It's quite simple, really." She looked at him. Her eyes were huge, luminous. Her complexion had become parchment-pale, as if all the woman's force was drawn into that bottomless gaze. "I want you to marry me."

CHAPTER 22

Rae stopped at her favorite sandwich shop for lunch. The line was out the door, but one of the counter staff recognized her and brought out her regular to-go—sun-dried tomato and mozzarella with spouts and whole-grain mustard on sourdough, and fresh-brewed green tea. Only today she wasn't in any hurry, so she slipped into an empty chair under the window's awning. She wasn't considering next steps with John, not really. Questions rose and faded unanswered. This vacant hour was given over to accepting what Amiya had said was real.

Safe.

The tragic script of a potential wrong move, the solemn warning, had been written on Amiya's lovely features. Rae sensed a driving need to be brutally honest with herself. At long last.

Rae made a mental list of all the questions and doubts she had previously done her best to ignore. She took the related issues as far as she could, then rose and started toward her office. She didn't have answers. Not really. But taking aim at a decision, recognizing that this was a problem she had to face, left her feeling almost calm.

Then she turned the final corner, and her day took on a drastically different course. One tight glance was enough for everything to snap into frantic clarity.

She jerked back out of sight, took out her phone, and hit the speed dial for Dana Bowen's personal cell.

The Raleigh attorney answered on the fifth ring, long enough of a delay for Rae's heart to approach redline. "Ninety seconds."

"I think the DEA is waiting in my office."

Dana might as well have confronted federal agents on the hunt every day before breakfast, she was that cool. "Tell me."

"Two black Tahoes parked outside my office door, a lady in a dark suit standing on the sidewalk."

"Definitely Feds. Okay, here's what's going to happen. My number two will take over here long enough for me to serve as your attorney of record."

"Thank. You. So. Much."

"I'll shoot you a Zoom connection. If this is for real, text me, then Zoom connect. Don't say a word except to identify yourself until I'm on-screen."

"Dana, I can't tell you—"

But the woman was gone.

As Rae approached, the woman on sentry lifted her wrist and spoke softly. She then stepped back and silently watched Rae enter the building.

Her office was on the second floor. There was a cranky elevator tucked down the service corridor behind the clothing shop. Rae had never used it. She climbed the stairs and found two agents planted on either side of her door.

"Rae Alden?"

"That is correct."

"Candice Styles, DEA. My associate is Carter Rice."

The man said, "How about we do this inside? Assuming your office has a/c. I'm baking out here."

She drew out her phone and texted Dana a single word: Go.

Rae unlocked her door and ushered them inside. She waved them into seats, then entered her private office and returned with her laptop.

Her outer office was a windowless chamber twice the size of her own room, and held an oval cherrywood table she'd found in a garage sale. Rae's part-time assistant was off today, which meant there was no need for them to switch offices.

As she waited for her laptop to boot up, Rae inspected the agents. It was strange to consider them a matched pair, since the woman was Black and the man some mélange of Latino and Anglo. Yet, as she coded in the Zoom connect, that was how Rae thought of them. DEA clones. Same agate-hard gazes, poorly fitting and rumpled dark suits, both already carrying the scent of hard days—at one in the afternoon.

The woman started, "You know why we're here. We want everything you have on Landon Barrett."

Rae shifted her chair so she was seated on the same side of the table as the agents. She positioned the laptop so the agents were the focus. And waited.

The woman continued, "It would go better for you in the long run if you didn't force us to go for a warrant. Which we will."

Soon as Dana appeared, Rae said, "Allow me to introduce Dana Bowen, my attorney. These are Agents Styles and Rice, DEA."

"Have they shown you their IDs?"

"No."

"Which is a breach of ethics, and possibly the law," Dana said.

The agents moved in robotic slowness, presenting the leather wallets first to Rae and then the screen.

Dana demanded, "Why are you here?"

Rae replied, "They want all of my Barrett files."

"We know that is not happening. Rae, shift the camera slightly to the left. Good. You, male agent. Stop trying to slide out of my sight. Now, then. The director of Homeland for the Carolinas is a close personal friend. I know full well he would *never* countenance agents to appear unannounced and demand access to *confidential client files.*"

"We have full authority—"

"I'm not done. This stinks of high-handed Washington tactics. Let me guess. Some ambitious junior deputy assumed you could traipse into a young, small-town attorney's office and bully her into releasing *confidential client files.*"

Silence.

"Please assure your Deputy Director Tyrant this is not happening. Is that clear, or should I ask the regional Homeland director to call and emphasize to your superior how you are all *breaking the law.*"

Neither agent responded. Their only movement was for Rice, the male agent, to slide his chair a fraction farther out of range.

"Please tell me this is not just some federal fishing expedition. That you actually have evidence of this individual's wrongdoing."

"A lot." The woman responded without unclenching her jaw.

The man added, "Two and a half years' worth."

"Sir, if you are going to speak *one word*, you are going to move your chair back where I can see you." Once he complied, Dana asked, "What is the target of your investigation?"

The two agents exchanged a silent communication. The woman replied, "Money laundering."

Dana huffed. "Which probably means this is actually tied to some larger investigation. Correct?"

"No comment." This from Styles.

"So, what you're really after here is a link tying this attorney's client to a bigger fish. Isn't that the real reason why your superior ordered you to travel down here and *break the law*." When neither agent responded, Dana snapped, "*I'm waiting.*"

Both agents remained silent.

Rae broke the stalemate. "All I've done for this client is purchase a property. And now sell it."

Both agents jerked in their seats. Styles demanded, "It's sold?"

"The contract was finalized in my presence," Dana confirmed.

Rice said, "We need to report in."

"What an excellent idea," Dana said.

Styles asked, "Who is the buyer?"

"Sorry," Dana replied. "You are welcome to that information once it becomes part of public record. Until then, these tactics of yours have earned you absolutely nothing. This meeting is now concluded."

"It is perfectly within our right—"

"Good *day*, Agent Styles."

Rae remained seated and mute as the two agents rose and departed. She could almost see the trail of smoke and cinders left in their wake.

Soon as the door closed behind them, Dana said, "You need to warn that young man. Your buyer."

"Curtis Gage."

"And his superiors. Inform Gage I'm fairly certain they'll be coming after him next."

The screen went blank.

CHAPTER 23

Curtis parked in Emma's front lot and rose because Amiya was already out of the car. His body moved, he might have even spoken to the young woman staffing the bookstore, but he operated on autopilot. He followed Amiya down the connecting hall to where Emma was seated at the kitchen table, her computer and sales slips and bills of lading spread over the surface.

Emma greeted them both with a smile and told Curtis, "Why don't you give me and your lady a moment?"

He didn't mind leaving. Emma's smile said it all. Rae and Amiya's conversation back there on the avenue in Atlantic Beach had been about this. Of course, Rae's first phone call after their departure had been to her aunt.

Of course.

Today of all days.

His phone pinged as he walked back through the bookstore. The text was from Jiyan, an Iraqi from a northern Christian tribe, the Yazidi. His family was spread all through northern Iraq, Turkey, and parts of Iran. Jiyan was in his fifties, a former colonel in the Kurdish militia, who had served as Kurien's go-to guy and sole guard since the year after Amiya's mother died. Curtis liked and trusted the man, who was smoothly efficient and clearly devoted to his boss.

The text said simply that Kurien's plane would land in New Bern at eleven the next morning, and this timing included the necessary stopover in Washington to clear customs. Curtis responded with an okay, then asked if an ambulance was required. The response was a long time coming. He entered the sunlit front yard and stood drenched in heat and the magnolia tree's cloying fragrance.

Finally Jiyan responded: No ambo.

Curtis knew he should run through a summary of what they'd lined up. But the phone weighed a thousand pounds, and his fingers simply wouldn't obey his simple commands. His thoughts slowed. Congealed.

Amiya wanted to marry him.

He should have been framing the list he would offer in response. All the reasons why that was a terrible idea. Wrong from every angle.

Except one.

The looks she had been giving him. The way she spoke. The one element he should have recognized before now, which changed everything.

She loved him.

He might have stood there, trapped in the sweltering heat for the rest of his human existence. But his phone rang.

Rae.

He swiped it to voice mail.

Ten seconds later, she called again.

And again.

On the fourth time, he gave in and connected. Curtis wanted to shout at her. No. Scratch that. First he'd demand to know exactly what she had told Amiya. Then he would shout.

But it just wasn't in him.

In the end, it didn't matter.

Rae declared, "I have a problem. A big one. Tomorrow it's most likely going to become a full-blown crisis for all three of us. And Dana agrees."

"Rae—"

"This is urgent, Curtis. And confidential. I'm making this call on Blythe's phone. Despite it being totally off-the-wall illegal, there's a chance my line is being surveilled, or about to become. Where are you?"

Rae's tension washed over him and left him untouched. "Emma's."

"That won't work. I need to discuss this with you and Amiya, now and in private. How fast can you get back to the hotel?"

"No idea."

"I'll meet you there." When he didn't respond, she came close to shouting. "This impacts everything you're trying to put in place. Get a move on!"

Amiya was ready when Curtis reentered and told her that something urgent had come up, they needed to leave. Emma motioned him forward. She pushed herself to her feet, one hand maintaining a trembly grip on her chair's back. When he was within reach, she hugged him. When Emma released him, she settled one hand on his cheek. Just held it there.

Then Amiya received the same. An embrace, a hand to her face, the caring look that had seen him through so much. They departed without a word being spoken.

As they left the kitchen, Amiya slipped her hand in his. Like they had been doing it for years. Like it was natural to pass through the bookshop and enter daylight, with Amiya so close her own heat defied the afternoon.

Chapter 24

Rae parked in the Fortunate Harbor main lot and walked the path around the central buildings, following the text Curtis had sent with Amiya's suite number. When she arrived, Amiya opened the door. Curtis was seated at the dining table, his back to the wall. One glance was enough for Rae to know they had discussed the issue foremost in Amiya's mind and heart.

Amiya asked if Rae wanted anything, then seated herself on the sofa and tucked her feet up underneath. She then looked at Curtis, clearly wanting him to join her. If he even noticed, Curtis gave no sign.

Just so like a guy, Rae thought.

Amiya, on the other hand, exuded a stately calm. It was all out in the open now. The decision was up to him.

Amiya asked Rae, "What is so urgent?"

Amiya's oceanfront suite was similar to the other rooms Rae had seen, only here everything was kicked up a notch. The suite's furniture was polished mahogany and cherry, the oils adorning the walls appeared to be original, and the floor was a lacing of marble and some black ornamental stone. Rae thought onyx. The high ceiling held two blown-glass chandeliers with hand-painted wooden sailing vessels. The floor-to-ceiling glass sliders were open to the ocean's gentle wash. The sea breeze and rattan ceiling fans kept the room fairly cool.

Rae supplied heat of her own.

She paced the room as she described the agents and their confrontational attitude. At the time, Dana's equally severe response had been comforting. A strong ally had put the agents on the defensive. Where they belonged.

Or so Rae had thought then. Now . . .

Rae's recounting of events acted like a tonic on Curtis. He lost the waxen complexion, his eyes cleared, his demeanor and body both tightened. Amiya noticed it as well. His transition gradually impacted her own state. By the time Rae finished speaking, Amiya had swung fully around to observe both him and Rae.

When she went quiet, he asked, "Are you happy with how things stand?"

" 'Happy' is definitely not a word that applies here."

"You know what I mean." Curtis was back in his element. Focused. Intent. "On the surface, Dana has resolved your situation."

"For now," Amiya said.

"Longer than that," he replied, without even glancing her way. Keeping his gaze tight on Rae. "Any plans for future confrontation have been permanently altered. A move regarding either your files or the property will require them jumping through multiple hoops. If you want, Dana can stonewall them forever. So back to my question. Is this what you want?"

His words impacted her on a very deep level. As if his observations began fitting together her jumble of emotions and unfinished thoughts. She actually felt relieved to respond, "I'm not sure."

Amiya asked Curtis, "You have an alternative in mind?"

"I do. Yes." His response was directed at Rae. "But only if you agree."

Rae said, "I want to hear the alternative."

Amiya patted the sofa beside her. "Rae, come sit down." When she settled, Curtis took Rae's place on the tiled floor and started pacing.

"It all comes down to something Kurien loves to say," he began.

"Why make an enemy when it's possible to forge an alliance," Amiya said.

"I'm not suggesting Dana's response was wrong," Curtis went on. "Dana did what was required. A show of strength was absolutely necessary at that point in time."

Rae asked, "And now?"

He nodded, reached the wall, swung around. "Now is different. Assuming your files on this guy are as clear as you claimed."

"Sanitized."

"In that case, why not let them see?"

"I can't . . . and stay inside legal parameters."

"Sure, I get that," Curtis replied. Eyes on the wall up ahead. "But what if a third party could act as a go-between? Say . . ."

"A judge," Rae said.

Amiya asked, "Is that possible?"

The answer was, a certain friend in the Beaufort court-house had already sprung to mind. "In theory."

"An ally of yours goes through the files," Curtis said. "Then on the record, he or she tells the agents there is nothing of interest."

"I like this," Rae said. "A lot."

Amiya asked, "What about our property?"

His response was to circle around the sofa, walk to the open sliders, and stare out over the sunlit sea. "If you ask me, this is the real reason why they came after you in the first place."

Rae said, "I don't follow."

"This is just a guess. But given what you've told us, I think they've found something. Evidence that is tied to one of your client's properties. Right now, they're not certain which. If they knew it was hidden at Cape Fortune, their tactics would have been totally different. Warrants, raids, seizure. The property would have been lost. Permanently."

Amiya's tone sharpened. "We can't let that happen."

"No. We can't."

Rae felt as if the internal fragments suddenly snapped into new focus, completely rearranged by what Curtis had said. "The way those agents came at me, you're saying it was all a blind?"

"That's my take."

In this moment, the real sense of comfort came from how Dana had missed this as well. "They played me."

His eyes remained on the sunlit ocean. His voice sounded beyond calm. As if he was removed from them and the room. Searching. "I could be completely wrong. But I think, yes, they came after you so strong because they need to search the house."

Amiya noticed it, too. "Curtis, what is it?"

"If I'm right, they're off somewhere looking for another way in. And there's a very real risk that whatever they're after is there. Hidden inside that house. So they'll circle around, fashioning some other way to break through these legal barriers Dana has thrown up." He nodded slowly. "They're still on the hunt. They haven't given up. Not by a long shot."

Amiya asked for her, "So, what do we do?"

"There's only one course of action that I can see." He faced the ladies. "We tear it down."

"That makes sense," Rae said. "The house is pretty much a wreck."

"No, Rae. This isn't some pipe dream we put in place when it suits us. Our only hope is to get rid of their reason to seize the property while they're still recovering from Dana's counterattack. We tear it apart *tomorrow.*"

Both she and Amiya responded with an indrawn breath.

"You alert your judge. Then you contact the agents. Tell them you're making these arrangements for them to see the files. It needs to happen tomorrow."

Amiya realized, "This time, it's us who are preparing a blind."

He nodded. "The judge's preview of Rae's documents buys us a little time. Takes their eyes off the target. Momentarily. Nothing more. In the meantime, I alert all the contractors working on the resort property. Drop everything. Bulldoze the Cape Fortune house. Tear it apart. Raze it to the ground. And cart it all away."

Amiya said, "Stripping away any reason they have to search and seize."

"Right." He still had not looked her way.

Rae started to rise. "I need to get things rolling."

"Wait, I'm not done." Once she had settled, Curtis asked, "What if they're right? What if the items they're after are inside the property? Sooner or later, that might come out. There's a risk you'd be permanently labeled as a threat. A lawyer working for the dark side."

Amiya said, "We can't let that happen, either."

"No. We can't," Curtis agreed. "Which means we have got to search the place. *Now.* This afternoon. Because whether we find something or not, the dozers have got to start at daybreak."

CHAPTER 25

Curtis left to begin making plans with the contractors on-site. In order for the demolition to start first thing tomorrow, he needed to handle this in person. Make them understand he was paying for their time. Whatever it took, this had to happen.

Before departing, he passed on Jiyan's text with their arrival details. Amiya suggested she remain at the hotel, try and speak with her father, see if there was anything of a personal nature she might do for him. Curtis said it was a good idea and left.

He had still not met Amiya's gaze.

When the door shut and it was just the two of them, Rae said, "I'm so sorry."

"For what?"

"You told Curtis." It was not a question.

"I went one better. I asked him to marry me."

"You *proposed* to him?"

"What did you expect? That I would say I held him in high regard?"

"No, of course not, it's just . . . You *proposed*." Rae marveled at Amiya's matter-of-fact tone. "And?"

"Just as you saw. He hasn't responded."

"To me, he looked absolutely shattered."

"Which is the best thing I could have hoped for." Amiya managed a weak smile. "Correction. The second best."

"I don't follow."

"Curtis did not dismiss my proposal out of hand. He is taking this seriously. He is examining himself. Facing the terrors he still carries. Asking himself if he is ready to step into a tomorrow shared with me."

Rae shivered. The risk that Curtis might refuse was there in her voice. Amiya did not quite sing the words. More like a poetic lament. "You are the bravest woman I have ever met."

Amiya was seated in a padded chair facing the ocean. She was calm, subdued in a manner that only heightened the woman's regal nature. Rae thought in a world where rest came easy, where her hours weren't shattered by events beyond her control, Amiya might very well be the most alluring woman she had ever known.

Rae was still searching for something more to say when Amiya changed subjects. "I wish you could have known his wife."

That was enough to drive Rae over and settle into a chair of her own.

Amiya was silent so long, Rae thought the woman wasn't going to continue. Then, "Lorna was my very closest friend. A sister I never had. Losing her and the baby robbed the air from both our worlds."

She stared at the ocean, the sky, and scenes lost to Rae. "It happened so fast. When I arrived at the hospital and heard the news, I didn't believe them. I thought the doctors were playing a cruel joke. Two days before, we were shopping for a stroller. She started having cramps while we were driving back. Lorna reluctantly called the doctor, only because I insisted. When I spoke with Curtis that evening, he said she had gone to the hospital for a couple of tests. As unconcerned as I felt. The next thing I heard, she'd been kept there for observation. Nothing more. And then I arrived, thinking I would drive her home. And the doctor told me she was gone. This simply wasn't possible. Lorna and the baby were stolen away? No."

Rae felt as if she had been granted an unwanted glimpse into the transition that had reforged the man she had once loved. The words opened a wound that was not even hers to claim. She watched Amiya because she could not turn away.

"When I went over to help prepare for their funeral, the breakfast Curtis hadn't eaten three and a half days before was still there on the table. Smelling Lorna's perfume in the air left me collapsed on the floor." A struggle; then, "I recovered because I had to."

Rae could no longer see Amiya. Not clearly. "For him. For Curtis."

"My dearest friend could not go forward unless I gave him strength I did not have."

"He loved her so much," Rae said. The words might as well have been scripted in the blurred sunlight.

"In the weeks that followed, he tried to quit, leave our company. I don't even know how many times he submitted his resignation. But my father wouldn't let him. I really didn't understand how important he was to us both, what a role he played in our lives, until my Curtis was not there."

"How long?"

"Four hard and endless months. I almost lost hope. Finally we spoke, and he let me in. And we turned that dreadful corner together." A very hard swallow. "He and Lorna helped me rebuild my world after my divorce. I felt as though I had survived that awful time for this. So I could be there when she was gone from us."

Amiya's words dislodged any number of crystal tears.

"For him to even consider my proposal, my prayer for our tomorrow, Curtis is the brave one. Not me."

CHAPTER 26

The suite's kitchenette held a chromed-out Nespresso machine, and Rae found single serving–sized containers of fresh milk in the fridge. She didn't ask if Amiya wanted a coffee. It wasn't so much about having a beverage as offering comfort. The woman did her best to smile her thanks when Rae handed her a mug and a moist hand towel. Rae cleared her own face as she made a second cup.

When she was ready, she texted Blythe and apologized for not being able to accompany her and Emma on this afternoon's shopping expedition. Emma knew her tastes and size. Her aunt would just have to shop for her.

The text to Emma was even shorter. Rae basically just begged her aunt to find her something that would both fit and suit the occasion. And not to forget shoes.

Rae then phoned the office of Judge Jodi Dwyer, her closest friend on the state bench. Thankfully, the woman was available. Rae's request took less than three minutes. Even so, she had to stop twice and clear her throat. That done, she finished her coffee and placed the call to Dana Bowen.

Describing her conversation and the ideas Curtis had put forward silenced the Raleigh attorney. Dana needed a long moment before she finally said, "That makes perfect sense."

"I agree."

"Actually, I should have thought of this myself."

"That makes two of us."

"So." Another moment. "You've had time to think this through. How do you want to handle the next steps?"

"Judge Dwyer is a friend on the regional bench."

"I know her. Not well. But we've met."

"She's agreed to review the client files. On the record."

"When?"

"Eight-thirty tomorrow morning. I'd appreciate it if you'd call the DEA agents yourself and act as my attorney of record. Tell them we're volunteering this assistance in discovering what role, if any, my client played in a major drug-trafficking case. I've spent hours going through Landon Barrett's files. They're totally clean. I'd like one or both of them to be present so the judge can confirm this."

"Sounds good." A silence; then, "They'll probably want confirmation that the judge had access to Barrett's bank records."

"No problem. Everything related to his Cape Fortune acquisition and all related payments were handled through Wells Fargo accounts. I'll have those with me."

"Okay. Anything else?"

"Yes. Judge Dwyer might be a friend. But she still has hoops of her own to jump through. She required extenuating circumstances to justify her involvement. A simple request, without a warrant to back it up, wasn't enough. I suggested we use this as the starting point to have the court declare Barrett legally dead. He's been gone four and a half years. Vanished off the face of the earth. No living relatives. I know because I've checked thoroughly." She hesitated, then added, "I've wondered about that. You know, asking myself if maybe that wasn't his real name. It would be great if you set that as a condition to their participation. If they discover anything about who this guy really is, they request clearance from Washington to tell us."

"On the record."

"Right. We need them to keep thinking our focus is totally on their original request. Everything comes down to their interest in the files. As if we have no idea what their real motives might have been."

"That definitely works." A breath; then, "This is excellent work, Rae."

"All because Curtis pointed us in the right direction."

"You're the one doing what's required to protect your clients' interests. It's a pleasure working with you, counselor."

She and Amiya were silent as they left the suite and settled into Rae's car and left the hotel. It was the quiet of two friends with no need for small talk. Rae felt increasingly comfortable in the woman's company. As if they had known each other for a substantial portion of their lives. Long enough to have endured the sort of memories that forge unbreakable ties. Which, in a sense, was already the case.

Rae turned north onto the island's main highway, then took the next left into Landon Barrett's former property. She had the same thought she always did when entering Cape Fortune. Tall imperial palms had been planted either side of the long drive, accompanied by blooming shrubs and head-high ornamental lights. But the trees were canted now, as if a giant's hand had swept haphazardly down the rows, tilting them at drunken angles. Most of the light stands were snapped, their lantern tops dangling from exposed wiring.

"This place could be so lovely," Rae remarked.

"It will be," Amiya replied. "If Curtis has anything to do about it."

"He places a lot of importance on locating the marina in this particular cove." Rae gestured to her right. "Which is kind of strange, since the resort already has over half a mile of intracoastal frontage."

"The marina is only a small part of his vision," Amiya said. "But he doesn't want to discuss it with anyone until my father has a chance to see and decide." She pointed ahead. "The marina will go to the right, along with a small secondary clubhouse. Curtis wants the major portion to become a family compound. My father loves his privacy, and he loves people. Since he was injured, his mobility has become very limited. Curtis wants a main house with a large rear deck, where Daddy can sit and watch people enjoy his development. Happy families doing happy things."

Rae was about to say how much she loved the idea, when the house in all its ruined splendor came into view. Three dump trucks and a full-sized bulldozer were already stationed by the home's northeastern corner. But the only person in sight was Curtis. He made no sign he even noticed as Rae pulled up and parked. Rae thought he looked a thousand years old.

Amiya asked, "Would you mind giving us a minute?"

"Of course." Rae rose from the car and headed for the house. The glass wall fronting the ground-floor foyer had been utterly demolished. She did not remember seeing that the last time she had been here; but just then, she could scarcely think beyond the man rooted in the home's ruined garden. As she started to make her way up concrete steps jammed with storm clutter, Rae glanced back. Amiya approached Curtis and started to reach out, then stopped, her hand an inch or so from his shoulder.

Rae climbed, feeling like a child who had glimpsed an adult world that frightened her terribly. She thought of John, her strong and handsome would-be fiancé. The word echoed with every careful step.

Safe.

Curtis stared at the house, but all he could see was his own ruined life.

He knew Amiya was standing beside him. Waiting. Planted by choice in the same muddy earth that held him fast. Because she wanted to be there for him.

He had always admired the way Amiya used her regal calm and astonishing beauty to hide an incredible mind. How she had allowed him and Lorna to witness her at her weakest, when the world shattered her image and her life. How it had been a genuine honor to help her recover and reknit her fractured world. How he had felt a deep kinship to Kurien as well, being there for his only child. How there was no one in his world who meant more to him. How it would be so easy, so natural, to . . .

Coming face-to-face with the raw truth forced the words out. Not much louder than the warm breeze drifting through the trees. But she was close enough to hear him say, "I can't handle losing another love."

Now that the words had emerged, they sounded so lame. So feeble. He hung his head, feeling the old pain clawing at his heart. The fear. The shadows.

Amiya swept him up in an embrace as gentle as it was complete. She kissed his neck, stroked his hair, sang to his ear, " 'To have and to hold, for better or worse, in sickness and health, till death do us part.' I can't promise you more than that."

It was enough to fill his world. The feel of her arms and breath and body was a soothing unguent that silenced his fears. For the moment, it was enough.

They might have stood there for hours, Amiya embracing and Curtis doing his feeble best to respond. But Rae called through the shattered window overhead, "Sorry to break up your tryst. But you both need to get up here."

CHAPTER 27

The ground-level chambers were a mess. Curtis did his best to focus on the structure. Even though it felt as if Amiya's arms still held him.

The first hurricane had struck in the standard central-Atlantic pattern, crawling up the coastline until high-altitude atmospheric pressure shoved its course inland. All the east-facing walls took a hammering, but Curtis thought they had probably held.

The basic rule of thumb was, a hurricane's direct impact aged a structure ten years. But the problems with Cape Fortune only started with this aging process.

The necessary repairs weren't done because the money wasn't there, and the insurance payout had not yet arrived. That was another rule of life among homeowners in a hurricane zone: Never wait for the insurance check. Get it done. Get it done. Roof and windows first, then mold, then everything else. Get it done.

Then the second hurricane struck.

This time, the eye hovered over the island's northern region for almost nine hours.

Hurricane winds are strongest around the eye, and almost as damaging as the winds are their direction. As the eye slowly drifted northward, the house was first struck from the east, and then from the west.

Hour after hour of being trapped and exposed and hammered. The inland waterway developed ocean-sized waves that wrecked the piers and bulkhead, then flooded the grounds and weakened the support pillars.

Up close, Curtis could mentally track the pattern of destruction. The home's ground-floor walls were a jumbled wreck. Two sides of the four-car garage were gone entirely. Which was probably what forced the outer pilings to give way. The water turned the walls and support beams into battering rams, shoving at the pillars until they bent, tilted, and dragged the entire house to an angle.

Rae called down, "I'm waiting here!"

"Coming."

The garage had taken up most of the downstairs, and resulted in the main entrance being placed significantly off-center. The glass entryway was history. The laundry room, storage facilities, and what had probably been a workshop were in tatters.

The foyer's interior wall and the home's main staircase were all steel-reinforced poured concrete and formed part of the upper floor's support. They were riven with cracks where the foundations had shifted, but otherwise remained intact.

Curtis stepped through the glassless front door. Amiya followed. As he threaded his way through the debris, Rae called, "Hold it there!" She aimed her phone at them. "Okay, one more step toward the stairs. Amiya, move in closer to Curtis. Good."

She fiddled with her phone, then started, "This is Rae Alden, attorney for clients . . ." Rae lowered the phone. "Who should I state as the property's buyers?"

Amiya asked, "Is this necessary?"

"Yes, it absolutely is, and you'll soon see why."

Curtis said, "Use my name. I'm signatory on the deed and purchase contracts."

"Okay, here we go." She aimed the phone, gave her name, identified Curtis, then waved them forward. "My client is entering the property for the first time."

Three steps up, Curtis realized what was the problem.

Chapter 28

Four hours later, Rae was seated at the desk in her home office. The final remnants of a lovely spring sunset scattered rose-tinted clouds beyond her window. Down below, tourists laughed their way along the island avenue. She emailed the court reporter, who also served as Judge Dwyer's personal assistant, and alerted her to an incoming video that would be required at the hearing. She went through the edited video a final time, tweaking a couple of places, shortening it down to seven minutes and eleven seconds. Judge Dwyer was notoriously impatient when it came to evidence and testimony.

Her phone rang.

The screen said it was John Anders.

She hesitated a long moment, mostly gauging her own response. What she mostly felt was a mild irritation over his wanting to insert himself into an overfull day.

When the call went to voice mail, Rae attached the recording to a brief email and sent it off.

John called again.

As she closed her laptop, Rae found herself thinking back to the scene she had witnessed outside the property. The way Amiya's words and embrace had somehow reshaped Curtis and his world. At least for that one brief moment.

The phone went quiet. This time, John called straight back.

She answered and did her best to sound glad to hear from him. "Sorry, sorry, I was in the middle of something. How was today's hike?"

"Fine. It was fine." John's voice was quiet. Somber. "Crowded with thoughts. Sometimes I think best when I'm pushing myself. You know how it is."

Something about his tone, the directness, whatever, elevated Rae's heart rate and stripped away any need for a cheery tone. "Yes, John. I know."

"What you told me, it's made me look at what I've done my best to avoid seeing."

Rae opened her mouth, but no sound came. No apology, no desire to reassure and avoid what she knew was coming. Nothing.

"You were right, what you said. And what you didn't say. But this time, I heard it anyway. We're just not meshing like we should." He coughed. "You're pushing hard as you can toward goals that . . ."

"They don't mean anything to you," she completed for him.

"No, they don't." Knowing she was there with him accelerated his words. As if he could hear her racing heart and tried to match its speed. "It's more than that, Rae. Every now and then, I catch sight of where you're headed."

"John—"

"Let me finish. Please. Otherwise, I'll never get this out."

"Okay."

"You know where you want to go. And that's the big difference between us. For you, it's out there ahead of you. But with me, it's totally the opposite. You know what I mean?"

She wiped her face. "Yes."

"I'm already there, Rae. Right where I want to be. Right here, right now, this is it. And the longer we're together, the more you're moving away. I don't mean you're running from me."

"I know what you mean."

"But you are running. And I'm running, too. Only, we're not running the same race."

"You're a good, good man, John."

"But I'm not the man for you and your race, am I?"

When she did not respond, he said, "Goodbye, Rae. Thanks for, you know, the run."

CHAPTER 29

When he left Cape Fortune, Curtis returned to the resort and spent another hour with the four construction crews currently working there. To emphasize the project's urgency, he insisted on writing out checks covering all their estimated costs. Then he promised a massive bonus if they completed the demolition by next sundown. When he drove away, the chiefs and crews were moving at their lumbering version of warp speed.

He drove to the Morehead City supermarket and filled his cart with basics—coffee, milk, bottled smoothies, cheese, fresh bread, herbal teas that Kurien preferred, and so on. Standing in the checkout line, Curtis recalled earlier days, prepping for his boss's arrival, doing what he did now. Excited about the time they would soon share. Happy. Which was crazy in a way, how delighted he was to be Kurien's personal assistant. So many of his business school buds would have considered it an insult, one step above serfdom.

For Curtis, though, it was a chance to move into Kurien's intimate space, be with him for hours when all barriers between them were dropped. He was granted an opportunity to observe and study a business genius, an incredible strategist, a diplomat. Sitting with Curtis and sometimes Amiya, occasionally with Lorna, other times just the two of them, analyzing the day and the people involved and their aims. Both sides. What they want, what they are after, how to bring the sides together in long-term harmony. Or not.

At the newly rented home, Curtis unloaded his groceries, then took a long, slow walk through the place. He made mental note of the extra furniture Kurien would probably require, starting with electronically adjustable easy chairs and bed. All in all, though, he was pleased. The home was in pristine condition, everything he tried worked as it should; and beyond the rear glass wall, boats sliced through the evening waters in an illuminated parade.

He made a salad he didn't particularly want and took it out to the broad rear deck. There was nothing left for him to do but face the inevitable.

Amiya might as well have been seated there beside him. The woman's heat, her strong embrace, formed an enduring presence. And allure. Curtis ate slowly, wondering at their relationship's sudden transition.

Until that very day, Amiya's beauty, her intelligence, her drive, had simply been part of who she was. This incredible woman had been both his boss and his dearest friend. While Lorna had been alive, personal times with Amiya had been both intimate and distant. His late wife had always called Amiya her sister. Curtis had felt precisely the same.

And now?

He had read somewhere about the earth's magnetic poles occasionally shifting. The words had been meaningless until now. The way she had held him, the invitation, the love she revealed . . .

If he allowed, it would shift his world on its axis.

The prospect terrified him.

Curtis found himself utterly incapable of asking the simple question: What did he want?

Every glance in that direction brought him back to the look in her eyes. The brief embrace. The words she had almost sung to him.

The invitation.

Curtis carried his unfinished meal back inside. He closed up the house and prepared for bed, moving by rote. When he cut off the lights and lay down, he felt encased in a surreal calm. It reminded him of the run-up to a major blow. The air turned blisteringly hot and filled with a humidity that made breathing difficult. The air crackled with such energy the old-timers liked to say the sea was ready to boil. All the while, the hours remained windless, the ocean utterly calm.

Waiting.

Eventually Curtis fell asleep, his dreams fractured, his fear a very real force. Until a woman's voice came to him, perfumed whispers, her every breath a lilting melody.

Curtis woke just before six. He ate a bowl of slow-cooked oatmeal with berries and raw cane sugar, Kurien's favorite. He cleaned up, then stood watching the daylight strengthen, listening to the house breathe around him. It was a good home. Open and yet private. He hoped Kurien would find it a place of healing.

He dressed and went for a run.

Beaufort occupied a mini-peninsula surrounded by water on three sides. In many places, the depth extended right up to the docks. This was extremely rare along the entire eastern seaboard, as most of the Intracoastal Waterway was marked by shifting sandbars and dangerous shallows.

Yachting Magazine regularly named Beaufort the number-one small town in America, and for good reason. The Beaufort Channel offered safe passage around the Shackleford Banks and into the Atlantic. Coastal islands blocked the worst of ocean-born storms. The long string of islets shielded the town's ocean-facing bulkheads and marinas.

Curtis ran the town's long waterfront promenade, past shuttered restaurants, cheerful shopwindows, and beautiful yachts. The original builders had buttressed their structures with frames of live oak, the same hardwood used by eighteenth-century shipwrights to make the vessel so impervious to cannon fire it had become known as Old Ironsides.

He was jerked to a halt by the realization of where his mind had wandered. Without conscious thought, he had been mentally sharing a lazy cruise with Amiya, dining with father and daughter . . .

A family.

He came to a halt and shuddered hard. Staring out over the sunlit waters, what he really saw was an internal vista forged by terror. The dilemma was as stark as the growing heat. Did he have what it took to enter a new relationship?

Curtis started back, his every step echoing the real crisis issue. He had no idea what he really wanted. Twenty paces later, Curtis was halted once again when his phone pinged with an incoming message.

Jiyan's text was nineteen words. Long enough to change everything.

In a strange yet satisfying way, Jiyan's message was exactly what this moment required. The day's course solidified in the few moments required to plan his next steps. He set aside all the questions and fears and doubts surrounding Amiya because he had no choice.

Curtis pocketed the phone and kept running.

Back at the house, he brewed another pot, stretched, showered, and dressed.

When he was ready, he texted a three-word response to Jiyan.

Then he phoned Dana Bowen's personal cell.

*   *   *

To his great relief, Dana answered on the second ring. He started, "Rae is with Amiya. Something has come up. I'm fairly certain Rae would agree this call is important, and we're going to need your help."

"Why don't we pretend seconds count," Dana said. "Skip the windup and dive straight in."

Curtis needed ninety seconds to lay it out.

She responded the instant he finished. "Leave it with me. Soon as I'm done participating in your hearing, I'll be spending another day tied up in court proceedings. I'll coordinate things with Rae. She'll serve on point."

"Was I right to call?"

"Most certainly. Good luck today. Keep me informed."

CHAPTER 30

Rae woke to find a text from Amiya, asking if they could travel to the courthouse together. Amiya was standing outside the hotel entrance when Rae pulled up. Amiya's slacks, blouse, and jacket were three shades of midnight blue, fashioned from what Rae suspected was shantung silk. Rae wore one of her three courtroom suits, which under other circumstances might be considered severely fashionable. As they drove back through Atlantic Beach, headed for the island's bridge, Amiya described how Curtis had spent the night in the home they had rented. Making sure everything was ready for Kurien's arrival.

When Amiya had confessed she'd been too nervous to eat breakfast, Rae stopped in town for smoothies. Which was when she found herself describing her conversation with John. The one that had played on a continuous loop in her head all night.

Amiya heard her out in silence, then asked, "How do you feel?"

Rae braced herself. She took a firm two-handed grip on

her cup, determined to maintain her control. A gentle wind laced with sea salt puffed through her open window, sighing the lament as she replied, "Lonely."

"I can't help but worry that my silly comments have caused you pain."

"Amiya, no, it's not like that at all. Talking with you helped me to see things clearly. Besides, John was the dumper, not me."

"Don't call it that. He told you farewell. And from the sounds of things, he was hoping you'd tell him he was wrong."

"Maybe. I don't . . ." Rae found it necessary to clear her throat with the smoothie. Incredible that her hands were steady. Amazing, actually. "All I could think of after was how this news was going to break his parents' hearts."

"You should call them later today. Or tomorrow. Just as soon as you're ready. You tell them they are special, and you want to maintain the friendship that has meant so much." The woman's strange combination of formal speech and caring tone fit this moment perfectly.

"Thank you, Amiya."

"I'm so sorry, Rae. But to tell the truth, I haven't heard you say anything about regretting your changed status."

"No. Emma will be delighted. She never said much, but I know she didn't think John was right for me."

"Your aunt is a truly remarkable woman. I can't wait to introduce her to Daddy." Amiya smiled at a thought. "She told me I needed to learn how to dress down. That it would help me fit in and be accepted by the locals."

"Not just you. When Curtis showed up at the assembly discussing your resort, every eye in the place tracked him. This stud muffin, dressed for some Paris runway, didn't fit Atlantic Beach and never would." Rae pointed at a trio of women strolling toward them. "Those three could be company executives down for a long weekend. Gallery owner, perfumer, pediatric brain surgeon, whatever. Soon as they arrive, off go the city suits. Now they're dressed for island life. Supercasual clothes that have never been introduced to an iron. Comfy sandals, big sunglasses, and they're ready for the day. This is the one time in their crazy-hectic life when they can enjoy simple pleasures. It's family time here. People are friendly and simple in their greetings. This defines life on the Crystal Coast."

Amiya watched them pass. "If Daddy saw me in denims cut that high, his poor heart would finally give out."

"Curtis might like it, though."

She laughed. "In that case, he and I will go shopping soon as we bring Daddy in from the airport."

Rae started the car. "Where is our guy?"

"He spent the night at the new rental. He wanted to make sure everything is okay."

"You know, that actually makes a lot of sense."

"Yes." Amiya was still smiling. "Maybe if I wore a pair of those shorts, he would have let me go with him."

As they approached the bridge, Rae's phone pinged with an incoming message. She handed it to Amiya and said, "Read it to me."

"What if it's a client with something confidential?"

"Do it with your eyes closed."

"Look at the funny lady." Amiya read, and almost instantly the car's atmosphere shifted.

"What is it?"

"Curtis. Something's happened."

"Read it."

" 'We have an unexpected and potentially serious development. I have communicated directly with Dana Bowen. If your schedule permits, I would ask that you accompany us to New Bern. Dana agrees. Please wait and let me tell Amiya myself.' " She passed back the phone. "I guess I should have kept my eyes closed, after all."

CHAPTER 31

The Carteret County Courthouse in Beaufort was a stunning antebellum structure, red brick with white pillars and lacing. Adjacent to this was a secondary building that could best be described as a 1980s-era necessity.

Through seniority and stubborn grit, Justice Jodi Dwyer's chambers occupied what Rae considered the finest portion of the original building. High ceilinged and marble tiled, its brass light fixtures dated back to the time of whalers and clipper ships.

They gathered around a century-old conference table in a mini-chamber adjacent to the courtroom. Judge Dwyer sat one chair off the table's head so as to view Dana Bowen, who now appeared on a wall-sized screen. Rae's files on Landon Barrett made an eight-inch stack beside the judge's left hand. The court reporter occupied a lone position at the table's far end.

Dwyer called the meeting to order, then requested they go around the table, identifying themselves and stating for the record what role they played in the proceedings.

The two agents handed over their badges without being asked. The woman served as spokesperson. "I'm Agent Styles and this is Agent Rice, DEA. We seek information on Landon Barrett that might be relevant to an ongoing investigation."

Judge Dwyer was not a large woman, but well-padded in a manner that made her robes very unflattering. Her silver-gray hair was cut in a pageboy style that had gone out of fashion decades ago. Rae thought she looked like someone's favorite grandmother, except for the icy sharpness to her gaze. When angered, she revealed a tone to match, capable of eviscerating anyone she considered out of line.

Like now. "It has come to my attention that your initial contact with Ms. Alden may have crossed a legal line in the sand. At Ms. Alden's request, I am taking this no farther." She handed back their badges. "I want to be absolutely certain you both are fully aware of what I mean when I say, you are only being granted a temporary pass."

"That is absolutely clear, Your Honor."

"Very well." Two chairs separated the agents from Amiya and Curtis. "Next?"

"Amiya Morais, Your Honor. Daughter of the Morais Group's chief executive. I serve as the board's deputy chair and oversee our North American operations."

"And your presence is necessary because . . ."

"Our first U.S. acquisition is the Fortunate Harbor Hotel and the adjacent land, where we are now building a resort housing estate. We acquired the Barrett property in order to build a marina for the resort."

"I see. Next?"

Before Curtis could respond, Amiya replied, "Curtis Gage is executive vice president of the Morais Group, and managing director of our U.S. operations."

His jaw dropped. "What?"

Amiya offered a smile, softly saying, "Surprise." She told

the judge, "My father arrives this afternoon from Delhi. He intended to tell Curtis himself."

"In that case, congratulations are in order." The judge looked at Rae, who was seated directly across from her, three seats removed from the court recorder. "Ms. Alden is known to this court and an attorney in good standing." She turned to the screen. "Ms. Bowen, I'm not clear on why you are participating."

"Your Honor, Ms. Alden requested that I supervise the Barrett property sale, as she also has the Morais Group as clients."

Rice, the male agent, muttered, "She represents both Barrett *and* the buyer? That's just great."

Judge Dwyer swung around, her motion slow as a battleship cannon taking aim.

And waited.

Rice cleared his throat. "Sorry, Your Honor."

Dwyer resumed her position and settled one hand on the top folder. "I have made a thorough examination of Ms. Alden's client files and find her work to be of absolute impeccable quality. Were I to have been named attorney of record, I see nothing here that I would have handled differently."

Rae managed, "Thank you, Your Honor."

She glanced at the agents. "It may interest you to know that for the past eight months, Ms. Alden has not been paid for her services. The hours she spent trying to locate her client and doing the necessary repairs have left her out of pocket to the tune of—"

"Eleven thousand four hundred dollars."

"Which she will now recover, as the sale has been concluded. I also hereby award her a further five thousand dollars for the hours and effort she no doubt expended without marking them on her time sheet."

It was Rae's turn to be silenced by the proceedings.

"As far as your investigation is concerned, there is not one shred of evidence to link the property's sale or Ms. Alden's activities to anything remotely illegal."

The agents were glumly unresponsive.

"I therefore declare this matter to be permanently . . . Yes, Ms. Alden?"

"Your Honor, there is something else I respectfully ask the court to place on the record."

The judge glanced at her watch. "Proceed."

"The Barrett property cannot be repaired. Yesterday my clients toured the home for the first and last time."

Agent Styles asked, "Why last?"

Curtis spoke for the first time. "Because we're in the process of tearing it down to make way for our new marina."

The male agent huffed as if he'd taken a body blow. Styles shot him a look. Rice settled. Angry. But silent.

Rae said to the court reporter, "Run the video, please."

Dana Bowen's head shrank to a tiny square in the screen's right-hand corner as the home's cluttered staircase came into view. Rae was shooting from the top of the stairs, which meant the demolished foyer and entryway were all visible. Her phone's software included an option to reduce unsteady motions, which was very good indeed. Even with the app on maximum adjustment, her body's tremors remained clearly visible.

None of those gathered seemed to mind.

Rae listened as she identified herself and her clients. She thought her voice sounded courtroom crisp—a strong hint of nerves, but her speech precise and sharp. She kept the camera focused on the pair as they clambered across the foyer and started up the staircase. Rae aimed mostly at Curtis, who climbed first, pausing now and then to help Amiya over the worst bits. Watching it now, she could see the complete disparity in their expressions. Amiya was confused, unsettled, perhaps a bit frightened.

With each step, Curtis seemed to grow more aware. His expression was grim. Intent. Then he reached the top step. And nodded slowly.

Rae heard herself ask, "Can you tell me what you think has happened?"

"Robbers. No question. They used the storm damage to mask their entry." He pointed back down the stairs. "I wondered why glass from the door and front wall was inside the house. The major storm damage came from the second hurricane, and that blew in from the rear, over the Intracoastal Waterway. That should have blown the glass outward."

Amiya reached the top step and gasped.

Only then did Rae turn and reveal the main room.

Curtis offered, "No storm could have done this."

The room took up more than half of the entire main floor—living and dining and bar and kitchen and television alcove, flowing in easy lines with small indentations or single stairs offering suggestions where one chamber ended and the next began. With a long glass wall overlooking a broad balcony and the bay beyond, it must have been a beautiful home.

No longer.

Every wall was torn out. Sledgehammer blows had crushed the bar, the kitchen cupboards, the tables, television, the sound system. Nothing was left intact.

"Look here." Curtis walked to the wall formerly holding floor-to-ceiling shelves. The central portion was simply gone. A gaping hole, three feet square, was dug through to the master bedroom.

Amiya asked, "What was it?"

"A safe. No question."

The two agents groaned as Curtis kicked aside rubble and pointed to the floor. "You need to get this." He waited as Rae shifted over and focused on deep gouges dug into the floor. "Something seriously heavy was dumped here." He continued to shove the debris aside, pointing to where Rae needed to focus, following a broad scrape in the floor. Together they made their way over to where a sliding glass door dangled from one last hinge. "They took it out by way of the balcony. No, don't step out there, it doesn't look safe."

Judge Dwyer said, "Pause it here, please." When the video froze, she asked Rae, "Before yesterday, when was the last time you visited the property?"

"I haven't been inside since I brought the contractors and insurance adjusters to obtain an initial estimate."

"When was that?"

Rae thought back. "I'd have to check my records to give you an exact date, Your Honor."

"Ballpark."

"The second storm hit the third week in September. I managed to get a roofer in ten days later to do emergency repairs over the three main holes. Then I waited for the adjuster to fit me in. The second week of October, give or take."

"And you didn't notice any such damage at the time?"

"The home was a ruin, Your Honor. The contractor refused to even give an estimate, but the insurance adjuster . . ." Rae waved that long-standing argument to one side. "If you mean this theft, no, ma'am. A hole in the wall that size would be hard to miss."

The male agent demanded, "What about security cameras?"

"They are everywhere," Rae answered. "Or rather, they were. And the garage held two generators the size of freezers. But both of them were flooded when the bulkhead was breached. The power lines were repaired within a week or so. But the house electrics remain a total mess."

Dwyer said, "So at some point during the past six months, this home was burgled. Clearly whatever was hidden in the wall safe is gone." She looked down the table. "Do the current owners have anything further to add?"

"We toured the house," Curtis replied. "All except the two bedrooms teetering on collapse. It was more of the same, except the office, which was totally demolished."

"They even shredded the leather office chair," Amiya said. "They smashed the desk to splinters. The walls and paintings were ripped apart."

Dwyer planted a hand on the table. "All right, I've seen enough. Questions, comments, anyone?"

Agent Styles asked, "Can we have a copy of that video?"

Rae looked at the judge, who replied, "I see no legal reason why they shouldn't. That is, assuming Ms. Alden is in agreement."

"They're welcome to it, Your Honor."

"Let it be noted for the record that Ms. Alden has gone out of her way to be of assistance. Despite the confrontational and potentially illegal manner of the DEA's initial approach."

When the agents remained silent, the judge snapped, "Now is the time when you express your gratitude."

Both agents offered reluctant thanks. Rae thought they sounded like schoolyard bullies being caught in the act.

Dwyer clearly thought the same. The judge did her best to hide a smile as she declared, "This hearing is adjourned."

CHAPTER 32

As they left the courthouse, Curtis asked if Rae was able to join them for the trip to New Bern, then suggested they take his SUV. His demeanor was oddly formal, enough to erase Rae's high spirits from the courtroom. When he opened both passenger doors, Rae slipped into the rear seat. She wanted another chance to study the two of them together.

Curtis waited until they joined Highway 70 to say, "This morning, I received a text from Jiyan."

Rae asked, "I'm sorry, who?"

"Jiyan is as close to a guard or butler or personal aide as Daddy will come these days," Amiya replied. "Why a text? Why not call?"

Curtis nodded agreement to her question. "I suspect because he didn't have time to call and keep it secret."

Amiya stared at him. Finally she said, "Ajeet."

"Yes."

"Same question," Rae said.

"My cousin," Amiya said. "Go on, Curtis."

"Ajeet met your father's plane in Washington. He is flying down with them."

"Oh no."

When the pair went silent, Rae said, "If I'm supposed to be playing a legal role here, somebody needs to tell me what's going on."

When Curtis did not respond, Amiya said, "Ajeet is a dangerous, ambitious fool. The man is poison. As a result of the kidnapping, Ajeet inherited his father's shares and now sits on our board." Amiya's reaction was interesting. Rae thought she could actually see the woman come into her own. Her entire demeanor sharpened as she told Curtis, "We need to take this very seriously."

"I agree."

"There is a specific purpose to his meeting Daddy."

"Why Washington?" Curtis confirmed. "Why now?"

"I suspect the second issue is the more important," Amiya said.

Curtis nodded with his entire upper body. "Why now?" he repeated. "Why would Ajeet choose this particular moment? What purpose does it serve?"

"Tell me what you're thinking," Amiya said.

Curtis hesitated, then said, "I will if you insist. But I think it would be better if we hold off guessing."

"Wait until they arrive," Amiya said. "See the man for ourselves."

"Why Washington? Why now?" Curtis said again. "Once we have the answers to those two questions, we can chart our next steps. Not before."

Rae could see Amiya wanted to argue, but in the end, she merely asked, "Did Jiyan say anything else?"

"Yes. Ajeet is traveling with four bodyguards."

Amiya hissed.

Curtis glanced in the rearview mirror. "I contacted Dana. I hope that's okay."

"Of course."

"She has enlisted a group she's used before."

"Bodyguards," Amiya said. "Daddy will hate it."

"They're not just for your father," Curtis replied.

They arrived in New Bern early enough to stop at Gail's for a lunch no one wanted. But Curtis insisted, saying they had no idea when they might have another chance to refuel. Throughout the meal, he and Amiya continued to speak in terse bites, their few words reflecting a turmoil shown on both faces. Rae played the willing observer.

Seated in the pizzeria off Highway 70, Rae began seeing the entire situation in a different light. On the surface, nothing changed. Three attractive young people picked at food no one seemed particularly interested in eating. Twice, the waitress came by and asked if everything was all right. Rae doubted the pair seated opposite her even noticed. They remained deeply involved in the unfolding dilemma, their words emerging like bursts of steam.

As they waited for the bill, Curtis began working his phone. Frowning.

Amiya asked, "What is it?"

Curtis gave a fractional shake of his head, kept working.

"Curtis, tell me."

He rose from the booth. "I can't access our accounts."

Amiya's eyes widened. "Ajeet?"

"Has to be." He stepped away. "Take care of the bill, I'm going to try and reach our banker."

When Rae and Amiya emerged, Curtis was already behind the wheel of the car and the motor was running. Soon as they were underway, he announced, "Our bank received a court order an hour ago, freezing all our accounts. Corporate and personal."

Observing them was like staring into a mental prism. Rae saw them, their worries, their fears. But mostly, what she studied was her own future. Here was a dividing line. She could not logically spell out why she was so certain. Even so, down deep where it mattered most, Rae was absolutely certain. This moment marked a life transition. Perhaps for all three of them. But most definitely for herself. The small-town world she had been content to claim as hers, all this was about to undergo a seismic shift.

If she wanted.

Which she did.

Rae felt the same gut-level draw she had experienced before turning down offers from the big-city firms. Only now, she had the chance to become involved in major corporate affairs, spread across multiple time zones and nations, while remaining part of her beloved Crystal Coast.

Amiya asked, "What should we do?"

"We have to tell your father. He needs to be a part of whatever comes next."

Amiya stared at him. "He's ill and he's bound to be exhausted from the journey. Not to mention Ajeet bullying his way onto the plane."

"This can't wait. You know it, as well as I." Curtis gave her a chance to object, then went on, "There's a hidden reason for Ajeet being on that plane."

"What?"

He shook his head. "This isn't logic talking. It's my gut. But I'm certain. Denying us access to our accounts is only the tip of Ajeet's blade."

Rae knew these two were not shutting her out. Their terse half-spoken conversation had nothing to do with confidentiality. They were simply testing the mental waters.

Rae felt no need to insert herself. Her time was not coming. It was already here.

When they were ready, they would ask her help. And she would spring into action.

Their trusted ally.

CHAPTER 33

Rae's attitude toward the New Bern airport was complicated. All the soldiers in uniform, all the farewells and cheerful hellos, granted her a tiny glimpse into a different world. One where children wept with the intensity of answered prayers when their mother or father appeared in the arrivals hall. Where a goodbye tore strong people apart, and soldiers walked away with stonelike expressions, even when their hearts were shredded.

As usual, the arrivals terminal was crowded, noisy. Parents tried futilely to rein in children who ran about, shrieking to hear their echoes bounce off high ceilings. Laughter was a constant refrain. As were tears. Rae surveyed the balloons, the signs, the uniforms, the embraces. Under different circumstances, she would have considered it a nice introduction to the region she called home.

Not today.

Curtis stopped close to the exit and told Amiya, "You should greet him alone." When she looked ready to argue, he added, "Don't give Ajeet a reason to mar Kurien's arrival. You ride back with your father."

She nodded acceptance. "Not Ajeet as well. Please."

"Ajeet goes wherever Ajeet wants under his own steam," Curtis replied. "Once we're all underway, we need to hook up by phone and plan. It may be our last chance."

"Very well." She pointed to the welcome desk. "I'll just go see when Daddy's flight is expected."

Curtis asked Rae, "Could you text Dana, see if she can join us for that call?"

As Rae drew out her phone, a slender man in his thirties approached them and said, "Mr. Gage?"

"That's me."

"Holden Geller." He offered his hand. "Ms. Bowen said you might need help taking out the trash."

Curtis liked that enough to offer the day's first smile. He pointed to Amiya and said, "The lady's name is Amiya Morais. She's on point. Her father is arriving from Delhi by way of Dulles, where an unwanted gentleman insisted on joining him. With security."

Rae thought Holden Geller resembled many young officers she had known. John's hyperfit crowd contained any number of such people, trim and intelligent and very aware. And handsome. Which Holden was. Very.

Holden glanced her way, offered an eyes-only smile, there and gone in an instant. He said, "Ms. Bowen mentioned the gentleman at the center of this task is Kurien Morais. Did I say that right?"

"Close enough."

"How many in the uninvited guard detail?"

"The text I received said four."

"Okay." He turned to a woman Rae had not even noticed until then, a dark-haired Asian, so still she managed to vanish in plain sight. When she stepped up, Holden said, "This is Number Two. Her actual name is Elena, but nobody remembers that. If you can't find me, ask for Two. Or just point in her general direction."

"Only if you want to lose your finger," Elena replied.

The pair managed to be stern and serious and cheerful, all at the same time. Clear-eyed, dressed in dark gray slacks and pearl-colored shirts and black lace-up boots. No weapons Rae could see, no radios, nothing to declare themselves as security. Or dangerous. Except for an air of tight readiness, strong as scent.

Holden asked Curtis, "What's your role here?"

"If possible, I'm just part of the scenery." Curtis gestured to Rae. "Ms. Alden serves as our regional attorney. She will also handle your billing and accounts."

"Good enough. Ms. Bowen will be glad to hear you made it." He pointed to the arrivals gate. "A private jet from Dulles landed . . ."

"Eight minutes ago," Elena offered.

"The FBO terminal is still under construction, so . . . Hang on a second."

A bulky gray-haired man in USMC fatigues, with colonel's eagles on his lapels, walked over, surveyed the pair, and said, "So the rumors are true. You've gone for the big bucks."

"We're also on the clock, sir."

"It's Dwight to you now, marine." He nodded to Elena. "Sorry to have lost you both to the dark side."

Rae noticed a trio of other officers standing five paces back. They were all of a similar breed, same muscular builds, tight gazes, catlike ease.

The colonel said, "You need reinforcements, give us a shout."

"Roger that, sir." Holden waited until the officer and his crew moved away; then he asked Curtis, "What's the name of your superior's uninvited guest?"

"Ajeet Morais." Curtis spelled the name. "He likes to

dominate. Which is the real reason for his security detail. Ajeet is happiest when he's playing the bully. And he despises me. Hates the ground I walk on."

"Other than protecting Mr. Morais and your good selves, what's our role here?"

"We need to separate Ajeet and his team from Kurien. If you can."

"There is no 'if,'" Elena replied. "Only do."

"You heard the lady," Holden said. "That takes care of the airport. And after?"

Amiya joined them and confirmed the flight's arrival. Curtis made a swift round of introductions; then, "Mr. Morais was recently injured in an attack that killed Ajeet's father. There's a risk Ajeet intends to use Kurien's weakness as an opportunity."

"What exactly are we talking about?" Holden asked. "Another physical assault, business deal, what?"

Curtis replied, "We don't know anything for certain."

"We know enough," Amiya said. "Ajeet will seek to dominate now, control later."

"We can't let that happen," Curtis said.

Amiya said, "The very instant Ajeet appears, he needs to be separated from my father. Put in his place. Shown that he is not, and never will be, the one in control."

Holden told his number two, "Give our team the sitrep."

Curtis asked, "How many are you?"

Elena replied, "Many as you need." She moved away.

Holden asked, "So we isolate Mr. Kurien Morais the instant he arrives. Anyone else to be included in our zone of protection?"

"Jiyan," Curtis replied. "Kurien's PA. Sort of. The reason you're here is Jiyan managed to shoot off a text unseen."

"Jiyan. Good guy. Noted."

Amiya warned, "Ajeet won't like your people separating him from my father."

"What Ajeet and his team like or don't like are not part of our equation," Holden said. "Slick, smooth, fast. They enter, we take control, we leave. Your ride or ours?"

"What are you driving?"

"Two Land Rovers and an armored Navigator."

"Your ride. Definitely."

Amiya stepped away. "Here they come."

CHAPTER 34

As soon as the old man appeared, Rae knew he was Amiya's father. He shared his daughter's slender build and striking features. Kurien's skin tone was marginally darker, his face craven. But neither his wounds nor age erased the man's looks. And magnetism.

Rae stood near Curtis, back by the main exit, with a clear view of faces turning and watching as the daughter rushed over and embraced Kurien. He leaned heavily on an ivory-handled cane, so only one hand was free to hold his daughter. But the pleasure and joy and pain were all evident.

Rae did not notice the second man until Amiya turned and greeted him. It had to be Jiyan, a gentleman in his late fifties whose deeply lined face rearranged itself as he smiled. He kept close to Kurien, but did not touch him. Jiyan searched the terminals hall, spotted Curtis, and nodded a greeting.

Then the third man appeared.

Ajeet's similarity to father and daughter only went skin

deep. He was immaculately groomed, not a single hair out of place. He accented his skinny build with the latest fashion—tightly tailored trousers and half-zip cashmere sweater and pointy-toed boots. His clothes might have looked beautiful on a Paris runway, but here in New Bern, they were almost clownish. But there was nothing humorous about his expression. Or gaze.

Four men stepped through the arrivals gate behind Ajeet. The four all wore the semiofficial black-on-black security uniform that only added to Ajeet's evil-clown persona. They were all overly tall, overly bulked-up. The largest was a brute whose hands could not fit through Ajeet's briefcase handle, so he carried it with two fingers. They all wore earpieces with the dangly wires. Rae heard Curtis snort softly.

Then she realized Holden Geller, their own security guy, was laughing. When she looked over, he said, "Stick those jokers between slices of sourdough, my guys have lunch all taken care of." He asked Curtis, "I'll stay with our incoming guests. We'll travel in the Navigator. One of my Rovers will be on lead. Elena will stay with the second Rover and handle the luggage. You coming with us?"

"No. I'll follow in my vehicle. Once we're underway, I need to connect with Amiya, have everyone on a conference call."

"No problem." Holden waved his crew forward and moved to join them.

The closer Holden and his people came to the hulking four, the smaller they seemed. Rae thought it was dangerous how Elena was the one going up against the largest guy. Holden's crew looked too young, too clean-cut, too . . .

They connected with the four, and Rae found herself breathless.

Holden's group flowed like water, or so it seemed. They streamed around the much larger men, smooth and fluid, and suddenly the four were halted. Little more than rocks in the stream. Holden and his crew determined the currents. It was *their* flow. *Their* operation.

Elena looked like an elfin sprite next to the brute. Just the same, she formed an effective barrier between the guard and Kurien. The man tried to swat the lady. Again. Both times, she simply flowed the assault away. Water and rock. The guard snarled loud enough to attract attention. Elena gave no sign she heard.

The brute dropped the briefcase and grabbed at her. Elena laughed and flowed around those massive hands, deflecting without giving an inch.

All the while, Holden and Jiyan ushered father and daughter toward the exit. Moving them farther and farther away from the four. And Ajeet.

The colonel sauntered over, accompanied by several of his fellow marines. Rae heard him ask Holden, "Everything good here?"

"Just another day at the office, sir." Holden followed the officer's gaze back to where Ajeet stood and steamed. He pitched his voice loud enough to carry. "I was about to explain to the gentleman there how he didn't want to make a scene."

Ajeet barked a single word Rae did not need to understand. The four reluctantly disengaged and stepped back.

The colonel kept his gaze locked on Ajeet. "You need any help with that crew, give us a shout."

"Roger that, sir."

Ajeet scowled, tried to move toward the pair, and was halted by a trio of Holden's team. Outrage grew as he realized what was happening, his team blocked, father and daughter moving slowly toward the exit.

Then he spotted Curtis.

Ajeet's outrage had a target. "You!"

The terminal went so quiet, Rae heard Amiya softly tell her father, "Please let me help, Daddy." Kurien appeared so intent upon Curtis, he might not even have heard his daughter. "My dear young man."

"Hello, sir."

Ajeet swatted futilely at the three blocking his progress. He stabbed the air between him and the departing pair. "You're not going anywhere with *that man*."

For the first time since entering the terminal, Kurien addressed his nephew. "It is time you recognize 'that man' for who he is. *That man* is *family*."

Rae watched the nephew stagger back a step. As if Kurien's words carried physical force.

Kurien went on, "If you wish to continue our conversation, *that man* will supply you with my address."

Ajeet's fury mounted at the realization that Kurien was traveling without him. "I *demand* to come with you!"

"You 'demand.' How interesting." Kurien waited until Jiyan positioned the wheelchair, then allowed Amiya to help him settle. "Do you actually wish to declare yourself my enemy? In public? Here? Of all places?"

Ajeet seemed to become aware of the watching faces, the people treating this as rare theater. "That is not what I said!"

"Is it not?" Kurien reached for Curtis, gripped his arm, and continued. "*That man* will arrange an appointment when you and I might speak. Be on time. And, Ajeet, take careful note. Your goons are not welcome. Not in my temporary home or in my hotel. *That man* can assist in finding them a suitable alternative."

Soon as father and daughter departed, the rest of Holden's team effectively vanished. Rae watched as they stepped back, flowed away. Water.

Which granted Ajeet the opportunity to stalk over. Rae might as well have been miles away. Or invisible.

The man could only see Curtis. He clearly did not care who watched now. Or heard him say, "You think you've *won*? You think those words from a feeble old man mean anything *at all*?"

The emotional display created a new lens. Rae viewed this man she once loved at a level far below skin and sinew. She saw how similar he was to Kurien. And to Amiya. Down where it mattered most. The strength, the goodness, the integrity. The ability to stand there, the focus of this man's wrath, and not even blink.

"You think you *matter*?" Ajeet's laugh carried a manic glee. "You think you have a *job*?"

Curtis remained silent. Unmoved. "I've taken the liberty of reserving you a room at our—"

Ajeet chopped the air, silencing Curtis, then waved his guards forward. "You see this man? *You see him?*"

But the guards were very much aware of what Ajeet chose not to notice. How the colonel and others in uniform remained close at hand. Watchful. Ready.

Ajeet formed a meaningless smile and lowered his voice. "Your days of groveling for crumbs dropped from your master's table are over. You just don't know it yet."

When Ajeet and his security departed, Curtis approached the officer and his team. "I'm very grateful for your presence here today, Colonel."

"For a minute there, I thought I was back in Kabul." He watched Ajeet shout his way into a waiting ride. "Don't see that level of theatrics very often around here."

"We have a history."

The colonel grunted. "Let's hope you also have a future."

Curtis took a card from his pocket, wrote swiftly. "You know the Fortunate Harbor Hotel?"

"Heard of it."

"I'm head of the parent group." Curtis offered a tight

smile with the card. "For the moment anyway. I want you five and your families to come be my guests. Full access to the beach club, plus dinner in the main restaurant. My private number is there on the back. Call or text and I'll make all the necessary arrangements." He started away, then paused long enough to add, "As you've just heard, it's probably a good idea to take up this invitation sooner rather than later."

CHAPTER 35

Curtis waited while Holden's crew stowed the luggage, then asked Rae if she'd drive. Once they were underway, he asked, "Could I take a couple of sheets from your pad?"

Rae pointed to her shoulder bag. "Reach in the side pocket, I always carry an extra. Need a pen?"

"No, thank you." He made a couple of notes, then said, "Maybe we should bring Dana up to speed before connecting with the others."

"Go ahead."

Curtis made the call and connected with the car's system. Rae then listened as Curtis summarized the confrontation. He might as well have been making a shopping list, for all the emotion he showed. That completed, Curtis placed the second call, this time adding Amiya's phone to the mix.

Soon as they came on the line, Curtis said, "Holden, I need to know everything said here remains confidential."

"It's amazing how deaf we are when it comes to a client's discussions," he replied.

Curtis introduced Dana to Kurien, explained the role

she'd played in the acquisition of Cape Fortune, the court proceedings, and in putting their security in place. As far as Rae could tell, he remained utterly unfazed by the airport confrontation. Soon as he finished, Dana said, "I need some background on this Ajeet."

"He is my cousin," Amiya replied. "Since his father's death, Ajeet has served as cochair of the executive board."

"Kurien and his brother were a matched pair," Curtis said. He remained focused on his pad, writing and drawing and flipping pages as he spoke. "Kurien handled strategy and planning and acquisitions. His brother was an expert at day-to-day operations. An engineer at heart. A lover of detail."

Dana asked, "And the son?"

"Ajeet cares about neither," Amiya replied. "He wants to wield power while his minions toil in the trenches."

Curtis shook his head, but all he said was "We need to prepare." He flipped to a new page. "There are two questions we need to answer while we have time. First, why now? Second, why here?"

Kurien spoke for the first time, his voice clear, precise, and very weak. "Ajeet said the board wanted him to view the hotel."

"No, Daddy. Ajeet wants to see *his* hotel. *His* resort."

Curtis nodded in agreement, but did not speak.

"I don't understand," Dana said. "You told me the North American operations are run as a completely separate group. No connection whatsoever to the Indian group."

"This is correct," Amiya said.

Curtis circled a number, leaned back, and repeated, "Back to the core issues. Why now? Why join Kurien's flight in DC?"

Kurien murmured something.

"Sorry," Curtis said. "I didn't catch that."

Amiya said, "Daddy says, you've learned the lessons well."

"I had a good teacher," Curtis replied. "The best."

Kurien spoke louder this time. "You see it, don't you?"

"Yes," Curtis replied. "And so do you. And Amiya. She understands now, don't you?"

In reply, Amiya said, "Tell the others."

Instead, Curtis asked, "What else did Ajeet have to say on the flight?"

This time, it was Jiyan who replied, "He was most concerned about Kurien's health. Many, many questions. Doctors, tests, why this trip? Was it in the board's best interests, Kurien coming here now?"

"The *board's* best interests," Amiya said.

"Always the board," Jiyan confirmed.

Amiya asked, "Why did you even let him on the plane?"

Kurien answered, "I received a text when we landed in Washington. The board demanded we make room for Ajeet on our flight."

Amiya huffed softly. "It was Ajeet's way of declaring he now controls the board."

"An hour into the flight, Kurien demanded time to rest," Jiyan said. "This pleased Ajeet the most. He told us that he was here to offer all the assistance the board requires."

"Back to my questions," Curtis said.

Amiya said, "It's all tied to our accounts being frozen."

"I agree," Curtis said.

"Hang on a second," Dana said. "Explain what you mean by that."

Curtis swiftly recounted his online discovery, confirmed by the bank manager.

When he was done, Dana said, "You're telling me the board of directors of an *Indian* company has frozen accounts of an *American* corporation?"

Rae said, "This defines illegal overreach."

"This isn't about the executive board overreaching their power structure," Curtis replied. "They have obviously taken this to the courts and to their allies within the Indian political system."

"The court where Ajeet and his allies on the board control the judge," Kurien said. "As they control the politicians who are involved."

Dana asked, "Is that possible?"

"If I'm right, Ajeet and his allies have turned it into a political issue," Curtis said. "They have claimed that the chairman of a major Indian conglomerate is secretly relocating much of their company to the United States. As a result of this, Kurien threatens to steal away Indian jobs. Which is enough for the politicians in Ajeet's pocket to demand action."

"When everything is in place, they will go public," Kurien said. "Ajeet's politicians will declare this a national outrage. We've siphoned off funds from India. We've stolen jobs."

"There is only one thing to be done," Amiya said. "I must fly to Delhi tomorrow and personally speak with our allies on the board—"

"No," Curtis and Kurien said together.

"Ajeet will have anticipated this very move," Kurien said.

"It puts you in the crosshairs," Curtis said. "There's no telling what might happen."

Kurien said, "I would rather travel back myself—"

"No." This time, the immediate response came from Amiya and Curtis and Jiyan.

Kurien said, "There, you see?"

In the silence that followed, Dana said, "I'm assuming you don't wish to fight the Indian courts from here."

"Impossible," Amiya replied. Glum now. "The Indian courts are notoriously backlogged. Corporate cases have languished for years. For generations."

"Unfortunately, my young friend is not finished," Kurien said.

"Why now and why here?" Curtis inquired. "Because the Indian embassy has reached out to their allies among the Washington power structure. Ajeet has requested an injunction be set in place, forbidding us from using any and all corporate funds on these new ventures."

Amiya said, "Because the origin of these funds is India. And the Delhi board members are opposed to this. And so Ajeet's allies in the Indian government have officially requested their U.S. allies to put an injunction in place, barring us from this nefarious use of Indian funds."

"Now that we can fight," Dana said.

"Which is exactly what Ajeet wants," Kurien said.

"The accounts will remain frozen throughout the appeals process," Curtis said. "Which would force our Carolina project into bankruptcy."

"Ajeet has arrived now because he holds all the cards," Amiya said. Resigned. "Which explains his questions about Kurien's health. He wanted to gauge Daddy's level of strength, his ability to fight back. He found what he hoped for."

Dana said, "That you're too weak to fight."

Curtis turned to the side window. Shook his head. But he remained silent.

Amiya replied, "That Daddy will accept his terms."

Dana asked, "Which are?"

"We'll find out tomorrow," Kurien replied, sharing his daughter's somber tone. "So you are aware, I brought all the cash I had on hand. Four hundred eighty thousand dollars U.S. Curtis, given our current commitments and funds outflow, how long do we have?"

Rae watched Curtis work the numbers. Finally he circled a figure on his final page. "Given how much I've committed to the Cape Fortune home's demolition, we have five weeks," Curtis replied. "Forty days max to turn this around."

CHAPTER 36

Rae was exhausted from a very long day, but she knew she wouldn't sleep. After Curtis dropped her off, she decided to go see if Emma was awake. The woman kept the oddest hours of anyone Rae knew. The bridge was empty this time of night. She drove with all the windows down, wishing the warm island breeze packed enough punch to wash away her stress. Then the phone rang. Dana.

Rae rolled up her windows, turned on the car's a/c, and put the call on speaker. She said in greeting, "I hate what's happening to them worse than turnips. And I hate turnips a lot."

"Let's not go crazy," Dana said. "At least, not yet."

"I don't see how you can be so calm. Unless you've come up with a secret plan to give the good guys more time."

"I've been in situations like this all too often," Dana said. "And what I heard in their discussion was the same thing I saw in my conference room. They're a team. A good one. If there's any way out of this mess, they'll find it."

Rae felt the band of tension around her chest loosen a trifle. "Okay, now maybe I can sleep tonight."

"I'm in court most of the day, but you need to call me with an update tomorrow afternoon at four sharp. How did my security team do?"

"They were amazing." Rae pulled into an empty space by the Morehead City boardwalk and described watching them halt the larger team in their tracks. Water and rocks. "Who are they?"

"When Holden left the Marines, he was recruited by one of the big agencies. He loved the security work, but hated the egos. He pulled together some of his fellow POGs and left. More efficiency, less aggression."

"What did you call them?"

"POG. It's gyrene speak. Stands for 'personnel other than grunts.' Change the subject. Did anything happen after the conference call I need to know about?"

"As a matter of fact, Curtis handed me all the funds Kurien had brought with him. I'm to set it up so all incoming expenses would pass through me."

"Smart," Dana said. "Ajeet's attorneys will be reluctant to go after funds held by outside counsel."

"Curtis also asked if the purchase of Cape Fortune had gone through. I said it had, but there might be time to retract funds on the Beaufort property. He said no, it was a sound investment and increased the value of the entire resort."

"In case he has to go for outside funding," Dana said. "I am liking this young man of yours more and more."

"He's not my anything."

Dana's voice took on a lilting note. Teasing. "Might be time to trade in your current model on this new and improved version."

Now she was smiling. "Too late. John broke things off."

"Well, now."

"Plus, Amiya has asked Curtis to marry her."

"You think or you know?"

Rae watched a midnight shrimper plow a silver furrow through the moonlit waters. Heading out to sea. "I saw it happen."

Dana was laughing now. "Let me get this straight. She used you, the guy's former flame, as official witness."

"It wasn't like that. At all."

"This is one smart lady."

"I'm hanging up now."

"Good luck handling the bad guy. And remember. Call me at four. I want the long version of whatever happens next."

Rae cut the connection, reversed from the space, and headed back for the bridge. Going for her island home and bed. Talking with Dana had been as helpful as bothering her aunt. Almost.

As she pulled up in front of her aunt's apartment, Rae's mind became snagged by the last thing Curtis had said.

He had personally escorted Rae upstairs. As she had unlocked her front door, Curtis told her, "You've always been a good friend."

"Curtis, it sounds like you're saying goodbye."

"No, it's just . . ." He studied her, then continued, "We've been moving so fast, it's easy to leave things unsaid. I'm glad you're involved, Rae. It's so good having a chance to work with you. See you…"

"As an adult," she finished for him.

"As a top-notch attorney," he corrected. "Someone I can trust." He started to add something, but then his phone chimed. Curtis pulled it from his pocket, checked the screen, said, "Ajeet wants to meet us at ten."

"I'll be there."

"Thank you, Rae. For everything."

"Curtis, wait. What were you going to say?"

"Before this is all over, you think maybe we could go diving for treasure in Cape Fortune?"

"I'd like that. So much."

"I'd like us to show Amiya what it's like to hunt for doubloons."

The stress and worry in his gaze cut deep.

"Let's go tomorrow," Rae suggested.

"Our dance cards are a little full. But soon." He started back. "Good night, Rae."

Four o'clock that predawn morning, Curtis left his hotel room and walked to the beach. He greeted the guard from Holden's crew and headed north. The moon was up, the breeze gentle. Clouds like silver ships sailed the starlit sea. Phosphorescent algae sparked each wave, transforming them into gentle washes of light and mystery.

Everything was different now.

All his plans had been transformed during the drive. The answer to that key question accompanied him down the moonlit shore.

Why now?

The answer was so clear, so simple. Now Curtis had a reason for why Ajeet had always despised him. Right from that very first meeting. The one element Amiya had failed to mention when she reminded him of that first day in Delhi. When she had walked Curtis down the line of family photographs, introducing him to her own lineage.

Ajeet had stepped through the doorway, realized what Amiya was doing, and flown into an astonishing rage. In that instant, Curtis had become the new threat.

Ajeet had already known Amiya's marriage was failing. And he was ready to step in. Claim the prize he had probably spent his life secretly wanting.

No matter that Curtis was married. Amiya had always been open with her affection for him and his wife. She cared for him.

The answer was as clear as the night sky. Ajeet finally had

the necessary lever. He would release the funds. Reverse the board's opposition to their North American operations. In exchange for Amiya's hand in marriage.

In the face of such a move, all the hesitations Curtis had over accepting Amiya's proposal vanished. Dust in the wind.

He wished his mind and heart were clearer. Amiya was a truly wonderful woman. She deserved a man who was totally, utterly hers. A man who came to this marriage with a whole heart, a future open to all the joy and life they could make together.

Someone better than him.

The empty sand stretched in both directions like a silver ribbon. Curtis settled on a high dune and turned his face to the moon.

Lorna would have loved this place. This hour.

She was the night owl. Not him.

Lorna managed happily on four hours' sleep. Less. She had always been his Energizer Bunny. She would go and go, then bounce happily into sleep, smiling her way through dreams she never shared, then up and running delightedly into another day.

She called Curtis her grumpy bear, always looking for his cave, always wanting to hibernate. That was how she referred to his need for nine hours' sleep. His daily hibernation fix.

She loved to walk in moonlight. She called the hours like this her midnight escapades. She claimed the night winds sang to her in a language she never shared.

Delhi had enchanted her from the moment her plane landed. Portions of India's cities ran to a twenty-four-hour clock. Some market was always open. Many religious festivals continued noisily to dawn. Others started before daybreak. She had arrived in Delhi three days before the start of Diwali, one of the nation's largest festivals, and treated it as her very own personal welcome. Times like these, Lorna was defined by a joy that was both childlike and enduring. Long before they were married, Curtis had known she would make the very finest of mothers.

And then, in silent abruptness, Lorna was with him.

Such events had occurred in the weeks following her funeral. Gradually over time they had faded to mere passing clouds of remorse, and then departed altogether.

Tonight was as distinct as any of those earliest experiences. Yet entirely different.

There was a distinct solemnity to this moment. A calm as potent and as deep as the moonlit sea. This was Lorna's other face, the timeless wisdom she had shown him so often, and with which she had guided him so well.

After a time, Curtis spoke to the night, the sea, and to her. "I understand."

The breeze touched his eyes, his upper lip, his heart.

She was gone.

Curtis sat on the miniature dune and waited until he was ready. When dawn painted the eastern sky with golden promise, Curtis walked back to his room, showered, and dressed for the day. There was a formality to his movements now, checking his appearance in the mirror and walking to his car and starting for the mainland. Actions this important required a certain solemnity.

He would honor Amiya. And her father. He would love her as much as was possible. Give her all he could manage. Despite everything.

He could do no more.

CHAPTER 37

Sometime after midnight, Rae woke from a dream about Cape Fortune.

Such moments still came occasionally, when the past sparked into candle flames that lit her lonely bed. Usually, she woke with an image of Curtis holding the gold doubloon, the two of them shouting their joy to the cloudless sky. The memories always carried into the next day, sometimes longer, leaving her with a unique blend of joy and unshed tears.

Tonight was different.

In this particular dream, she was back inside the Barrett home, standing by the bar with her client. There was a party out on the rear deck, people drinking and talking loudly around a smoking grill. Rae made it a point never to be alone with the man. Even here in her dream, her client's dark side lurked in the hidden reaches.

In the dream, Barrett wore a New Yorker's version of Carolina casual. Landon was a skinny man, with oversized hands that were never still. Rae had always suspected his diminutive build held a tensile strength and the speed of a striking snake. His tailored shorts were overlarge for his bony frame, kept up by an alligator belt with a tooled silver buckle. Over this, he wore a loud silk shirt in floral pastels that only heightened the unhealthy cast to his features.

They were seated to either side of the bar, with Rae's semifake pirate map framed on the wall behind him. In her dream, the map glowed brightly, as if lit from behind. Landon had loved hearing her tales about buccaneers and buried treasure. It was the one time when his nervous energy stilled and he listened with unblinking intensity.

Rae rose from her bed and realized she had left the a/c running. The fact left her unsettled, as if the previous day's troubles had shoved their way into her night. This time of year, the habit of opening all her windows was a natural part of her daily cycle. If she left the a/c off all day, her upper-floor apartment was an oven when she arrived back. The place then took forever to cool. But nights like these were magic, especially when the breeze came off the ocean. It was a natural part of her nightly routine, cutting off the a/c and opening all her windows before slipping into bed.

She padded to the living room and hit the controls. As she approached the rear windows, an idea began whispering. Rae felt the hairs on her arms lift, not fearfully so much as sparked by the unseen. Her senses were on full alert as she opened the living room's two windows, then went back to the bedroom and reached for the window latch . . .

When it hit her.

Rae waited until a few minutes past five to call Amiya. "I'm sorry to wake you."

"I'd have to be sleeping for that to happen. What is it?"

"I have an idea. Crazy, lunatic, utterly bonkers."

"Does it have anything to do with the mess that's robbed me of sleep?"

There was no reason why such a question should send Rae's heart into overdrive. "Where are you?"

"I spent the night at Daddy's."

"Is Curtis there?"

"Huh. No. More's the pity."

"I've called and texted him a dozen times. He doesn't answer."

"Let's hope he's sleeping for all three of us. Rae, tell me what's going on."

"I'd rather show you. And I need your help. Can you meet me at Cape Fortune?"

Rae had never been particularly worried about snakes.

But tramping around the Barrett property the hour before full sunrise, while shadows were still deep and the place was utterly quiet, all her childhood boogeymen-fears crept out and slithered. Not to mention gators, which she'd heard all her life didn't make it this far north. The softest rattle of palm fronds in the dawn wind had her searching for monsters creeping out to swallow her whole.

When she heard tires scrunch down the long drive, she ran out to meet the Land Rover. "What took you so long?"

Amiya rose from the Rover's front seat. "What are you talking about? I came straight here."

"That's impossible. I've been waiting hours." She waved to Holden and his two smiling crew. "You brought reinforcement. Excellent."

"We also brought coffee," Holden said.

"Even better. Are you armed?"

"Always. Who needs getting shot?"

Rae gestured toward the rubble-strewn expanse where the house formerly stood. "Anything you see slithering in my direction."

Amiya retreated toward the car door. "There are snakes?"

"I haven't seen any. Yet."

Holden turned to the nearest guard. "You're hereby volunteered to tromp around the property."

"Ha." The guard walked over and handed Rae a steaming plastic mug. "No."

A young man built like a human tank began passing around power bars. "That is definitely the boss's job."

"Not a chance," Holden replied. "I'm a lead-from-behind kind of boss when it comes to snakes."

Amiya told Rae, "I am hereby ordering you to tell us what we're doing here."

"There I was," Rae told them, "standing by my bedroom window, listening to the night. All of a sudden, Landon was right there beside me."

"You and the money launderer," Holden said.

"Allegedly. Right."

"In your bedroom together. Three-thirty in the morning."

"Just stop, okay. It wasn't like that."

"Still," Holden said, grinning at his mates. "You got to admit, there's a definite hint of the deviants."

"You sound like a ten-year-old," Amiya said. To Rae, "Then what?"

"All the time we talked about pirates and buried treasure," Rae said. "Barrett never went hunting himself. Not once."

Holden said, "Maybe he couldn't swim."

"No idea. And it doesn't matter." Rae never took sugar with her coffee. Now her mug was sweetened by too much sugar and condensed milk. Somehow the combination tasted right. Perfect. "What if he saw himself as a modern-day version of those same buccaneers?"

"News flash," Amiya said. "Barrett's safe was ripped out. And the rest of the house isn't there any longer."

Holden inspected the two ladies. "Okay. I'm lost."

Rae turned from the rising sun and inspected the empty

lot. "Something I haven't thought of in years. Barrett brought in a contractor from Jersey. A number of owners use builders they know. What made this totally unique was how this guy didn't work on the house. He poured the foundation and vanished."

The four of them formed a motionless tableau.

Rae went on, "He came down, dug the hole, set the steel supports in place, poured the concrete, and left."

Amiya said, "That is definitely strange."

"I know, right?"

Holden asked, "Who built the house?"

"Local guy. He died from a heart attack during Covid." Rae waved that aside. "Doesn't matter."

"Matters to him," Holden said.

Amiya told the security chief, "Let's try and focus here, okay?" To Rae, "The foundation."

"Why would he bring in this guy from Jersey, unless—"

"He's hiding something," Amiya said.

"Maybe, yeah. It's what woke me up." Rae stared at the house that was no more as she told them about the destruction they had found, the video they shot for the judge.

Amiya was with her now. "You think the wall safe was just a decoy."

"'Think' is too strong a word," Rae replied.

"A modern-day buccaneer buries treasure under his own house, and then vanishes," Amiya said. "This is just so totally off-the-wall crazy good."

"*Maybe* he did," Rae corrected. "Call it one chance in a hundred billion."

Holden said, "And here I thought this was going to be just another boring security gig."

"There's a problem." Rae pointed to the garden shovel and kitchen broom. "That's all I have for tools."

In response, two of Holden's crew walked back to the Rover and drove away.

Amiya demanded, "Where are they going?"

"Doing what they do best," Holden replied. "Making things appear out of thin air."

Ten minutes later, they returned, the SUV's hold so jammed with gear the rear gate stood open. The grinning pair started handing around industrial-strength gloves, shovels, construction-grade rakes, wire push brooms.

The human tank told Rae, "You owe us three hundred bucks."

"Probably best if you don't ask why," Holden added. "Our accountants pretend blindness to things we stick in the miscellaneous column."

In addition to the equipment they had bribed off a night watchman, the guy had also offered them a cheerful description of demolishing the house. The watchman had actually called it a gleeful day's work. Being given just twelve hours to tear down the home meant all the tedious bits were set aside. There was no time for salvage. Speed was everything. The crew had been offered triple pay, plus bonus, for completing the job by sundown. Which they did by employing all the heavy equipment they had on hand—a dozer, two excavation diggers, and a half-dozen dump trucks. They were done by four.

Over where the support columns had been tilted by wind and the waterway's flood, the foundation was riven by deep cracks. Otherwise, the concrete slab was largely intact. All the support beams had been sawed off and carted away, leaving dark stubs rising six inches or so from the foundation. Holden and his crew got busy shoveling and raking away the blanket of rubble, while Amiya and Rae followed behind with the construction brooms.

The sun rose; and with it, the heat. The concrete slab became a reflector for both. An hour or so after full sunrise, the wind died altogether. Every push of the broom lifted more dust and grit that drifted in the still air. Rae became drenched with sweat and coated in grime. Holden passed around bandanas, which she and Amiya tied around their noses and mouths. The cloth helped. Not a lot. But some.

Then she realized Amiya was humming.

"You can't possibly be having fun," Rae needled.

Amiya timed her words to pushing the broom. "This is so much better than not sleeping."

Push.

"And being captured by the helpless feeling of losing a battle."

Push.

"I'd pay money to be here."

Push.

"If I had any."

Push.

"Which I don't."

Push.

"Even if this is all we gain from today, it's enough."

Push.

Holden tossed another shovel load of rubble off the slab. He told his crew, "Let's all pretend we didn't hear that bit about the boss being broke."

Half an hour later, Rae was beyond ready to call a break, admit defeat, say they needed to get back and clean up and ready themselves for what would definitely be an awful meeting with Ajeet. Anything to get off that slab and out of that baking heat.

Then Amiya managed to sing the words "I think I've found something!"

CHAPTER 38

Curtis pulled up to Kurien's new home and parked. He planned to walk around back, sit on the patio until Kurien woke up. See if maybe Jiyan or the guards had coffee brewing. There were worse ways to prepare for the coming declaration of love. However fractured.

But when he rose from his SUV, Elena emerged from the lone Land Rover and walked over. "Where have you been?"

"Walking the beach. Why?"

"The lawyer lady has been trying to reach you." She waved at the house. "Ms. Morais came bouncing out of the house about an hour ago. Holden and two of our guys were hard pushed to keep up. They jumped in one of the Rovers and off they went."

Curtis knew immense relief at knowing he could first speak with Kurien alone. The prospect of doing this with the both of them, together, all at once, had made the drive over an endurance contest. "Can you call and see what's going on?"

"I can try. But nobody tells me anything." Elena pulled

out her phone, hit speed dial, spoke softly. Then, "Holden says you should hang tight, and treat that as an order from on high. Don't go anywhere."

"I wasn't planning to."

"Then I guess I don't have to cuff you to a post." Elena pointed at the path leading to the boat dock. "The old man is on the back patio."

Six-fifteen in the morning, the heat was a growing force. As Curtis started around the home, he heard a man singing.

Or rather, a man singing badly.

As he entered the backyard, a woman standing in the boat dock's shade offered Curtis a two-fingered wave. Up ahead, Kurien was seated by the patio railing, coffee in hand, singing to the gulls and rising sun. The living-room stereo blared out a show tune from *South Pacific.*

" 'Some enchanted evening, you may see a stranger.' " The man could not carry a tune in a forklift.

Kurien waved his mug in greeting. "No one has ever designed a melody like Rodgers and Hammerstein. No one!"

"Now I understand why Amiya ran away."

Jiyan appeared in the doorway. "He's been like this all morning. Coffee?"

"Please."

"It's the air," Kurien explained. "The light. The wind. And Amiya promised to make me green eggs and ham for breakfast."

Jiyan stepped out, bearing a second steaming cup. "He means, baked eggs and green harissa."

"Amiya learned the recipe from her mother." Kurien watched Curtis pull over a chair. "She loved the dish even as a young child. She renamed it after her favorite story."

Curtis sipped, breathed, drank again. Steeling himself. "You're in a good mood."

"I feared the board would not let me leave. Of course, I understand now why it happened. They wanted me away so they could vote in Ajeet's schemes for taking control." He used his mug to point at the shimmering waters. "Then I woke up this morning, dragged these old bones out here, and was greeted by a dawn that promises better days to come."

Curtis decided he would not ever know a finer starting point. He set his mug on the floor by his feet and felt the day's disparate elements click into place.

It was time.

He asked Jiyan, "Could you cut off the music and make sure we're not disturbed?"

Kurien's hands whitened as they gripped the mug. Curtis knew the old man feared more bad news.

He hoped desperately he was about to prove Kurien wrong.

Curtis rose to his feet, took a hard breath, and said, "Sir, I have loved your daughter since my earliest days in Delhi."

"My dear friend, please—"

Curtis used a single uplifted finger to silence him. "I loved her as a friend. I loved her as a colleague. I loved her as someone I could trust with my future and my life, just as I do you."

He watched Kurien use the chair arm as a means of steadying his mug, so his free hand could cover his eyes.

Curtis went on, "Then we both went through our very hard times, and I came to love her as a sister. Now the time has come to take the next step. I respectfully ask your permission to marry your daughter."

CHAPTER 39

Rae and the others arrived back only a few minutes shy of their ten o'clock appointment. They were filthy, sweaty, exhausted, and so merry that it defied their physical state. Rae's hair was plastered with sweat, her clothes a mess. It was a very odd way to enter a crucial meeting with her client's number one opponent. She could not have cared less.

Elena rose from the Rover parked in the drive and asked, "Whose party did you destroy?"

Holden waved her over. He handed Elena a credit card and an address the construction watchman had given them. He carefully explained what they needed, and finished, "Go spend whatever it takes." He turned to one of his grinning mates and added "Your job is to keep the lady's purchases within screaming distance of reasonable."

Elena started the car, gunned the engine, and said through the open window, "Boss, I was born for this gig."

Jiyan waited for them by the front door. He smiled a welcome and almost formally ushered them inside. He gave no sign he noticed their state. "Ms. Amiya, please to come with me." He closed and locked the front door. "Everyone else, wait here."

Rae pointed to the wall clock. "The meeting—"

"All such matters must wait." Jiyan started for the open rear doors. "Ms. Amiya, please."

Rae stepped into the living-dining area, from where she had a clear view of the deck. The patio held an odd sort of tableau. The two men, Curtis and Kurien, were seated with their backs to the house.

They were holding hands.

Curtis leaned forward, so intent on what Kurien said that he was unaware of Amiya's approach. She floated over, or so it seemed to Rae. Not so much walking as drifting, cloud-like.

Curtis jerked in surprise at her appearance. He rose to his feet and offered Amiya his chair. Kurien reached out one hand, welcoming his daughter. Smiling broadly.

Curtis knelt beside her.

Holden stepped up close to Rae and murmured, "This day just keeps getting better."

"Quiet now," Jiyan whispered.

Amiya flung herself into Curtis's arms.

CHAPTER 40

Which was why, when Ajeet and his minions arrived less than five minutes later, he found them all on the back patio. A happy, sweaty, filthy bunch. Laughing and chattering and all of them talking at once. Amiya and Curtis molded together in a joyous new union.

Kurien forced himself to his feet, ignoring Ajeet's sheet-white astonished fury. "You're just in time! Come celebrate my daughter's betrothal to this fine young man!"

The only sign their group even noticed his speechless rage was how Holden took a single step forward, watching not Ajeet but his security. Ready.

Ajeet wheeled about and stormed back through the house, roaring invectives in a language Rae didn't need to understand.

Only when his guards followed did Rae notice the two men in suits. She walked over and asked, "Can I help you?"

The older gentleman said, "Carl Waters, partner in Waters and Stewart."

Rae knew the name, of course. A megafirm based in DC with satellite offices in half-a-dozen cities around the world.

She started to apologize for her filthy state, decided it didn't matter. "Rae Alden. I represent the Morais Group in all matters relevant to your presence here."

Waters and his younger minion took in her appearance, the joyous crew ignoring them entirely, the empty space where their client had previously stood. "I see. Or rather, I don't."

Rae chose her words carefully. "Whatever spurious case you might have helped put in place, I respectfully suggest you withdraw your support."

The senior attorney continued studying the happy group. "That is an interesting word you chose. 'Spurious.'"

"If you'll give me a few hours, I'll supply you with further details as to why you should remove your firm from these proceedings," Rae replied, hoping desperately she was right.

He started to respond, but something he saw on the back porch made him keep his comments unspoken. "In that case, perhaps you'd be so kind as to arrange transport to the hotel."

His legal minion offered, "Fortunate Harbor."

Rae signaled to the ever-observant Holden. "No problem."

She and Jiyan and Holden and a crew member walked them out. Jiyan and Holden's crew held open the Rover's doors and ushered them inside. Polite, courteous, utterly at odds with Rae's state. She stood there until the Rover vanished around a bend in the road, then told Holden, "You were right. This day is amazing."

When she returned to the patio, Curtis asked, "Who were those two?"

"It doesn't matter." Which was valid only if their impossible hopes and wishes were about to come true. "You need to come with us."

"What, now?"

Amiya disengaged herself. Stepped back and took hold of his hand. "Yes, my love. Right this very instant."

CHAPTER 41

They all crammed into Curtis's SUV basically because they had no choice. The bulletproof Navigator was off on another gig. One Rover was carting the baffled attorneys to the hotel, the other was with Elena doing whatever. There was a considerable amount of whining and major-league complaining by the pair left behind on guard duty, while the others packed sardinelike into the overloaded Caddy. Something in the suppressed laughter, the sparkling gazes, the way Amiya clutched his arm while Holden supervised the bodies curled and piled into the rear hold, kept Curtis from demanding answers no one would give.

Elena and her shopping mate were already there when they arrived at Cape Fortune. As they clambered out, Elena declared, "Boss, that place had everything."

"That's good," Holden replied, stretching his back. "Because that's probably what we're going to wind up needing here. Everything."

The crewmember who had traveled with Elena added,

"The lady ain't lying. She told the warehouse boss what we were looking at, then he walked us through Aladdin's cave."

"He offered us four options, didn't even blink an eye," Elena said. "Oxy-fueled flame cutter, that was first on his list."

"Nix on the flames," Holden said. "We don't know what's inside."

Curtis demanded, "Inside what?"

But no one was paying him any attention.

Elena agreed. "What I told the sales guy."

Her pal said, "Next came this major-league plasma torch. We nixed that, too."

"Ditto on the laser cutter," Elena said. "Which left us with option four."

Her pal said, "If we'd looked hard enough, we could've probably come back with a Stinger and a couple of Tomahawks."

Curtis asked again, "Will somebody finally, please, at long last, tell me why we're here?"

Amiya signaled to Rae as she pulled him forward. "Come with us."

The entire crew followed as the ladies led Curtis onto the home's foundations, over to just another stretch of poured concrete. The surface was moderately clean, though still streaked by the wire push brooms.

Curtis leaned toward where Rae pointed. "What am I not seeing?"

"Look." Rae knelt and used one finger to sketch a line. "Amiya found it."

Abruptly what he was seeing popped into electric clarity. "Oh. Wow."

Rae said, "I stared at it for ten minutes before I saw it."

Holden offered, "It's steel plate, inch or so thick, set in place with a watchmaker's precision." He stomped a boot on the surface. "Covered with a sheet of more concrete. Meant to blend in with the foundation for as long as the house stood."

Curtis traced a visual line around the square. "Amiya found this?"

"That is one amazing lady," Holden said. "I've been force recon with some of the world's finest snipers. I bet most would never have spotted a thing."

Amiya said, "The hurricanes and the dislodged pillars must have revealed the cracks."

Holden asked Elena, "How many crowbars did you buy?"

"Four."

"That should do it." He stepped back. "All my team who aren't already hot and bothered, you're hereby volunteered."

It took them almost an hour to chip away the surrounding concrete so they could manage a two-sided grip. Even then, the steel plate remained a sullen and stubborn foe. Curtis took his turn with the others and agreed with Elena that the cover had to weigh half a ton. After his third gig on the crowbar, Holden declared he'd rather be back in Afghanistan.

Elena worked on it until she dislocated her forefinger. She screamed at the pair who held her fast and popped it back into place, waited until it was taped to the neighbor, then went stomping into the distance. Finally, though, with strained muscles and enough swearing to silence the birdsong, they managed to shift the menace over to one side, revealing a shadowy hole perhaps two feet deep.

Curtis dropped to his belly and used Rae's kitchen broom to sweep away the surface grit.

Holden asked, "What do you see?"

"I can't make it out." He tossed away the broom and used his fingers. "More metal, for certain."

One of Holden's crew started off in Elena's direction. "That's it. I'm done."

"Here." Rae turned on her phone's light and passed it over.

A long moment, then Curtis rolled over and stared at the passing clouds. "Oh, man. Oh, man. Oh, man."

There was a general sweaty scrum as they all tried to cram their way into the hole.

"It's a safe," Amiya said.

"Yep," Holden said.

"Rae was right all along," Amiya said.

"Definitely," Curtis said, speaking to the passing clouds.

"The safe they stole was a decoy," Amiya said.

"Right again," Curtis said.

"Elena?" Holden straightened slowly. "Where's the lady?"

"Off kicking at stumps and nursing her sprained digit," someone said.

"Elena!" When she reappeared, he called, "After you nixed the fire-and-brimstone methods, what did the warehouse guy give you?"

This was what Rae and Holden and Amiya had been hoping all along.

Desperately wanting it to be true.

Central to the equipment Elena had rented was a Bosch professional-grade BITURBO cordless power drill. They positioned the stubby steel frame around the opening and levered the drill down to within an inch or so of the safe's dial. Two of Holden's crew now held phone lights to either side of where Elena served as drill operator.

She sat with her feet on the safe and told the others, "Unless somebody objects, I aim to drill straight through the face of the lock. That will position me by the drive cam lever. After that, I'll use the punch rod to shove them out of the way. That frees the locking bolts."

Holden squatted down beside her. "They rented you a punch rod?"

"I told you," her mate said. "That place has everything."

"Two rods," Elena confirmed. "And an assortment of titanium and diamond-tipped drill bits. You know, in case there's a cobalt plate I've got to work through."

Curtis and Rae and Amiya shared a confused look. Elena's pal suggested, "Situations like this, it's always best not to ask."

Holden stared into the hole. "What's the downside?"

"The safe might be shielded with relockers." Elena pointed at the dial. "Those would be tripped when my drill breaks a sheet of glass that's set over the locking mechanism. And that would trigger a set of auxiliary bolts. Then we'd have no choice but tear a bigger hole in the foundations and haul the safe out to where we can saw our way in."

"She brought those, too," her pal offered. "Two saws."

Holden asked Elena, "But you don't think that's a major risk, do you?"

"No, chief. I don't."

"Tell us why."

"Two things. The storms they told us about, the ones that ripped the pillars free, those kinds of vibrations would probably have cracked the glass."

"Something this dude would probably have thought about."

"Right. And two, the guy was after building himself a hidey-hole."

"Which he did."

"A good one," Elena agreed. "I think then he went for an old-fashioned safe. No extra risks that might wind up with him unable to open the thing when it mattered most. No electronics that could go wrong."

"Just a solid steel safe with mechanical locks, covered in more steel and concrete," Holden said.

"Holding buried treasure nobody else ever needed to know about," Elena said.

"Except us," Holden said. "Thanks to the lawyer lady here."

"Okay," Curtis declared. "Major chills."

Holden rose to his feet. "Objections, anybody? No? Okay, Elena, drill away."

Twenty minutes later, they were in.

CHAPTER 42

After she returned home, Rae showered and ate a bowl of fruit and yogurt, then conked out for almost two hours. Afterward, she made coffee and scrambled eggs with cheese and scarfed that down. She wished for a couple more days to fully recover, but the flow of events continued to sweep her along, unconcerned with her bruised, drained, weary state.

When she was as ready as possible, she phoned the Fortunate Harbor Hotel and asked for the room of Carl Waters. Once the DC attorney came on the line, Rae used her courtroom voice, solemn and formal, to announce, "I wish to inform you that my clients have established a massive line of credit."

Waters replied, "Define 'massive.'"

"Large enough to cover all operating expenses for the foreseeable future," Rae told him. "There are also sufficient funds to keep their North American expansion plans on schedule." She paused for effect. "And finance any and all necessary court actions to unfreeze their assets. Here in the United States and India. For as long as it takes."

"I see."

But she wasn't finished. "And once we have won these fraudulent legal actions, we will set in motion our own cases to recoup all relevant expenses."

"Your client's line of credit," Waters said. "This is a definite event, already in place?"

"The funds are being processed as we speak," Rae answered. "They are going into an escrow account I will personally oversee, along with Ms. Morais, the North American chairperson."

"Am I correct in assuming you are the group's legal representative?"

"I am."

Rae could almost hear the gears shifting, rearranging the man's legal horizons. "In that case, my colleague and I will have a word with our client in regard to next steps. Once that happens, assuming what you say is true, I believe our work here is done."

CHAPTER 43

Curtis woke to a silent house. He had showered and collapsed in the home's fourth bedroom because he didn't have the strength to drive back to the hotel. In the bathroom, he found a pair of drawstring shorts and a T-shirt bearing the Coca-Cola symbol and Arabic script. Jiyan. The shorts were too baggy and the T-shirt too tight. But at least they were clean.

He padded into the living room and discovered a Canali tux, along with dress shirt and tie and cuff links and shirt studs and shoes and socks, all laid out on the living-room sofa. He told the empty room, "I completely forgot about the gala."

The Nespresso was charged, and there was milk in a pitcher. A large bowl held fresh salad. A neighboring plate held sliced avocado and a selection of antipasto. There was dressing, a fresh-baked sourdough loaf, butter, cheese, honey, and marmalade. Trays, plates, silverware. The works.

He made himself a coffee and plate and carried it out to the rear deck. The afternoon was utterly still, the heat so fierce Curtis felt it in his bones. Even the ever-present flies were gone, defeated by the stifling temperatures. He ate and listened to the silence. The entire day held its breath. Waiting. Expectant.

Amiya emerged half an hour later. She wore an oversized Vikings T-shirt and gym shorts. Her normally perfect hair was a tousled mess. She tried to shield her eyes from the sunlight, but keeping her hand in place proved too difficult a task. She weaved in an uncertain line over to him, drank from his cup, took a slice of buttered bread, added cheese, started away. Curtis thought she had never looked more beautiful.

Curtis said, "Should we invite Jiyan to tonight's event?"

She shook her head no, then waved a hand over her head. Later.

"Amiya." Curtis waited until she reentered shadows and squinted in his general direction. "Thanks for the suit. Is your father coming?"

She took a bite, nodded, and winced at the effort.

"I need to go over, make sure everything's in place." He silently added, *And decide whether Ajeet should be granted a seat at our table.*

But she had already drifted away.

CHAPTER 44

Curtis carried his new finery to the car, then had to return for a towel, which he spread over the rear seat. His entire SUV was smeared with grit and smelled of too many sweaty bodies. Despite the heat, he drove with all the windows down. He was waiting at a Morehead City stoplight several blocks from the bridge when he realized he had not turned his phone back on.

Soon as it came online, his phone began chiming with incoming texts. Nine in all, each from the deputy manager in charge of food and beverages. Alvita was an attractive woman in her forties, half Jamaican and half French Canadian. She stood a trace under six feet, and when happy, she showed the world a wide and brilliant smile. Following the resort's multiple firings, Curtis had used the same detective to do a summary check on all the hotel's senior staff. Alvita had a master's in hotel management from Miami U. She ran a very tight ship and kept meticulous accounts. She was kind to the staff that met her exacting standards. To those unfortunate few who did not, she scorched the earth.

Alvita answered midway through the first ring. "This is how you treat your staff in such an hour?"

"I'm so sorry, this day has been—"

"Never you mind, your day. It's my day that should have you in a panic."

"Alvita, why are you calling me and not Simon?"

"Hmph. That is indeed the question. Especially when my boss and his assistant manager both ordered me never, never, never to speak with your good self."

This was news. "Simon instructed you not to contact me?"

"He tells me not to enter the same room with a certain Mr. Gage. That man, Simon tells me, is a monster. A giant snake in Gucci."

"I don't understand."

"Hmph. Well. I don't have time for that, either. Tell me the truth now, are you a monster?"

Curtis had the distinct impression the woman was trying hard not to laugh. Which made no sense. "No. I'm not. Where is Simon?"

"Oh, Mr. Gage. You will not believe what I have to say."

"Call me Curtis."

"Now that does not sound to me like the name of a Gucci monster."

"We're talking about Simon," he reminded her.

"Well. My two bosses, they spent hours this morning together in Simon's office with that man from India."

He reached the bridge's island side and stopped by the first light. "Ajeet met with Simon?"

"He did more than meet, good sir. They called my room service staff for this and that, and I was the one who personally made the deliveries. Which means each time I listened to a few words before Simon hissed the others to silence." The laughter bubbled closer to the surface. "I am thinking this Indian gentleman is the Gucci snake."

"You are an excellent judge of character, Alvita."

"Hmph. I need that ability to be doing this job, I tell you that straight up. Where was I? More important, where are you?"

"Heading north on the island highway. What happened next?"

"That Indian snake, what is his name?"

"Ajeet."

"Hmph. Well. Those two gentlemen who checked in with Ajeet, the ones in city suits, they come rushing into Simon's office. That is when the shouting starts. And the swearing. Oh, my poor scalded ears! Such language. Then these four goons come parading in. The office door had to stay open because there wasn't room for everyone. And then, the shouting changes to even more foul language, which stops the lobby, just freezes our guests in their tracks. I wanted to run around, plugging the ears of every child with napkins."

Now Curtis shared the woman's smile. "Sounds like something ruined Simon's and Ajeet's day."

"Hmph. Well. On this point, you and I are agreeing."

"And then?"

"That Gucci monster, he stomps out with his goons and that pair in their city suits. Ajeet keeps shouting, and I look inside the office before the assistant manager shuts the door. I see Simon just sitting behind his desk, his head in his hands."

"So Ajeet is gone."

"Did I just say that?"

"I have no idea."

"Perhaps you need lessons in listening. Yes. The man is gone. Him and the city suits and Ajeet's four monsters."

"And Simon?"

Finally the laughter emerged. "He's gone, too. Him and his number two. They are both about as far gone as they can be, and still be inside Simon's office."

"They're drunk?"

"Oh no. Those two left drunk a long time ago. Five bottles of the finest wine from tonight's event, those two have drunk. Five Lafites. Those two, they may wake up someday. When they do—oh, my—you'll see just how sick two poor souls can be after drinking five thousand dollars' worth of wine."

Curtis reached an empty stretch of island road and sped up. "The guest chef has arrived?"

"The chef, the food, the band, the wine." She kept up with the gentle laughter. Truly enjoying herself. "What's left of it."

"Use Ajeet's room, have some of your stronger staff cart them up," Curtis told her. "Alvita, can you handle the hotel?"

"Are you asking me to do this for the night? Or for tomorrow as well?"

"Which do you want?"

"You are asking me this for real?"

"I am."

"This is the position I have dreamed of since deciding Simon was a snake of the first order. Before even then. Since first setting foot in this fine place."

"The job is yours."

"Sir, Curtis, for a monster, you have made me very happy."

"Can you spare a staffer to make sure those two don't emerge during our party?"

"I will personally tie them up," Alvita replied. "Another dream I have had for so very long."

CHAPTER 45

Thankfully, all the necessary arrangements for the gala had been finalized days before; in some cases, weeks. Curtis dressed in a clean outfit and made a quick survey of the hotel's main rooms. Alvita was already stationed inside the manager's office. She paused in her discussions as he passed by her open door. She was joined by the headwaiter, the wine steward, and a white-uniformed woman Curtis thought he recognized from some television program. He assumed it was the visiting chef. Curtis nodded at her and kept walking. Soon as he was out of sight, he heard Alvita resume the conversation.

Of Simon and his assistant manager, there was no sign.

Curtis had two hours before the first guests were scheduled to arrive, so he slipped on trunks and a T-shirt. He was tempted to go for a run, but fatigue was already a weight that would only grow more burdensome as the night progressed. So he walked down to the shore, left his sandals by the crossover, and started north. He passed the housing resort's new beachfront club, where decorators were putting the final touches on what would soon become a shining pastel jewel. A hundred yards farther, the crowds were all behind him. He left his T-shirt on the sand and dove in. The water held a bracing edge in contrast to the day's unseasonable heat. He swam a few strokes, then turned on his back and watched the drifting clouds.

Events of the past few days crowded in on all sides. One event after the other, constantly accelerating, and changing his life in the process. All he felt now was a blur of emotions. The highs and lows blended together into a seamless gray.

He was engaged.

His boss and best friend had offered Curtis his blessing.

His company was solvent.

He was to become the head of their North American operations. Which was not about to begin a major expansion.

All because of what they had found buried in the Cape Fortune property's foundations.

His body jerked with each flash of memory. As if he actually experienced the shocking moments all over again.

When the chill started biting, he swam to shore and headed back. He returned to his room, showered, and stretched out on the bed. But trying to relax was futile, so he slipped back into trousers and knit shirt and sockless loafers and did another circuit of the main rooms.

Curtis entered the ballroom just as the band completed the sound check. A sea of starched linen, crystal goblets, silverware, and frosted wine buckets stretched out beneath a domed ceiling and sparkling chandeliers. He stood by the rear wall, opposite the long bar and its collection of uniformed staff. He watched Alvita make a slow circuit, adjusting a chair here, a knife there, smoothing the lapel on a waiter's jacket as her words drew smiles from her staff.

His life had held moments when he'd forged ahead on the path he assumed was his to claim. Then something happened. A sheriff was shot in the line of duty. A mother fell in love a second time and moved them from the only home Curtis had ever known. A young woman promised to love him despite everything and to wait for his return, which never happened. A man from a distant land opened his eyes to a world Curtis had never imagined might exist. An earthbound angel loved him fully and granted him a taste of eternity. Then she was gone, taking their child and his future hopes with her.

And now this.

A new course was set, their current crisis resolved.

And Curtis Gage was betrothed. To a lovely woman, intelligent and gifted.

He knew it was the right move. He knew he would do this. Walk the aisle. Stand before the world. Promise to give her everything he had left. All he could.

The commitment rested on his weary soul like a weightless comforter. He was doing the right thing. Taking the only step that honored her and her father and all they meant to him.

Holden entered the ballroom, spotted him, and walked over. "Everything appears totally calm. I've heard there's been a change in hotel personnel. Should we be expecting blowback?"

"Not tonight." Curtis felt the gray flow of events sweep him along, take him back into the stream of everything that was about to unfold. "I need to thank you," Curtis told him. "You and your team."

"Just doing our job."

"No, this is something else entirely. Working with us on this level, offering protection and help when you could have—"

"Don't even say it," Holden snapped. He waited long enough to be certain Curtis would not continue down that path; then he resumed his calm manner. "When we sign on, that is exactly what we do. It's how Elena and I select our crew. Hunting out individuals who can be trusted, no matter what."

"My job is to thank you in a way that holds meaning for everyone involved."

Holden's only response was to keep surveying the room's exits.

"Let me tell you what's going to happen," Curtis went on. "Your group will be put on a long-term contract."

"No need."

"Now is the time for you to be quiet and listen." He was rewarded with one of Holden's rare smiles. "We have to jump through a number of legal and tax hoops. Which means this payout will take a while. The disbursement also needs to happen so we don't attract the attention of possible watchers. Rae is setting up a shell company that will hold the new assets and serve as official lender to our group. How long all this will take to put in place, I have no idea. Your ongoing contract will form part of this. You and your team will be paid. And you will receive bonuses. Whether or not we actually need your help with anything more going forward isn't an issue."

Holden remained as he was, tracking the room, for a very long moment. Then he offered Curtis his hand. "I wish we had more clients like you."

"Thank you, Holden. For everything. You and your crew have saved our group."

"We played a role. The one we were born for. Nothing more, nothing less." He started away, then turned back. "Can I ask a personal question?"

"Seems to me that pretty much summarizes everything we've been discussing," Curtis replied. "Personal."

"This is different."

"You can ask me whatever you want. Now or at any point in the future."

Still the man hesitated. A long glance over the room, then Holden said quietly, "I've been wondering about Rae."

It was, Curtis thought, the right question asked by the right man, and happening at the perfect point in time. "She has just broken up with a man almost everyone thought made a perfect match. You know her Aunt Emma?"

"Never had the pleasure."

"She'll be here tonight. Emma told Amiya that John was a fine young man. But she owed Amiya a lifetime debt for steering Rae in a different direction."

Holden gave that the time it deserved, then, "Sounds to me like I should make a point of getting on that lady's good side. You know, if I'm going to try and introduce myself to the recently single Rae."

Curtis watched the solemn warrior cross the room, speak with Alvita, and shake the woman's hand, then depart through the exit used by the band members. He started across the room, taking comfort in the fact that the people accompanying him through life's next chapter were friends. That, in itself, was a gift.

Directly in front of the bandstand stretched a half-moon of polished elm flooring that made a lovely dance floor. Alvita and her team had made a remarkable job of adding the extra table, tightening the lanes between tables a fraction, encroaching on the dance floor to where the front chairs had only inches to spare. Alvita stood by what was now the head table, pretending to adjust this and that, all the while staring at what was now an empty chair.

"Allow me to introduce myself." He offered his hand. "Curtis Gage."

She managed to be both solemn and happy at the same time. "And I, good sir, am the happiest lady on this good earth."

"It appears we have an extra person accompanying us tonight. Kurien Morais is chairman and CEO of the hotel's parent group." He inspected the table. "Is there a Mister Alvita?"

His question sparked a new level of humor in those dark eyes. "His name is Raymond, and the man has come to love my stories of snakes and mystery guests."

"Can we fit fourteen places around this table?"

She waved her hand over the glittering array. "See for yourself. So long as everyone here are friends, there should be no problem."

He met her gaze. "Simon certainly did one good thing. Hiring you. Do you have an outfit that might suit the evening?"

"Oh, Mr. Gage—"

"Curtis."

"Curtis." She was tall enough to meet his gaze with a broad smile. "I have an evening dress that has been whispering to me all the day long."

"Would Raymond be willing to join us?"

"If the man knows what is good for him."

"Join us, Alvita. Please."

She offered a grinning little curtsey. "Oh, Curtis. You do know how to give a lady wings."

CHAPTER 46

Once she was done with the Washington attorneys, Rae packed a case with her cosmetics and other items, then headed out.

She dropped her case by the car, then walked down to the Wells Fargo island branch. Initially all she planned was to ensure her work regarding the new safety-deposit box was in order. The assistant manager found nothing out of the ordinary in her return, and personally escorted her into the safety-deposit cage. Once she was inside, though, just she and the banker staring at the wall of polished steel facades, Rae could not help herself. She had to look.

She and the banker inserted their keys; then she accepted his offer to help her carry the oversized drawer to one of the curtained alcoves. Once she was alone, Rae took a long breath, opened the top to . . . what they had found.

It was a very good thing that they hadn't used heat to cut their way inside.

Because the safe held a single slender file.

In the file were just forty pages.

Each page was a gold certificate drawn on a different bank: France, Germany, Liechtenstein, Luxembourg, Switzerland, and Singapore. The largest banks in each country.

A gold certificate was a guarantee drawn upon the bank's gold reserves. The bank promised to pay whoever presented the page in either gold or in cash. It was the client's choice. Such guarantees did not contain any names or dates. Possession of the paper meant ownership of the assets.

Each certificate was for a thousand ounces of pure gold.

Forty thousand ounces. Two thousand five hundred pounds.

At current prices, the value of those forty pages was a touch over ninety-three million dollars.

Rae drove straight from the bank to Emma's. The bookshop was closed for the day. A second sign in the window simply read: GALA. It was decorated with skyrockets and rainbows.

Emma was in the kitchen, and refused to show Rae the dress she and Blythe had selected until Rae told her about the treasure.

Rae protested. "I've told you already."

"Over the phone," Emma replied, pointing her to a chair and planting a plate of sugar cookies on the table. "This is different and you know it."

Rae, in fact, liked the retelling. She wasn't really hungry, but ate anyway. This was a special day, and overdosing on Emma's incredible cookies was simply part of the package.

When she was done, Emma asked, "Are you sure they'll be able to keep all that for themselves?"

"They'll pay taxes, but because of ongoing business expenses, their accountant and I can apportion . . . What?"

Emma stopped waving the empty mug, set it down in front of Rae, and poured in the aromatic elixir. "That's not what I meant and you know it."

"Yes, Emma. The treasure is theirs to keep."

"You think or you know?"

So sitting there at Emma's kitchen table, drinking herbal tea and devouring the better part of a plate of cookies, Rae told her about the landmark case that defined the ownership of treasure. The telling sparked memories of Dana and those amazing hours spent in her class.

The case of *Cesarini* v. *United States* began in 1957, when a husband and wife purchased a used piano at auction for fifteen dollars. While they were cleaning the piano's internal workings, they discovered packets of cash. The bills were over fifty years old and no longer in circulation. So they took the money to their bank and traded it for new bills. Then the fireworks started. In the end, the court established a precedent that still governed the discovery of any treasure on private property and the taxation that would potentially apply to it as gross income.

When Rae finished, Emma was smiling.

"What?" Rae asked.

"Look at you. All grown-up. I don't often have a chance to see you in lawyerly action."

"You're welcome to accompany me to court anytime you like."

"Really?"

"Emma, of course. I'd be honored."

"I would like that very much." She levered herself to her feet, took the pot of water off the stove, and refilled the pot. "More?"

"Please."

She refreshed Rae's mug, seated herself, and said, "Now tell me about Curtis."

Rae was glad to talk about it. "On one level, once we opened the safe, their reaction was crazy strange. Just this calm acceptance. No dancing, shouting, horseplaying, screaming, none of that. We all sort of hugged and smiled and then started talking about next steps."

Emma sipped, sighed, said more softly, "Tell me about Curtis."

"That's what I'm trying to say." Thinking about that time on the superheated concrete platform drew out the same hollow bloom at heart level as she'd felt at the time. "Curtis was really happy, you know, over the company being out of the woods. But he was very quiet. Just a silent ghost, lying there, smiling at the sky until Amiya made him get up. His quiet reserve was enough to make everybody else tone it down. I was worried about him. But I had the impression Amiya thought it was okay, so I didn't say anything."

"Amiya is correct," Emma stated.

Rae was glad for a reason to shove the remaining cookies to one side. "How can you say that?"

"Because I know the boy."

"He's not that anymore. The boy is gone."

"Hidden, maybe. But all good men keep hold of the boys they once were. Curtis grew into the fine young man who was worthy of your heart." Emma spoke with the quiet certainty that had framed so many of their conversations. "And now he is ready for the next chapter."

When Emma paused to sip from her mug, Rae was tempted to ask what she thought about her and John breaking up. But she stayed silent, much as she wanted to hear Emma's unvarnished take on the man no longer in her life. *John.* She sighed.

Emma went on, "Curtis has grown. He's suffered, he's survived. I know he has, because he's done right by Amiya, by Gloria, by the Dixons, and by you."

"You've only seen him once since he got back."

"Twice," Emma corrected.

"For how long, a few minutes? You amaze me."

"I amaze myself sometimes." She stood slowly. "I think I'll need the chair tonight. I don't want to, but I want to relax and enjoy myself more." She used both canes to start down the hallway. "Come have a look at the dress Blythe and I chose for you."

It was beautiful. And it fit perfectly. Just as Rae knew it would.

CHAPTER 47

Curtis stopped by the ready room behind the stage and introduced himself to the band. Then he returned to his room and dressed in his new tux.

He walked the path leading to the forecourt as dusk captured the scene. It was a beautiful evening. An ocean breeze drifted around the structures, perfumed by seaweed and salt. Overhead cirrus clouds created golden feather strokes in the evening sky.

He stood by the hotel's main entrance as two staff members lit torches now lining the long drive. Hotel guests brought children out to observe the flickering flames as the first visitors began to arrive. Curtis greeted them in turn, then directed them to the ballroom foyer, where a hostess checked their names. Waiters circulated with hors d'oeuvres and flutes of champagne. A local band played warm-up as the glittering crowd assembled.

The flow of new arrivals slowed and gradually the lane emptied; then two dark Land Rovers made the turning. The sense of drama was heightened when, through the open en-

trance, Curtis heard the band strike up a lovely rendition of
Nat King Cole's "When I Fall in Love."

Amiya was the first to alight. And in that firelit moment,
Curtis felt his entire world become rearranged.

Amiya wore an evening gown of gold and russet shades,
with a plunging neckline that framed an emerald pendant.
The torchlight danced over her bare shoulders. The fire
blazed dark and brilliant in her gaze, and her look was for
him. Only him.

Curtis walked forward, aware at some faint level that others rose from the vehicles and joined them. They were all
close enough to watch him take both her hands and read
from the script that was now written upon his heart.

"All this is for you, and you alone. The night, the people,
the music, the food, all of it. A celebration for you. And because of you."

"Don't you dare make me mess up my face." She stamped
her foot a trifle. "I absolutely won't allow it."

He kissed her cheek, stepped around beside her, and told
the others, "Welcome to Amiya's night."

CHAPTER 48

They made a slow procession into the hotel, with Kurien and Emma's wheelchairs in the lead. As they moved forward, Curtis realized he was no longer tired. Fatigue had no place in this fine hour. Amiya did not so much walk with him as flow; their arms and bodies and hearts so linked, they might as well have been joined. And perhaps they were.

Amiya and Rae took charge of the seating. Colton and Emmett appeared especially uncomfortable in their rented finery. When Rae said how handsome the two men were, Blythe said, "Getting Daddy dressed was harder than putting a tutu on my kitty cat."

Emmett said, "Every hour she wasn't messing with her playhouse, she was making that cat's life miserable."

Blythe started to respond, then noticed the man who emerged from the stage entrance. She pointed and said, "Isn't that Chris Compton?"

Indeed it was. What was more, the trumpeter and composer walked directly to their table and asked, "Mr. Dixon?"

When the architect remained frozen and silent, Blythe said, "He's right here."

The bandleader offered Emmett his hand. "I understand you're a fan of my work."

"He's been playing your music pretty much nonstop since we were invited here tonight." Blythe offered her hand. "Hi. I'm Blythe. I serve as Daddy's interpreter when he goes quiet."

The musician continued to address the silent architect. "Was there any melody, in particular, you'd like to hear tonight?"

Blythe smiled at her father as she replied, "Anything from your *Slowing Down the World* album would just be a dream come true for us both."

"In that case, I'll sprinkle a number of them throughout the performance." He nodded. "Nice to meet you both."

As he departed, Blythe said, "Okay, Daddy. You can breathe now."

Emmett looked at Curtis. "All those nasty and awful things I've spent weeks thinking about you. I have no choice now but take them back."

Alvita watched the bandleader disappear backstage and said, "I never knew a trumpet could sing a lullaby until that man showed me."

There was an imbalance to the table, far too many women for an easy seating arrangement. Not to mention how two guests were seated side by side in wheelchairs.

Emma chose that moment to tell Kurien, "A little bird mentioned something about how you're both rich and single."

Rae gasped, looked horrified, turned fiery red, and said, "You'll have to excuse my aunt. She never fails to embarrass me every chance she gets."

Kurien, however, looked utterly unfazed. He asked Emma, "Did your songbird also happen to mention I'm dying?"

Emma took hold of his hand. "Honey, none of us is perfect."

"Say the word," Rae told him. "I'll shift my aunt into the other room."

"Nonsense." Kurien continued to smile at his neighbor. "For the first time, I am very glad I came."

"Well, now," Emma said.

"And I don't mean just to this particular event," Kurien said. "Are all the people of this fine land so open and welcoming?"

"No," Rae said. "Absolutely not. Thank the stars above."

And suddenly they were all smiling.

Comfortable.

Friends.

Kurien stood, then accepted a microphone from Alvita, and spoke a few words. Curtis tried hard to listen, but the speech formed a gentle wash. Then Kurien said something that brought cheers from their table and applause from the room at large. Curtis assumed it was about their betrothal and felt a chill run though his body as Amiya told him, "Smile and raise your glass."

Then the wine expert rose from the neighboring table and was joined by the lady chef Curtis had seen earlier in Alvita's office. Together they spoke about the evening's pairings. Curtis assumed what they had to say was both interesting and entertaining, because the audience remained attentive and smiling. As they spoke, servers circulated with chilled bottles wrapped in linen napkins and filled glasses. Another toast, and a brief time of conversation; then the first course was served.

Those plates were removed, a different wine served with the second course, and the third. Curtis pretended to listen as happy talk circulated around his table. But just then, all he could really focus on was the simple unutterable fact that he was in the presence of change. Another alteration of his life's course was taking place. And there was only one word to describe how he felt.

Content.

As the plates were removed, Amiya said, "It's time, my darling."

"Time?"

She must have seen what she wanted in his gaze, for she leaned over and kissed him. Which drew another cheer.

Friends.

Amiya said, "They're waiting."

He realized she was talking about the room. "Nobody said anything about, you know. Talking."

"Shall I speak for us?"

"Are you kidding? You absolutely have to do this. Please."

Amiya rose to her feet, waited for the room to settle, then began, "I've only been here a very short while. But my fiancé was born here. Curtis called the Crystal Coast home for the first seventeen years of his life. Most of what I know about this region comes from him. But the new friends I have made only amplify what I love most about this dear sweet man.

"I understand why some people are opposed to our project. They fear we will seek to change the nature of this remarkable place. I can only hope that with time they will recognize and accept that we intend to do no such thing.

"The Crystal Coast is a world apart. This region holds a very special, very delicate quality. There is a fragile element here, a sanctity of family and friendship. People do not keep returning simply for the beach. There are thousands of miles of shoreline, hundreds of coastal towns. They recognize, as do I, that the Crystal Coast is unique.

"They come here to savor a simpler life. To take stock. Heal. Walk these streets and recognize that the past is alive in all of us. And only by accepting this can we be ready to face tomorrow."

She lifted her glass, toasted her fiancé, then told the room, "To our new home, and sharing our tomorrows with you."

CHAPTER 49

A final course was served, followed by coffee and petit fours. Their table was rimmed by happy chatter and punctuated by bursts of laughter. Curtis remained focused on the hand holding his. Soft and subtle and strong. A lifetime grip.

He shivered at the prospect, then realized, "I don't have an engagement ring."

"Daddy is wondering if he can give you one. It was his *amma's*."

"Amiya, he wants you to have your mother's ring?"

"No, silly. My grandmother's. His mother."

Kurien leaned forward to smile around his daughter. "Engagement rings are not strictly traditional in India. But my parents spent their honeymoon in Paris. My father bought her a beautiful ring from a jeweler on the Place Vendôme."

"Daddy was conceived there," Amiya added. "In Paris. Not the jeweler's."

He told father and daughter, "I don't know what to say."

"It would please Daddy very much," Amiya said.

"Of course. Yes. I'm honored."

"My mother and I were very close," Kurien said. "Amiya has so many of her finest qualities, I'm happy to say. My *amma* lives in her."

Curtis was still searching for something more to say, when Chris Compton and his band stepped onto the stage. As his team settled, Compton approached the microphone, smiled to the applause, and said, "We've had a request for a first song that isn't normally part of our repertoire. When I asked my band members if they'd be willing to give it a try, I discovered, to my surprise, every one of them count it among their favorite numbers of all time. So we're treating tonight as a trial run for what will most likely be included in our next album."

He counted them down, and the band launched into a sparkling rendition of "Some Enchanted Evening."

Curtis took a long breath, doing his best to fit himself into this newly expanding universe.

He rose to his feet and held out his hand to the woman determined to reknit his life, his heart, his world.

He asked, "May I have this dance?"